THE
BRAZEN

WILLA NASH

THE BRAZEN

Editing & Proofreading:

Elizabeth Nover, Razor Sharp Editing

www.razorsharpediting.com

Julie Deaton, Deaton Author Services

www.facebook.com/jdproofs

Karen Lawson, The Proof is in the Reading

Judy Zweifel, Judy's Proofreading

www.judysproofreading.com

Cover:

Sarah Hansen © Okay Creations

www.okaycreations.com

OTHER TITLES

Calamity Montana Series

The Bribe

The Bluff

The Brazen

The Bully

———

Writing as Devney Perry

Jamison Valley Series

The Coppersmith Farmhouse

The Clover Chapel

The Lucky Heart

The Outpost

The Bitterroot Inn

The Candle Palace

Maysen Jar Series

The Birthday List

Letters to Molly

Lark Cove Series

Tattered

Timid

Tragic

Tinsel

Tin Gypsy Series

Gypsy King

Riven Knight

Stone Princess

Noble Prince

Fallen Jester

Tin Queen

Runaway Series

Runaway Road

Wild Highway

Quarter Miles

Forsaken Trail

Dotted Lines

The Edens Series

Christmas in Quincy - Prequel

Indigo Ridge

PROLOGUE
KERRIGAN

"ANY NEWS ON THE FARMHOUSE?" Dad asked from his recliner.

"Nope."

"What about the studio apartment?"

"Another nope." My answer was the same at this Sunday's family dinner as it had been last week.

I kept scrolling through my phone. Maybe if I didn't make eye contact, it would spare me from the conversation that had come after last week's questions about my vacant rental properties.

"You know . . ."

Ugh. Not again.

"Any time you want to come and work for me, I've got a spot for you."

"Thanks, Dad." I gave him a tight smile. *But no, thanks.*

"You could work in finance," he said. "Or be an assistant manager like Zach. Use that business degree of yours and teach us all a few things."

My brother's jaw clenched from his spot beside me on

the couch. I was the first in our immediate family to have earned my bachelor's degree. Larke had hers too for teaching, but Zach was the oldest sibling and his lack of higher education was a touchy subject.

"Or you could—"

"I'd better see if Mom and Larke need help in the kitchen." Zach shoved off the couch and strode away before Dad could toss out another job opportunity for me at his car dealership.

Great, now he was in a mood. Dinner should be fun. Especially if Dad didn't drop this subject before Mom served her lasagna.

Why had I told my parents I was running low on money? Why? I should have kept my damn mouth shut.

A couple of weeks ago, Mom and Dad had stopped by my house for an impromptu visit. I'd answered the door wearing two sweaters and my wool socks because I'd been keeping my thermostat at sixty to lower the power bill. By the time they'd left an hour later, Mom had been shivering and Dad had convinced himself that I was penniless.

I considered it more desperate than destitute. Funding three vacant properties didn't exactly lend itself to a cushy cashflow position, and trimming expenses had been my only option. But it was going to be okay. I was nearly broke, but not broken. And after my conversation with Gabriel on Tuesday, I wasn't as freaked out as I had been.

He'd given me the pep talk I'd needed. He'd promised that all successful entrepreneurs hit their peaks and valleys. I was just suffering through my first low. And he was extending my loan. The paperwork hadn't come through yet, but I was sure his lawyer would send it over shortly.

Gabriel Barlowe was a billionaire and the most

successful man I'd ever met, so to have him tell me that everything would be okay, to have his financial backing, soothed a lot of my fears.

I went back to my phone, pulling up the news. The first three stories were of no interest, but then a headline caught my attention.

Four Killed in Rocky Mountain Plane Crash.

Oh, God. I opened the article and its words hit me like a bullet to the chest.

My eyes blurred as I kept reading. It couldn't be true. This was wrong. It had to be. He wasn't . . . gone.

"You might like sales," Dad said. "Always good commission income."

I stood from the couch and left the living room, my phone clasped in my grip as I hurried to the bathroom and closed myself inside. Then I dabbed furiously at my eyes before forcing myself to read the article again.

And again.

And again.

I lost track of the number of times I read those tragic words, hoping and wishing they weren't true.

"Kerrigan?" Zach knocked on the door.

I swiped at my cheeks, drying the tears that wouldn't stop. "Yeah?"

"Dinner's ready. Mom wants to know if we should wait or . . ."

"I'll be right there." I waited until my brother's footsteps retreated down the hallway before burying my face in my hands and letting out one more sob.

Gabriel.

He was gone.

Killed in a plane crash two days ago.

No one had told me. No one had called me. I had just spoken to him and now . . .

He was dead.

Gabriel.

My mentor. My investor. My unwavering advocate.

My friend.

He'd never doubted me. He'd championed my ambitions rather than questioned them.

And now he was gone.

Another sob escaped followed by another and another.

My family ate dinner without me.

CHAPTER ONE

PIERCE

THIS WOMAN WAS SHOUTING at me, and I couldn't stop staring at her mouth.

Her lips were a perfect shape. A proud upper lip, not too plump and not too thin. The bottom was lush with a slight pout that deserved to be traced by the tip of a tongue. They were coated in a gloss that made their natural peach color look as sweet and juicy as the fruit itself.

"You can't do this." Her arms flailed in the air.

She was beautiful. Of course she was beautiful. My grandfather had had impeccable taste.

According to him, she was as sharp as a tack too, and while I should probably be paying attention to the fire in her eyes or the words she was throwing at me like knives, I couldn't seem to focus on anything but that mouth.

"Fuck you!"

My gaze shot to her pretty brown eyes. *Fuck you* was pretty hard to ignore, especially as it echoed off the store-fronts of downtown Calamity, Montana.

The letter I'd handed her moments ago was clutched in her hand. It stated, plainly, that she was in default of her loan and had one month to pay it in full. It was a loan my late grandfather had given her to fund some investment properties in this small town. A loan to a girlfriend. Mistress. Booty call? I didn't have a damn clue how she'd fit into his tangled web of women.

The notion of his mouth on the perfection of hers made me cringe. Maybe because of their relationship, she'd assumed her debt would be forgiven.

Never.

Yes, that made me a vindictive asshole, but she wasn't the only one freaking out at the moment. My grandfather had fucked me over while he'd been alive. His death had brought about round two.

All I wanted was to erase that son of a bitch from my life, starting by collecting on his loan to this breathtaking woman.

Kerrigan Hale's eyes blazed. Her face was turning red, either from her fury or from shouting at me for a full minute.

We were causing a scene. Well, she was causing a scene. I was simply standing here staring at her mouth, hating myself for thinking she was beautiful.

People emerged from their tiny shops. A woman wearing a black apron came out of the coffee shop, looking up and down the sidewalk until she spotted the source of the commotion. *Us.* A couple rushed out of the art gallery and came jogging our way.

Spectacles weren't all that appealing, so it was time to wrap this up before we drew a crowd.

I opened my mouth to reiterate the message I'd come here to deliver, but before I could speak, Kerrigan took the letter I'd handed her and began ripping it to pieces. Tear after tear, a snarl formed on those pretty lips. Maybe she was envisioning me as the paper. One moment she was shredding, the pieces getting smaller and smaller. The next, the fragments flew in my face.

I blinked and let them fall to the sidewalk. Tearing up that letter wasn't going to change the facts.

We were both fucked.

"Thirty days, Ms. Hale."

Her nostrils flared.

The couple from the gallery reached us, standing beside Kerrigan as they both looked me up and down. Since I had no desire to meet the locals, it was time to go.

"Thirty days." I spun away from Kerrigan before she could throw anything else in my face—another curse, a wad of spit, her fist.

My polished shoes clicked on the sidewalk as I made my way toward my gleaming gray Jaguar, ignoring the daggers being glared into my spine.

Kerrigan could hate me all she wanted. *I* wasn't the one who'd put her in this position. That award belonged to my grandfather. But had she cursed his name? No. Once again, Gabriel Barlowe emerged the victor.

Without a backward glance, I slid behind the wheel and pulled away. The Jag's engine purred down First Street. The leather steering wheel was warm beneath my palms from the sun. Even after spending most of the past two days in the driver's seat, the car still had that new-car smell.

I'd owned the Jag for months. It had been a gift to myself the day my divorce had been finalized. But I hadn't driven it much. I rarely needed to drive.

Until this trip.

The eleven-hour journey from Denver to Montana had consumed all of yesterday. I'd stayed in Bozeman, wanting to see the place where my grandfather had spent so much time. Then this morning, I'd driven to Calamity to deliver Kerrigan's letter.

A letter that was now littering the sidewalk as confetti.

The phone rang and my assistant's name came up on the console. "Hello."

"Good morning," Nellie said. "How are you today?"

"Fine." For being cussed at before noon.

"How did your meeting go?"

"Fantastic," I deadpanned. A negative reaction from Kerrigan had been a given. I'd expected tears and begging. Instead, I'd gotten a *fuck you* with paper thrown in my face.

She had steel, I'd give her that.

"Tell me again why you insisted on driving to Montana when that letter could have been mailed," Nellie said.

"I wanted to reinforce my point." And I'd been curious about the woman my grandfather had adored.

"Uh-huh," she muttered. Had I been in my office, I would have earned Nellie's famous eye roll. "Now what?"

"I'm going to stay here tonight."

"Really? I thought you were going to head to the cabin."

"Change of plan." I wanted to scope out this little nowhere town that Kerrigan Hale called home.

As I drove down First, creeping along behind a flatbed truck with the license plate *GoNCTRY*, I scanned the businesses that lined the street. A metropolis, Calamity was not. Yet my grandfather had invested a pile of money in this small community. Actually, he'd invested a pile of money in *her*.

Why? Why Calamity? Why Kerrigan? Why couldn't I stop thinking about her mouth? And why hadn't she cried? I'd really expected tears.

Curiosity aside, the real reason I wasn't going to the cabin tonight was because I wasn't ready. The idea of sleeping there made my stomach churn as much as the idea of Grandpa's hands on Kerrigan's supple breasts.

I could stay in Calamity and head to the cabin tomorrow. Then after a quick stop to talk to the caretaker, I'd get the hell back to Denver.

"Should I find you a hotel room?" Nellie asked.

"Please."

"In Calamity or Bozeman?"

"Calamity."

"Okay. But I doubt whatever motel they have has a star rating," she teased.

"I don't need a star rating."

She scoffed. "Liar."

Nellie had been my assistant for the past five years, and in our time together, I wasn't sure if she'd ever seen me as her boss. In most ways, it was the other way around. Not once had she looked at me like anything more than the guy she'd outscored on every high school math and English exam.

Maybe that was why she'd lasted five years. Her predecessors had an average tenure of only six months. The longest had made it a year, the shortest just two weeks. Each had annoyed me and when we'd parted ways, it had been with a sigh of relief.

If Nellie quit, I'd lose my goddamn mind.

Nellie didn't kiss my ass or call me Mr. Sullivan. She didn't bite her tongue when she disagreed with my decisions.

She didn't temper her opinions because I signed her paychecks.

"Anything come up in the office I should know about?" I asked.

"Nothing I couldn't take care of."

While she was technically my assistant, her title was vice president to the CEO and there wasn't much she couldn't handle. Which was why she made more than any other vice president at Grays Peak Investments. Now that we were taking on so much more, I'd need her. "Thank you."

"You sound tired."

I shifted, rubbing the back of my neck with one hand while driving with the other. "I am. It was a long drive."

"You could have flown."

"No, it was good. I needed to clear my head."

"Not much to clear. You could have done it with a thirty-minute trip along the Front Range."

"Funny," I muttered.

"You know I'm kidding. But I feel like I should have gone with you."

"No, I'm good," I lied. I hadn't been good in months.

"Your parents called."

I swallowed a groan. "And?"

"And maybe you'd know what they wanted if you returned their calls."

I'd been avoiding Mom and Dad since the funeral. Mom especially, because she'd want to talk about everything I didn't want to talk about. "Are they still in Hawaii?"

"Yes. Your mom invited me to fly over next weekend."

I chuckled. They loved Nellie more than they loved me, which was true for most people who knew us both. "Go for it."

"I need more vacation time."

"You negotiated for that last time I screwed up."

"I did?"

"Yes." She had one month a year. Soon it would be six weeks. Eventually I'd do something to piss her off and she'd get another two weeks out of me. I was only holding out for my ego's sake.

"When's the last time I got a bonus?"

"Ten months ago."

"Right," she drawled. "The day you took Kris's side over mine in our discussion about the Christmas party."

And I'd paid for that decision. Nellie had told us that an open bar would be more fun for the employees. Kris, our attorney, had argued that an open bar would lead to drunk employees and regrets come Monday morning. Given the party had ended an hour early and I'd been called cheap in a few hushed conversations, Nellie had been right.

She hadn't let me live it down.

"Anything else going on today?" I asked.

"Jasmine called."

Shit. "Tell her I'm busy. I'll call her back." We both knew I wouldn't.

"Pierce—"

"I'm busy, Nellie." This was one area where I didn't need her input.

Nellie sighed. "All right. For the record, let it be known that I think you're making a huge mistake by avoiding her."

"Noted. Next subject."

"That's all for now. I'll call if anything comes up. When are you driving back?"

"Tomorrow. I'll be in the office Wednesday morning."

"Okay. I'll talk to you later."

"Bye." I ended the call and turned off First Street, easing down a side street lined with homes. One block away from the downtown area, I pulled over and parked the Jag along an empty sidewalk.

Green lawns stretched down the road. Trees dotted each yard, their colors beginning to change much like they did in Colorado in early September. The homes themselves were quiet, most people likely at work this time of day. When I'd passed the school on the way into town, its parking lot had been crowded with vehicles.

Hopefully my own would be fine parked here for an hour or two. There were areas in Denver where I wouldn't dare leave a luxury vehicle, but I doubted carjacking was common in Calamity, and I didn't want to park on First. The Jag drew too much attention parked next to large trucks with mud flaps. Today, I wanted to explore without flash.

"Probably should have worn jeans," I said to myself, taking in my standard three-piece suit.

I unbuttoned my charcoal blazer and the vest underneath. Then I laid them in the passenger seat, covering my briefcase. I undid my titanium cufflinks, a birthday gift from my mom, and stowed them in a cupholder. Then I rolled up my shirtsleeves, tugged off my tie and loosened my collar.

The slacks would stand out since nearly everyone else I'd seen today had been in denim, but suits were all I'd brought along. This was a business trip, after all.

Leaving my car, I walked toward First Street, shoving my hands in my pockets. When I came to the intersection, I glanced left, then right. Left would take me toward Kerrigan's gym—the scene of the crime. Right would land me at a hardware store. I went right.

A bell jingled as I pushed the door inside. A clerk

wearing a red vest over his white polo nodded from behind a cash register. "Mornin'."

"Good morning."

"Help you find anything?"

I walked toward a hat rack not far from the door. It was teeming with caps of various colors, each embroidered with *CALAMITY, MONTANA*. Tourist markers. "Are these all you have?"

"Yep."

Calamity it is. I swiped a black version buried beneath the blood reds, bright blues and kelly greens.

"Bag?" the clerk asked.

"No, thanks. Mind if I rip the tags off and put them in the trash?"

"I'll do you one better." He plucked a pair of scissors from a vegetable can beside the till, cut the tags and handed over the hat I'd be ditching the moment I made it home to Colorado.

"Thanks again." I gave him a nod, then headed out the door, pulling on the hat as I walked.

With my sunglasses and the hat, maybe I wouldn't be recognized by those who'd witnessed Kerrigan's show earlier.

Grandpa had always told me how she *entertained* him. Considering it had been my grandfather speaking, I could guess exactly what entertainment meant. He'd gushed about Kerrigan for years, but he'd left out a few details, hadn't he?

He hadn't mentioned how beautiful she was. He definitely hadn't mentioned that mouth.

I should have known she'd be a surprise. Everything since his death two weeks ago had been a shock, and that wasn't counting the many unwelcome blows he'd landed during his life.

There wasn't much to do other than deal with them, one by one. I'd put them to rest and move on with my damn life. Including cutting all ties to Kerrigan Hale.

She had fire. Hopefully that fire could pay her debt.

I walked down the sidewalk, nodding at passersby. I glanced through the windows of the shops and restaurants, only slowing to take a closer inspection of the real estate office. They had their current listings displayed in their front window.

"Guess the market isn't hopping in Calamity," I muttered after scanning the few printouts taped to the glass.

Most of the properties of any size had been on the market for months. And the prices? Kerrigan would have to sell two or three properties to pay her loan.

Not my problem. A sliver of guilt pricked my spine but I shoved it aside.

This was the only way to move on. A clean break.

By October third, Kerrigan Hale would either pay off her loan or I'd assume ownership of whatever assets necessary to cover her balance. I made a mental note of the realtor's name before continuing on. I might need to sell a property or two in the coming months.

There was little foot traffic as I made my way down the sidewalk. Or any traffic, for that matter. Besides the occasional car or truck, First Street was quiet. Though most places would be compared to downtown Denver.

Without people bustling by in a rush, I settled into an easy pace. The air smelled clean rather than of city exhaust and concrete. Walking was almost . . . relaxing. When was the last time I'd walked with no destination in mind? Was it always like this here?

I'd done a bit of research on Calamity before my trip.

Located in the heart of southwest Montana, this community was home to roughly two thousand residents. The town was nestled in a mountain valley, and at the end of the street, indigo peaks rose in the distance.

The retail shops along First played up the Western element. Smartly so. It no doubt appealed to tourists. Most of the buildings had square, barnwood façades. Others boasted red brick and mortar. There was even a bar called Calamity Jane's. It was closed as I passed by. Otherwise I would have gone in for a drink and to scope it out.

I reached the end of First too soon when the road opened up to the highway. Tomorrow, I'd have to drive that way to get to the cabin, but for today, I turned and put Grandpa's sanctuary out of mind.

Looking both directions, I jaywalked across the road. Was there jaywalking in a town with only one visible cross-walk? Heading in the opposite direction, I set my sights on the building where I'd come to first this morning.

The Refinery.

Kerrigan's fitness studio. According to Grandpa's records, she'd bought the entire building. On the first floor, she'd created a gym. Above it was a studio apartment.

A vacant studio apartment. She also had a vacant two-bedroom farmhouse on the outskirts of town. And a vacant duplex on Sixth Street. With these vacancies, it was no wonder she hadn't made a single payment on Grandpa's loan.

Kerrigan had clearly overextended herself, and my grandfather had given her a safety net the size of Montana. He hadn't changed their contract to incorporate a payment plan. He hadn't called any portion of the loan due. From my vantage point, he'd simply tossed money at Kerrigan without any structure.

This was the worst investment in his portfolio.

My portfolio.

Grandpa had left me his company, though I'd expected Barlowe Capital to go to my mother—so had she. But he'd left it to me in his estate.

He'd given me the headache that was the gorgeous Kerrigan Hale.

Maybe he'd hoped she'd fail. Maybe he'd seen her as an easy target, a way to exploit someone young and score some easy properties in Montana. Or maybe she'd paid him by other means.

With that goddamn perfect mouth.

I gritted my teeth.

Whatever his reasons, I wasn't going to repeat his mistakes. I had no desire to own a studio apartment, a farm-house or a duplex in Calamity. If Kerrigan didn't pay, I'd liquidate and forget this town was even on the map. In a few months, I'd banish any and all thoughts of her just like I would Grandpa.

He'd been obsessed with Montana. I'd never understood it. Standing here, beneath the big blue sky . . . sure, it was pretty. The air smelled like evergreens and sunshine. But there were mountains in Colorado too. There was blue sky in Colorado too. There were small towns in Colorado too.

What was so special about Montana that he'd fly here instead of heading into the mountains outside Denver? It was just so . . . remote. It was like being in a different world. A world away.

Maybe that had been the appeal. Grandpa had been able to run away to Montana and ignore the roadkill he'd left in his wake. Isolated in the middle of nowhere, he could pretend to be a better man.

I passed the fitness studio, and the windows were dark. When I'd arrived earlier, she'd had the entire place lit up as she'd sat at the counter just inside the door. It was probably for the best that she was gone. Maybe others wouldn't recognize me, but she certainly would. And I didn't need another glimpse of that mouth.

I'd have a hard enough time as it was forgetting those lips.

With the gym behind me, I made my way back to the Jag. The walk hadn't taken long but now I had a better feel for Calamity. A mental image of the town.

And Kerrigan.

The clock on the dash showed it was still before noon. I had hours and hours of emails to work through, but as I started the car and returned to First, I found myself on the highway I'd sworn to avoid.

Go there tomorrow.

But I didn't turn around.

I'd delivered that letter to Kerrigan today. Maybe getting this visit to the cabin over with was the best way to round out an already shitty trip. Then tomorrow I could just go home.

Go home and get to work.

My focus was absorbing Barlowe Capital into Grays Peak. One loan at a time, I'd put my own mark on Grandpa's investments.

The bastard had put enough marks on what should have stayed mine.

Once the acquisition was complete, I'd be free of everything Gabriel Barlowe.

January was my goal. I needed to be free by January.

The two-hour trip to the cabin went quickly at first, then slowed when I hit the switchback road up the mountain. By the time I made it to the ski resort and the exclusive development where Grandpa had his place, I itched to turn around and leave.

The private road to the development was gated, and once inside the club's boundary, the only way to own a property on the mountain was to have a net worth of at least $20 million. My car was the only one on the road.

At any given time, less than a third of the properties were occupied. These were simply vacation spots where the owners would come for a week of winter skiing or summer hiking, then fly away home.

This *cabin* of Grandpa's was more of a mountain lodge considering it was over ten thousand square feet. Once, I'd loved it here too.

But that was before I'd disowned my grandfather. That was before my hero had stabbed me in the back.

I eased into the driveway and stared through my windshield at the cabin. The windows gleamed under the afternoon sun. The dark exterior blended with the surrounding forest. It was truly a gorgeous place. Top-of-the-line. Grandpa hadn't believed in half-assed.

My heart raced as I stared at the building. The keys to the front door were in my briefcase.

Except I couldn't bring myself to go inside.

Maybe because he was gone. Maybe because I was so fucking angry with him. Maybe because it would hurt too much.

Fuck this place.

I reversed out of the driveway and sped away from the

mountain as fast as possible. How depressing was it that I'd rather stay in Calamity?

The moment I reached town, I stopped at the nearest gas station because they sold liquor too.

"Anything else?" the cashier asked as he rang up my bottle.

"Unless you have a better brand of bourbon handy."

He blinked.

"Never mind." I inserted my credit card into the reader, signed the receipt and walked out of the store with my Jim Beam.

While I'd been driving, Nellie had emailed me the address to the motel where she'd made me a reservation. I drove straight there, checked in at the desk and disappeared to my room. Number seven.

With my bourbon in hand and my travel bag on the floor, I sat on the edge of the bed and tore off my Calamity hat.

"Shit." I raked a hand through my hair. I was ready for the day to be over. My plan was to drink, then collapse on this surprisingly comfortable bed.

The interior of the room belied the rustic edge of the outside. With the plush white bedding and soft tan carpet, there was a hint of fresh paint in the air like it had been remodeled recently. I toed off my shoes, then opened my bottle.

The bourbon would have been better with ice, but ice meant leaving the room, and the next time I walked through the door it would be to get the hell out of Montana.

The first drink burned, and I cringed at the taste, wishing I'd bought a can of Coke at the vending machine beside the motel lobby. With no other options, I settled for a glass of tepid water from the bathroom tap.

I relaxed on the bed with my drink in one hand and my phone in the other to check my emails. The bottle stayed close on the nightstand. I drank until the text on my phone was blurry and my head was spinning. My stomach growled as I opened the motel's amenities binder for a place that would deliver. I was just keying in the number to the pizza place when an incoming call flashed on the screen.

Area code 406. A Montana number.

"Hello." My voice was heavy from the alcohol. Not slurred, but anyone who knew me well would know I'd been drinking.

"Is this Pierce Sullivan?"

The woman's voice was . . . familiar. "Yes."

"This is Kerrigan Hale."

I sat up straight, swinging my legs over the edge of the bed. "Ms. Hale."

"Kerrigan."

I wasn't calling her Kerrigan. "Ms. Hale."

"Pierce."

"You can call me Mr. Sullivan. How did you get this number?"

She growled. "Your assistant."

Nellie? What the hell? Why would she give out my number?

"You gave me her business card with your *letter*." She slurred that last word a bit. Or maybe my ears were drunk.

Better to keep my mouth shut.

"Are you there?" she asked.

I hummed.

"Good. I just wanted to call and say that I hate you."

A laugh broke free. I'd expected her to beg, to plead for more time or for me to change my mind. But hate . . . hate was much, much better. "And?"

"And nothing. I hate chew." Okay, that was a slur. Right? Before I could find out, the line went dead.

I pulled the phone from my ear and stared at it. *Did that really just happen?* Yes. I wasn't that drunk. And I could definitely picture her snarling those words.

I hate you.

She was probably still in those black leggings she'd been wearing earlier. They'd wrapped around her toned thighs and trim calves. The top she'd been wearing had boasted her fitness studio's logo and had fit her like second skin, stretching across her full breasts. The curved neckline had dipped low enough to show a hint of cleavage and the edge of a peach sports bra.

Peach, like the color of her lips.

The mental image made my cock jerk.

"Fuck." I scrubbed a hand over my face.

Okay, I was drunk. I did not need to be thinking about Kerrigan Hale's legs or breasts or lips.

Food. What I needed was food. So I went back to my task, calling the pizza place to place my order, then pouring just one more bourbon.

I wasn't even three sips in when a knock came at the door. Calamity, Montana, had the fastest delivery on earth. Maybe that was its secret appeal. I dug a crisp hundred-dollar bill from my wallet and opened the door, expecting to be met with the scent of garlic and cheese and pepperoni.

Instead, *she* stood there.

And I might be drunk, but she most definitely was too judging by the way she swayed and worked to keep her eyes in focus.

"How did you find me?"

She rolled her eyes. "Small town. One hotel. Marcy at the front desk said you were here."

"So much for guest confidentiality," I muttered. "What do you want?"

"I . . . hate you." She gave me an exaggerated nod to accentuate her statement. "And . . . I'm not going to let you steal my dreams."

"All you have to do is pay. Then you can keep your dreams."

"I will." Her wrist twirled in the air between us, like she was conjuring up her next words. "I hate you."

"You said that already." And the constant repetition of those three words was beginning to bother me.

Why? No clue. I didn't care that she hated me. Did I?

It had to be the alcohol. I'd done a damn good job at shutting out any and all feelings since my grandfather's death. Being in Montana was screwing with me.

Or maybe it was just her.

God, she was beautiful. Kerrigan had thick, silky, chestnut hair. High, flushed cheekbones. Pretty brown eyes the shade of milk chocolate.

Those eyes might be hazed but there was no mistaking their fire. It hadn't dulled in the slightest from our confrontation on the street.

She was not the meek country bumpkin I'd expected to meet today.

Kerrigan opened her mouth, like she was going to say something, but stopped herself. I suspected it was another *I hate you.* Then she frowned, a crease deepening between her eyebrows. Hell, even those were pretty.

Grandpa, for all his faults, had excellent taste.

She shuffled forward, raising a finger to my chest. Her

gaze narrowed. Never in my life had I seen an angry woman I wanted to kiss so much. That mouth drew me in.

The bourbon was definitely in charge here because before I knew what was happening, I leaned in.

And kissed the scowl off her face.

CHAPTER TWO

KERRIGAN

"RISE AND SHINE," Larke singsonged as she came into my bedroom.

"Go away." I lifted my throbbing head from my pillow. The red numbers on my clock glowed six thirty. "Come back when time machines are a real thing, and you can take us back to yesterday and rip the vodka out of my hand."

"No time machine, but I did bring coffee." She sat on the edge of my bed, holding a steaming to-go cup. The aroma was enticing enough to rouse me from beneath my comforter.

"Ugh." I scooted up to a seat, shoving the hair out of my face. Then I took the cup from her hands for a heavenly sip. "This is good."

"I stopped at the coffee shop since you've become a cheapskate."

Because the good coffee was expensive, something my sister had no problem buying. But I was scraping together every penny these days.

Now more than ever.

"Oh, God." I leaned against the headboard, closing my eyes. Hangovers seemed to get exponentially worse with every birthday, and at thirty, this one would probably last all week.

A familiar meow came from the closet right before Clementine emerged, her white tail held high. She pounced on the bed and stalked my way, giving Larke a kitty sneer before plopping down on my lap.

"Hello, Mistress of Evil," Larke said to my cat, who simply purred.

Clementine hated Larke, but to be fair to my sister, Clem hated everyone. Even me at times.

"So . . . how bad is it?"

"Not that bad," Larke answered too quickly, which could only mean it was bad.

I cringed. "You're lying."

"Yeah, I'm lying. Everyone at the coffee shop was talking about it. The new barista, the one with the blond hair who is always drooling over Zach, asked me if you got arrested for assaulting that man."

My jaw dropped. "I didn't assault him."

"That's the story going around. People are saying that Duke arrested you at Jane's after you went there to get drunk."

"You're kidding."

"Nope."

"I'm going back to bed." I made a move to crawl underneath the covers and die, but Larke stopped me with a hand on my forearm.

"It'll blow over."

"Yeah, right." If that was the gossip before seven in the morning, it would only get worse from here. By noon, word around town would probably be that I'd murdered Pierce in broad daylight.

"Note to self," I muttered. "Move. Immediately."

Most days I loved my hometown. It was full of familiar faces and friendly smiles. But there were times when Calamity was too small for its own good. Gossip traveled at cheetah speed and I was a woman who preferred a turtle stroll.

There was no such thing as blowing over. The people in my community had memories like elephants.

"Did you at least clarify that I didn't get arrested and that it was Dad who picked me up from Jane's?" I asked.

"Of course. I don't know if they believed me but . . ."

I groaned.

"Hopefully after a few people stop down at the bar for a drink after work, Jane will reinforce that story."

"It's the truth, Larke."

"I know." She held up her hands. "I'm just the messenger."

"What else are they saying?"

"Nothing else about you. But there's a lot of speculation about him."

Him. Pierce Sullivan.

My stomach dropped and I willed my late-night snack— potato chips, Ritz crackers and pickles—to stay down.

Why did I drink? Never again. Not just because this hangover was going to suck, but because I made stupid, really stupid decisions.

Like calling Pierce's assistant. Like begging for his phone number. Like showing up at the motel.

Like letting him kiss me.

Like kissing him back.

He'd kissed me, right? Or had I imagined that in my drunken state? My hand drifted to my lips.

Oh, he'd kissed me, all right. I could still feel his mouth there, hot and smooth and delicious. I could still feel the scrape of his neat beard.

The last time a man had kissed me had been over a year ago. I'd gone on a second date with a banker in town who I'd never called back because our kiss had been . . . blech. My personal life was as exciting as a bucket of tar. Maybe I'd designed it that way to protect myself from being hurt again. When I worked all day, every day, there was no time for lukewarm romance.

But with Pierce? There was nothing tepid with that man. We could have sparked a wildfire with that kiss. His lips had been so soft, his tongue wicked, and he'd done this little nip-suck thing at the corner of my mouth that had turned me into a puddle.

But why? Why would he kiss me? Why would he come to Calamity, deliver that awful letter demanding payment on my loan and kiss me? My head was spinning, and it was only partially due to the alcohol.

"I did something stupid last night," I whispered.

"Was this dumb thing worse than verbally accosting a stranger on First and throwing a piece of shredded paper in his face before going to Jane's and getting plastered before noon?"

"Seriously?" I shot her a glare.

"What?" She feigned innocence. "I'm just asking."

"You're loving this."

She hid a smile behind the rim of her coffee cup. "Can you blame me? It's about time you did something gossip-worthy. Everyone's always talking about how smart and energetic you are. Now you're in the boat with the rest of us commoners."

"Please." I rolled my eyes. "No one gossips about you."

"Ha! Try working at the school. It's ten times as bad as it is everywhere else in town. Good thing those cute little faces make up for the assholes on the staff and administration. Now tell me what stupid thing you did because I need to leave for said school in fifteen minutes."

"I stalked him to the motel."

"Him?"

"Him."

"Kerrigan." She winced. "Okay, I need specifics."

I took a long drink of coffee, then shifted to face her. "After Dad brought me home, I passed out for a little while. When I woke up I was still drunk and mad so I called Pierce's assistant and begged for his phone number. Then I walked to the motel because his assistant mentioned he hadn't left town yet and . . . please don't make me keep going."

"Keep going."

"Marcy gave me his room number."

"And?"

"And when he answered the door, I told him I hated him." Then he'd kissed me. That part, I couldn't even bring myself to speak aloud. Not now. Not ever.

"You really shouldn't drink. Like, ever again."

"I know." I banged my skull against the headboard. "Why am I such an idiot?"

"What did he say?"

"Not much." He'd been too busy kissing me.

And damn it, that kiss had been good. Toe-curling good. Drenched-panty good.

"No more vodka," I declared. "Ever again. I mean it."

Not that I could afford another drunken vodka binge.

I had twenty-nine days to come up with $250,000. Miracles happened, right? I might have ripped up the letter Pierce had given me, but that had been after reading it. Twice. I had until October third to come up with his money.

"I can't believe this is happening." It had been two weeks since I'd learned of Gabriel's death. My heart was still aching.

And now to come up with all of that money . . .

"It's hopeless." The tears came flooding, and then I was crying into my younger sister's shoulder.

I'd secretly thought that whoever would take over Gabriel's estate would be kind and compassionate. That we could reminisce about what a wonderful man he'd been. That together, we could grieve.

Instead, I'd been stuck with the Antichrist.

"I'm sorry," Larke said as she hugged me.

"Me too." I sat up straight and dried my eyes, glancing at the clock. "You'd better get going."

"Yeah." Her lip curled. "There's a new teacher this year. High school science. He's such a jerk, and if I get there early enough, I can put my lunch in the teachers' lounge and miss him completely."

"Why's he a jerk?"

"Not sure. Small penis?" She stood from the bed, brushing out her slacks. "How do I look?"

"Beautiful. As always."

Larke was three years younger and had inherited my mother's nose. Otherwise, there was no mistaking we were sisters. We had the same chestnut-brown hair, the same oval face and full lips.

"I'll call you later." She kissed my cheek. "Most definitely brush your teeth today."

"You woke me up, remember? I think you should give me back my key."

"Never." She waved and disappeared.

As soon as the front door closed, I set my coffee aside and burrowed beneath the covers.

Clementine, irritated to be displaced, stood and leapt off the bed, disappearing down the hallway, probably in search of food.

"Oh, Gabriel." Even speaking his name hurt.

I wished I'd had the chance to tell him goodbye. To tell him how much his friendship had meant to me. I already missed him dearly. His laugh. His random surprise visits to Calamity. Our long conversations about my dreams and his advice on how to reach them.

Gabriel had loaned me a lot of money. The terms had always been set, but he'd been wonderful about giving me the flexibility to try new things. Not once had he required me to make an interest payment. Because even though I'd hit some snags lately, he'd always believed in me.

According to our original contract, the loan he'd extended me was due in thirty days. When I'd called him six months ago and told him I'd be selling my rental property, a farmhouse, in order to pay him back, Gabriel had told me to hold off on the listing. He knew the real estate market was slow moving and a rental property fit my business model best.

Then when I'd spoken to him the week of his death, explaining that I still had not gotten a tenant, he'd promised me an extension.

Don't sweat this, Kerrigan.

You'll come out ahead.

Lean on me, I've got you.

Our verbal agreement had been enough for me. I'd trusted Gabriel. He'd trusted me to repay him, with interest.

All would have been fine if not for that plane crash.

If not for his grandson, who'd inherited my loan.

Gabriel must not have told anyone about my extension.

I was flat broke. I had no way to come up with a quarter of a million dollars unless I sold a property, but the real estate market in Calamity was slow, especially now that the leaves had turned. I'd spent years studying trends around the area as well as in other small communities in Montana, and winter was consistently a sluggish season.

Sure, I could slash my prices and probably make a sale. But then I'd be selling multiple properties, not just one. I'd lose every dime I'd put into my properties, not to mention the hours and hours I'd spent on my hands and knees, cleaning and painting and remodeling.

Lost. My dreams lost.

Which led to my biggest problem at the moment.

Pierce.

I was so angry at him I wanted to scream. Why hadn't I slapped him when he'd kissed me? That man deserved a smack in the face. Instead, I'd kissed him back.

"Why?" I pulled the covers over my head. "What is wrong with me?"

Yes, he was handsome. Distractingly so. But I hated him. I distinctly remember telling him I hated him. And the son of a bitch had kissed me in response.

Did he really want to foreclose on me? I couldn't picture him, with the fancy suit and fancy shoes and fancy car, wanting to own a bunch of properties in Calamity. Unless he just wanted to steal my properties and sell them when the market picked up again in the spring.

The bastard.

He was going to ruin me.

"I hate him." I flung the covers off my head and rolled out of bed, marching to the bathroom to brush my teeth and take a shower.

By the time I got to the kitchen, my hangover was beginning to ease. Maybe that was just the rage burning it away. I stomped to the coffee pot to brew another pot of the cheapest of cheap coffee they carried at the grocery store. With a full mug, I took a drink and cringed.

Larke was right. This was awful.

My phone rang and I took it and my crappy coffee to my living room couch. "Hey."

"Hey." There was a smile in Everly's voice. "How are you feeling?"

"Embarrassed. Thanks for going to the bar with me yesterday."

"Anytime."

Yesterday, after the sidewalk incident, I hadn't been able to cope. With the grief from Gabriel's death. The shock of Pierce's arrival. The frustration with the letter.

The disappointment in myself because I could point my finger at Pierce all day, but the fact was, I'd gotten myself into this mess.

Yesterday had not been the day for cleanup. Instead, I'd just pulled up a seat at rock bottom and ordered a drink.

My friends Everly and Hux had been downtown. Hux was an artist and his wife, Everly, managed their gallery. When I'd gone to Jane's, she'd been gracious enough to hang with me at the bar. I was fairly sure Jane hadn't even opened yet when we'd shown up at her door, but she'd let me come in and get smashed anyway.

"Have you thought about what you're going to do?" Everly asked.

"Not yet." I slumped into the sofa. This couch doubled as my dining room table at the moment because my actual table was covered with a canvas tarp and painting supplies.

"Is there anything we can do to help?"

"No." I smiled. "But thank you for coming with me yesterday and listening."

"No thanks needed. Are you coming downtown today?"

"Do I have to?"

She laughed. "Can anyone else open the gym for you?"

"No," I grumbled. I really needed to find a backup.

My plan had been to hire someone to run the gym but per Gabriel's advice, I was being picky about staff. He'd cautioned me to put my processes in place before handing them over to someone else to follow. In a town this size, I couldn't afford to turn customers away.

So I'd been running the gym on my own, working from the counter during the various fitness classes. I'd hired two high school seniors to work in the evenings and weekends. But at this very moment they were in school, probably taking science from Larke's new nemesis, and I needed to get to work.

"Want to meet for lunch?" Everly asked.

"Sure. It will probably help squelch rumors if I act like everything is normal. My sister came by this morning, and everyone's saying that Duke arrested me at Jane's for assaulting Pierce."

"I, uh . . . heard. Hux went to the coffee shop about thirty minutes ago to pick us up breakfast this morning."

"Ugh."

"It's probably not that bad."

I loved Everly, but she hadn't lived in Calamity long enough to know just how vicious the rumor mill could be.

"White Oak. Noon?" she suggested. "I'll call Lucy and see if she wants to get out of the house and bring Theo."

Some cuddle time with my friend's new baby was bound to cheer me up. "Sounds good. Meet you there."

I'd be drinking water since I couldn't afford to eat out, but whatever.

Tossing the phone aside, I glanced around my living room at the partially completed projects. There was so much I wanted to do to this house. It had been built in the early 1930s and was brimming with character. Arched doorways. Hand-carved trim. Some fool had painted that trim green and covered the original hardwood floors with carpet.

This house was brimming with potential, but by the time I came home from working on an investment property, I was usually worn out. The last thing I wanted to do was pick up a paint brush.

Now that The Refinery was open, my next project was to fix the duplex I'd bought so both spaces could be rentable. The real estate market was sluggish, but there was a shortage of rentals in Calamity.

Once the duplex was finished, I'd planned time to work on my own home. To make it exactly how I wanted it. Except of all the properties I owned, the one I'd have the best shot at selling was this house. My own home.

The idea of letting it go made my stomach curl, so I shoved off the couch, needing to get to work. I made sure Clementine had food and water for the day, then went to the garage and climbed in my car, finding a yellow sticky note on the console.

LOTS OF WATER TODAY.
  Love you.
  xoxo
  Dad
  P.S. Think about the dealership.

THAT NOTE WOULD HAVE BEEN perfect and sweet if not for the goddamn P.S.

My dad had come to pick me up from Calamity Jane's yesterday. He'd taken a break from work to collect his drunk daughter and drive her home, where he'd tucked me into bed. But not before telling me all about the benefits of working at his car dealership. Literally, he'd outlined the health and retirement benefits.

Any opportunity to encourage me to work for his company and Dad would pounce.

I couldn't get too annoyed. He had come to get me. And he had arranged to bring my car home and park it in the garage.

He'd probably thought I'd actually stay in bed all night.

"Nope. Instead I hoofed it to the motel and kissed a stranger."

My headache came surging to life and it had little to do with yesterday's alcohol consumption.

As I drove, I caught the stares from people who recognized my black Explorer. I pasted on a smile and pulled into the alley behind my downtown building, navigating to my regular parking spot. Then, with my shoulders squared, I walked to The Refinery and flipped on the lights.

The studio was quiet. It smelled like bleach and eucalyptus air freshener. In such a hurry for a mind-numbing drink, I hadn't even thought about the gym yesterday.

I couldn't meet my own gaze in the mirrored walls.

What was I thinking? It was a good thing I had fantastic friends. I suspected that Everly and Hux had arranged to lock up the gym. The instructors and employees had keys, so they must have opened up for the evening classes.

Hopefully I hadn't pissed off any members. I really couldn't afford to lose a monthly fee right now.

I walked to the front door and opened my business, and after an hour where no one came in and ridiculed me for my behavior, I breathed.

"Good morning." My first encounter was with my yoga instructor. She swept in with a bright smile and warm hug. When she didn't mention a thing about my display with Pierce or the fact that I'd skipped out on work, I decided she was my favorite person in Calamity.

While she went to set up for her class, I ducked into the small office I'd carved out for myself at the back of the building. Most days, I sat at the front counter, working on my laptop and checking in members. But at the moment, what I needed most was time to run my numbers. So while the studio was occupied, I compiled a list of every asset to my name and estimated their individual values.

The grand total was over one million dollars. If I sold everything at market value, I could easily repay Pierce. But I couldn't exactly sell three houses that were currently being rented. I wouldn't boot those people from their homes.

I doubted there was anyone willing to buy my new gym,

considering the financials were in their infancy. There was a vacant studio apartment upstairs that Everly had lived in for a while but it couldn't be sold separate from the gym.

Then there was the farmhouse. The duplex. My car. My own home. Lastly, a checking account with a balance of $1,602.87.

"I'm screwed." I dropped my pencil and let my head fall into my hands.

Would Mom and Dad let me move in with them if I sold my house? Maybe Larke would let me crash on her sofa.

How was I supposed to do this? It wasn't fair. I should have had years to figure it out. Gabriel had promised me years.

But then he'd died.

I picked up my phone and went to recent calls, looking at the last number I'd dialed.

My hand was shaking as I hit the number and pressed it to my ear.

If I could just explain. If he would just listen to me for five minutes.

"Pierce Sullivan," he answered and damn it, that deep, rugged voice shot straight to my center.

Focus, Kerrigan. "Hi, Pierce. It's Kerrigan Hale."

Silence.

I blinked. "Are you there?"

"Ms. Hale. This is my private number."

I sat up straight. "Seriously?"

"I am serious."

"You kissed me."

"And I apologize. It was a mistake."

A mistake. Yes, it had definitely been a mistake. But did he have to say that word with such disgust? Was the entire world out to humiliate me today? Or just this man? "Yes," I said. "Yes, it was."

"Is there a reason for your call?"

"I had a verbal agreement with your grandfather in regard to my loan. I approached him the week he . . . the week of the crash. He gave me a verbal extension."

"Why is there no paperwork showing this alleged agreement?"

"Because he knew I would pay him back." But then he died.

Pierce scoffed. "My grandfather was a shrewd businessman. He wouldn't extend a loan without the necessary documentation or discussing it with an attorney."

"Are you saying that he was trying to swindle me?"

"It's possible."

No. "Never. He wasn't like that."

"Then clearly you didn't know him the way I knew him. The man was a shark, and you, Ms. Hale, are easy prey."

I flinched. There was such hatred in his voice. It was so raw and honest that doubts flooded my mind. Would Gabriel really screw me over? Had he made me a false promise?

No. I couldn't believe it. I *wouldn't* believe it.

"He gave me time. I need time."

"The terms are what they are. You have thirty days."

"Please, Pierce. It's not enough time."

"You may call me Mr. Sullivan."

The phone nearly fell from my hand. He'd said that last night too. I'd nearly forgotten because of the kiss but he'd told me to call him Mr. Sullivan.

The arrogant, selfish, brazen bastard.

"I cannot pay you back in thirty days." Admitting it,

though true, felt like an epic failure. Especially admitting it to him.

"Then you'll be hearing from my attorney. Any and all future communication must go through my assistant. Please don't make me block your calls, Ms. Hale."

And with that, he hung up the phone.

"What a—" I shoved to my feet, fighting back a string of screamed expletives that would no doubt echo to the studio and harsh the yoga vibe. I paced in front of my desk, wringing my hands.

For years, Gabriel had bragged about his smart grandson. The one who'd take over for him one day. The one who'd build an empire.

Considering that I was building my own empire—albeit on a much, much smaller Calamity, Montana, scale—I'd admired that about Pierce. I'd felt a kinship with him even though we'd never met. And whenever Gabriel had spoken of him, it had been with nothing but love and adoration.

But this was not the Pierce I'd pictured in my mind.

No, this was *Mr. Sullivan.* And maybe the man could kiss a woman dizzy, but that didn't change the facts.

He was enemy number one.

CHAPTER THREE

PIERCE

"STEVE, TELL ME YOU'RE JOKING."

My grandfather's lawyer shook his head. "I'm afraid not."

"Why didn't you tell me this when we went through his will and the details about Barlowe Capital?"

"It was part of his expressed wishes that I wait six weeks after his death."

I dragged in a calming breath. "And this is why when we had the initial reading, you said that he did not want a funeral service."

Steve nodded. "Correct."

My mom had been irritated by Grandpa's last requests, to put it mildly. She'd wanted to put her father to rest, but he'd specifically said no funeral service. Instead, he'd asked to be cremated and his ashes kept in an urn that he'd bought himself. The urn was currently at Mom and Dad's house outside the city.

I guess I'd be paying a visit to my parents this week.

"Why couldn't he do anything normally?" I pinched the

bridge of my nose. Even dead, the man was still pulling strings.

"Gabriel always had his reasons."

His fucking reasons.

Those reasons were sending me to Montana—again—to scatter his ashes at the cabin. A cabin that I'd decided to sell. It would be on the market already if not for the club's stipulation that a property not change ownership more than once per six months. They didn't want anyone to *flip* a property, not that those places were exactly fixer-uppers.

Since the cabin had just become legally mine, I was stuck with it for a while.

It had been nearly a month since my visit to Montana. Twenty-eight days to be exact.

I knew because that was how many voicemail messages and corresponding emails I'd received from the irritatingly beautiful Kerrigan Hale.

"My parents are not going to be happy about this," I told Steve.

"I've already discussed it with them. You're only taking part of the ashes. Gabriel asked that the other half be taken to his villa in Italy. While you go to Montana—"

"Mom and Dad are heading to Europe."

Steve nodded. "Exactly."

Christ. Why couldn't I have gotten the Italian vacation? The last place I wanted to go was Montana.

Of course, I could simply refuse this trip. It wasn't like Grandpa would know.

But would I? *No.* The bastard had me trapped. Even though I was furious with him, even after all he'd done to me, he must have known that I wouldn't ignore his final requests.

Sentimental as it was, once upon a time, I'd loved the man.

"Is this it? Or can I expect another surprise visit with another stipulation?"

Steve closed his leather padfolio. "See you soon, Pierce."

Shit. So there was more. "You could save yourself a trip. Tell me now."

"That wasn't what Gabriel wanted."

And *Gabriel* always got what he wanted, didn't he? No matter how much that meant fucking up my life.

"Thanks, Steve." I stood from my desk and shook his hand before escorting him to the door.

Nellie emerged from her office next door, smiling at Steve as he walked to the elevators. When he disappeared around the corner, she followed me into my office. "What was that about?"

I sighed and walked to the floor-to-ceiling windows of my corner office, taking in downtown Denver. "I am headed back to Montana."

"You are? When?"

"Soon." I gave her the quick recap of my meeting with Steve. "What's my schedule look like this month?"

"Actually, this week isn't bad. But the rest of the month is already packed."

Hell. That meant if I was going to fit in this trip, I'd be going immediately. Before Kerrigan's thirty-day notice expired.

She'd made no indication that she would be paying and though she still had two days left, I doubted it would make a difference.

"Let's just . . . get this over with," I said, turning to face

Nellie. "Block out the rest of my week if you can. Shove whatever can't wait to Friday."

"All right. Would you like me to call your pilot and get the flight arranged?"

"No, I'll drive." I hadn't been on my airplane since my grandfather's had crashed, killing him and his passengers. Though it would be faster, I couldn't bring myself to fly. I'd stick to driving for now.

"All right. Jasmine called. Again."

She'd tried me too. Twice. "I'll call her later."

Nellie arched her eyebrows. "Will you?"

No.

"You're running out of time."

I waved it off. "I have time."

"Pierce—"

"I need to return a few emails, then I'll go pack." The benefit of living in the same building where I worked was a short commute. "Would you mind making me a reservation at the Calamity motel?"

"Calamity? I thought you were going to the cabin."

"Not yet," I grumbled. There was a stop to make first. "Would you also call Ms. Hale and request a meeting, first thing tomorrow morning?"

Nellie opened her mouth but closed it before she spoke.

"What?"

"Nothing." And before I could convince her to tell me otherwise, she spun on her heels, her sleek white-blond ponytail practically whipping through the air as she scurried out of my office.

I turned to the windows again, taking in the city. The sun's rays bounced and glinted off the neighboring buildings in LoDo. Mine was one of the newest in this area of downtown. I'd wanted the best and though it wasn't in the hub of the business district like my grandfather's building had been, I preferred being close to the city's well-known restaurants, art galleries and boutique shops.

My company used seven of the twenty floors of the building. The lower levels were residential apartments, all top-of-the-line and many rented by my employees, including Nellie.

The building had an on-site gym and pool. There was a parking garage for residents and employees. Security was tight and the guards stationed at the entrance were paid well to ensure that no one unwelcome was allowed entry.

It was prime real estate, especially with the Front Range in the distance. The rugged mountains cut a jagged line across the horizon. Above them, the blue sky was clear and cloudless.

Why hadn't Grandpa wanted his ashes scattered here? A quick trip to the Front Range and I'd be done. Instead, I would make the long journey to Montana and, per Grandpa's wishes, invite *her*.

I groaned and returned to my desk. Like she knew she was on my mind, her name was at the top of my unread emails. Today's note read exactly like its predecessors.

MR. SULLIVAN,

Per my previous contact attempts, please consider a brief meeting to discuss the terms of our contract.

Sincerely,

Kerrigan Hale

. . .

DID she send the same email to annoy me? Because it was working. Every day, like clockwork, I'd receive an email requesting a conversation. The note would put a slight damper on my morning, probably because I ignored it and ignoring clients—even those I'd inherited from my grandfather—wasn't my style. Still, I ignored her, deleted the email and went about my day.

Then, the moment I had a break in my afternoon schedule, I'd get a phone call. It was like Kerrigan had direct access to my calendar and knew when I had ten minutes free.

I hadn't answered a single one of her calls. I'd let them ring through to voicemail. But the moment her message was saved, I'd replay it. The messages, like the emails, were always the same.

HELLO, this is Kerrigan Hale. Please call me back at this number at your earliest convenience. I'm looking forward to hearing from you soon, Mr. Sullivan.

THE WAY she tried to suppress her annoyance at my last name always made me chuckle.

Over the past twenty-eight days, hearing her voice had become a part of my routine, yet I hadn't once entertained the idea of returning her calls.

I didn't trust myself with Kerrigan. That was the problem.

The last time I'd seen her, I'd kissed her. And what a fucking kiss it had been. Probably the best of my life. As much as I wanted to blame it on the bourbon, the real problem was chemistry. My attraction to Kerrigan ran to the marrow, proving what I'd suspected the day we'd met.

Kerrigan Hale was a dangerous woman.

I'd suffered enough at the hands of another dangerous woman.

So I kept my distance. I ignored the calls and emails because nothing had changed.

If Kerrigan didn't pay her loan, the assets totaling the amount due would become the newest additions to Grays Peak Investments. I'd assign them to one of the junior members of my team, push for a quick sale and do my best to recoup whatever loss I incurred.

In the past month, I'd worked diligently to bring Barlowe Capital under the Grays Peak umbrella. It had been no small feat, but we were managing. Luckily, most of the Barlowe team had been willing to come to work for me.

Besides the cabin, Grandpa's properties and his cash accounts had gone to my mother.

Mom, being his only child, had never struggled for money. My grandmother had been wealthy in her own right. She and Grandpa hadn't been married long, and when she'd passed, Mom had inherited her estate. Dad had never hurt for money either, which had lessened the blow that Grandpa had bequeathed me Barlowe Capital.

Mom and Dad weren't equipped to run it anyway.

I came from a long line of successful businessmen and women who'd ensured my billionaire status would never be in jeopardy. But living off someone else's fortune had never been my style, and I'd started Grays Peak to build my own name.

Real estate holdings had provided a solid foundation for my company. Grandpa had specialized in real estate and I'd learned many things from him during my time working at Barlowe Capital after college.

When I'd branched out on my own, I'd started smart, with low-risk ventures. Then as my net income had doubled year over year, I'd diversified. My latest success stories were all in the technology sector. I'd also expanded into sports and entertainment.

We were becoming a powerhouse throughout the country, and there wasn't a state where I didn't have at least one interest.

Except Montana.

Ironically, the one area I hadn't established any sort of interest in was where my grandfather had filled the gap. He'd done it by giving a beautiful woman too much money.

He hadn't done her any favors. He'd set her up for failure by handing over that money. Maybe that had been his goal all along.

If Kerrigan took a step back and evaluated her business honestly, she'd see that she was overextended. She was smart and ambitious, but she'd tried to grow too fast, and her liquidity had paid the price. By selling some properties, lightening her debt load, she'd position herself for longer-term success.

I was doing her a favor by calling in my note.

Though I doubted she'd say *thank you*.

Nellie's line rang through to my phone.

"Yes?" I answered.

"Kerrigan, uh . . . Ms. Hale is on the line for you."

She'd called Nellie? This was new.

Granted, I'd told her to contact Nellie for any questions. Had she? No. She'd kept calling my personal number, and fool that I was, I hadn't blocked her. It was that damn kiss I couldn't get out of my head.

"What does she want?" I asked.

"You asked for a meeting tomorrow morning."

"Yes. For *you* to schedule it."

"Whoops."

"Nellie," I warned.

"What?" she asked, feigning innocence.

Christ. If Nellie was calling Kerrigan by her first name, then I suspected I wasn't the only one who got regular phone calls. Except Nellie must be taking Kerrigan's calls. "Tell her I'm busy."

"Then you can forget seeing her in the morning. She won't meet with you until you speak with her."

"Fine," I clipped, hitting the flashing red button for the other line. "Ms. Hale."

"Hello, Mr. Sullivan." That sugar-sweet voice was nothing like I'd been hearing in her voicemails. It was arrogant and taunting. The scales were no longer balanced in my favor.

I needed her time, something she'd been asking of me for nearly a month. And to get what I wanted, it was going to cost me.

"Nellie said you'd be in Calamity tomorrow and wanted to meet," she said.

For years, all my clients had referred to Nellie as Ms. Rivera. Apparently, Kerrigan and Nellie had become friends in less than a month.

"Yes, I'd like a few minutes of your time." Or an entire afternoon.

"Say please."

I gritted my teeth. "Please."

"In that case, no." God, she was loving this, wasn't she? The smirk in her voice was as clear as the Colorado sky.

"It's regarding my grandfather's last wishes."

"Oh." She paused. "In that case, I'll be at The Refinery by eight tomorrow morning. We can meet there."

I ended the call without a goodbye.

The details of Kerrigan and Grandpa's relationship were a mystery to me, though I had a vivid imagination. He'd always had a thing for strong, beautiful women, and she fit the mold.

Though at first glance, she didn't seem the type to screw an older man for money.

The idea of them together made my head spin and stomach crawl. He'd feasted on her lips. He'd known that she was soft and sweet.

I scrubbed a hand over my beard, wishing like hell I could forget my own kiss with that woman. But twenty-eight days later and there were times when I could still taste her on my tongue.

Had Grandpa actually cared for her? Or had he just lusted for a younger, stunning body? That was another mystery I didn't care to solve.

I shoved away from my desk, forgoing the work waiting, and left the office for my private elevator. With a swipe of my key card and a short trip up to the next floor, the doors opened to my penthouse.

Like my office, the exterior walls were mostly glass. The windows gave me the same view but even just one floor up, the city seemed quieter. Or maybe that was because here, in my home, I could breathe.

I'd spent a lot of hours staring out of my windows, pondering everything that had happened in the past seven months. The past seven years. And there'd been plenty of moments as of late that Kerrigan Hale had consumed my thoughts while I'd stood at the glass.

Why had I kissed her at the motel? Was it simply because she'd meant something to him? Had this need for revenge really turned me into such a miserable prick? Would I really have the nerve to steal her properties in two days?

Ruthless had been Grandpa's strategy. While I'd play that card when necessary—my letter to her had been one directly out of his playbook—I tended to take a fair approach with my clients.

Even before we'd met, Kerrigan had set me off-kilter. Why? She would be nothing to me. After this week, she'd be a distant memory. Did it matter what kind of relationship she'd had with Grandpa?

Now was not the time to search for answers. I jogged up the stairs to the upper floor, going straight for my bedroom and closet. With a travel bag packed, I returned to my office to grab my laptop.

Nellie was on the phone when I poked my head in to say goodbye, so I waved, then took the elevator to the garage.

After loading my car, I reversed out of my private space and used my personal entrance, then headed out of the city.

First, to stop by my parents' place and pick up Grandpa's ashes.

Then, to Calamity.

————

OTHER THAN THE colors of the trees, Calamity hadn't changed in the past month. Living in a booming section of Denver, I was used to seeing new construction. Window displays were constantly updated. Store signs were swapped out regularly as businesses failed and started.

But at first glance, nothing about Calamity had changed in a month. Nothing. It was oddly comforting.

I walked down First toward The Refinery, the street deserted except for the vehicles parked in front of the coffee shop and café. The sun peeked over the roofs from across the street and glinted off the shining windows of Kerrigan's gym.

The lights were on but the studio was empty. I went inside, escaping the morning chill, and stood by the reception desk, taking a moment to inspect the place. It, like the rest of Calamity, hadn't changed in twenty-nine days either.

Mirrors lined the longest wall on one side of the studio, making it seem twice as big. My shoes sank into the soothing gray mats beyond the tiled entryway. In the corner, a metal cage was stuffed with exercise balls. Stacked yoga mats were piled on one of the few shelves. Opposite the mirrors, a ballet bar had been mounted to the wall and it cut a honeyed-oak line against the white paint.

The studio was open, airy, and quite similar to many of the trendy fitness locations in LoDo. It didn't really fit in Calamity. It was too fresh. Too clean. Maybe it hadn't been designed for the town, but for the owner herself.

Kerrigan came rushing out of a short hallway at the back of the building and the moment she spotted me, her footsteps stuttered. "You're twenty minutes early."

"Good morning."

She frowned. "Morning."

Kerrigan was in another pair of yoga pants. The gray material wrapped around her slender thighs and made her legs look a mile long. She was barefoot and her sweater draped over her shoulders, the front forming a deep V and the loose sleeves falling past her knuckles.

"One minute." She held up a finger, then spun around, retreating the way she'd come.

With her hair twisted up, I had the perfect view of her top. The V cut just as low in the back as it did in the front. Beneath it was a bra with more straps than power poles had wires. They crisscrossed over her smooth skin, showing more toned muscle.

And her ass in those leggings was . . .

My cock jerked beneath my slacks.

"Fucking hell," I muttered, forcing my eyes away.

I hadn't been attracted to a woman in months. Why her? Why now?

Just don't fucking kiss her again. I sucked in a long breath, willing myself under control. Maybe that inhale would have worked, except her scent filled the air. The same scent I'd memorized when my lips had been on hers. Honeysuckle florals. Rich and sweet.

I could not—*would not*—get distracted by this woman. Any woman. I'd done that once and look where that had landed me.

"What a disaster," I muttered.

"Excuse me?"

I whirled around. Kerrigan was right behind me, her hands on her hips. "I said . . . what a disaster."

Her eyes flared and her mouth pursed into a thin line. "What, exactly, is a disaster?"

Me. I was the disaster. But answering her question with the truth would take more time than we had today. "This trip. It's doomed to be a disaster and before you start telling me how much you hate me, let me say that the disaster has nothing to do with you."

Not entirely true, but after a long drive yesterday and a fitful night of sleep at the motel, I didn't have the energy to argue with Kerrigan.

"Would you like to visit here or go somewhere else?" I asked.

"I was thinking we could go to the café."

I gestured to the door. "Lead the way."

She grabbed her purse from behind the reception counter. Then she pulled on a pair of tennis shoes and walked to the door, locking it behind us.

The walk to the café was short and silent. She crossed her arms over her chest and walked at a pace that would require anyone with a shorter inseam to jog. But the moment we stepped inside the café, her cold demeanor evaporated.

Well, not toward me, but toward the rest of the room.

A smile broke across her face and damn it, my heart skipped. The smile lit up her face and made those pretty brown eyes dance. My dick, swelling again, thought it was beautiful too.

"Hey, Kerrigan." A waitress waved as she carried a pot of coffee across the room. "Sit wherever you want."

"Thanks." Kerrigan waved back and led us to the only empty booth along the windows to the street.

I slid into my side of the table, ready to launch into the reason I was here. It would be better to get this over with before we could order and delay this meeting over the length of a meal.

"The reason—"

"Hi, Kerrigan." An older woman appeared at the end of

our booth. She bent low to give Kerrigan a hug, not sparing me a glance. "How are you, sweetie?"

"Good, Mrs. Jones. How are you?"

"Fine and dandy. I saw your parents at church yesterday. They look so well. I tried to convince your mom to tell me what skin cream she's using because I swear she hasn't aged a day in ten years."

Kerrigan laughed. "I'll raid her bathroom and make a list, then sneak it to you."

"You do that." Mrs. Jones laughed, then patted Kerrigan on the shoulder. "See you soon."

Kerrigan faced me and I opened my mouth, ready to speak, when once again, I was interrupted by a visitor. This time, it was the local sheriff if the badge and gun on his belt were anything to go by.

"Hey, Kerrigan."

"Hi, Duke."

He glanced at me and given the scowl on his face, I'd say he knew who I was. "All good here?"

"Yeah." She nodded. "Tell Lucy I'll call her later."

"Will do." He gave me one more stern look, then walked away.

I waited this time before opening my mouth, and sure enough, the moment the sheriff was gone, another person appeared to talk to Kerrigan about a raffle happening at the daycare and wondering if Kerrigan would donate a few classes at the gym.

Person followed person. Kerrigan was genuinely nice to each, even though it was obvious they were scoping me out. But she kept that breathtaking smile on her face for every conversation, seemingly unbothered by the intrusions.

It would be easier to deal with her if she weren't nice.

After another two visitors, the waitress finally got her own window of opportunity. She arrived with two ceramic coffee mugs, filled them both to the brim and left us with our menus.

"Popular today?" I asked when it seemed like the stream of endless guests had dried up.

Kerrigan shrugged and took a sip from her mug. "Not so much popular as just having lived here my whole life. Small town. It's hard not to know everyone."

"Ah." I took my own drink and leaned my elbows on the table.

The restaurant, like her gym, surprised me. From the outside, I'd expected a ghost-town-esque diner, greasy spoons included. But the interior looked to have been remodeled within the last decade. There was a chalkboard wall complete with today's specials. The white tile floor gleamed under the lights. And the tables, as befit the restaurant's name, were all white oak.

The waitress returned, a pad of paper in hand. "Ready to order?"

"I'll have the omelet special," Kerrigan said.

The waitress pivoted in my direction. "And for you?"

"Just coffee."

With a single nod, the waitress disappeared, leaving us alone.

"You're not eating?" Kerrigan asked.

"This won't take long." I held up a hand when she opened her mouth to protest. "I'm not here to discuss your contract."

"But Gabriel gave me an extension and—"

"My grandfather asked to have a portion of his ashes scattered at his cabin in the mountains."

She blinked and drawled, "Okay."

"He would like you to attend."

"Oh." Whatever irritation and frustration she had with me fell away. Her shoulders slumped. She swallowed hard. "I'd like that."

It was as clear as the Montana sky that she'd loved my grandfather. And for that reason, I needed to get the hell out of this booth.

Her loan was due tomorrow. We'd scatter Grandpa's ashes tomorrow.

And then I could forget about Kerrigan Hale.

CHAPTER FOUR

KERRIGAN

"THANKS FOR COVERING FOR ME, MOM."

"Of course. You know, if you worked at the dealership, you'd have a more flexible schedule. You wouldn't be tied to it like you are to this gym of yours."

I sighed, not wanting to get into this discussion. Again. "Do you have any questions? The first yoga class is at nine. Pilates at ten and barre at noon. Then the last yoga class at two. After that, it should be fairly quiet until one of the girls gets here at three thirty. They'll get everything ready for Body Pump tonight."

"You wrote it all down for me." She pointed to my sticky note. "I'll be fine."

"The instructors can always help if there's a problem." They were the real treasure at The Refinery.

We didn't have fancy treadmills or weight machines. There wasn't much walk-in traffic besides the occasional member who'd come in early to practice before the actual class began.

But the goal of this studio wasn't to compete with the

other gym in town. They could keep their machines and circuit rooms. The Refinery was a class-based facility like the ones you'd find in a city.

People of all ages were welcome here, including a once-a-week class for pregnant moms. There were a few men, but my membership was ninety-five percent female. Soon I hoped to offer something for kids, like karate or tae kwon do.

Or at least that had been the plan a month ago. As of today, everything was up in the air.

"You'd better get going." Mom shooed me toward the door. "Good luck and drive safe."

"Thanks." My luck seemed to have run out, so I wasn't holding my breath. "Call me if you need anything."

"I will." She took a seat in the chair behind the counter and pulled her Kindle from her purse. Before I was out the door, she was lost in her fictional world.

The familiar image of her, nose to book, was comforting on a day when my emotions were a tornado. How many books had Mom read over the years while working as the receptionist at Hale Motors? I could still see her there, so engrossed in a story that the only way to get her attention was to ring the bell on the front desk.

When I was younger, before the days of e-books, Mom hadn't gone anywhere without a paperback. Now it was her Kindle.

Mom was officially retired now—the day she'd decided to stop dying the grays out of her chestnut hair was the day she'd decided to quit. Dad was still as active as ever, working as the general manager. My brother, Zach, was one of the assistant managers. My uncle ran the shop. My other uncle was their accountant, and I had more than one cousin who worked as a mechanic. If I ever needed a job, they'd find a spot for me processing finance requests and parts orders.

But that was not my dream, something my family didn't quite seem to grasp.

Mom and Dad made sure to tell me how much easier my life would be if I took a nine-to-five at the dealership. My aunts and uncles said more of the same. The dealership had been founded by my granddad and he never missed the opportunity to remind me that the Hale family business could use another business-minded Hale.

Maybe that was my fate. As I climbed behind the wheel of my Explorer, I took a long look at my building. I rarely parked out front of the gym, not wanting to take a customer's space, but I'd left the spot in the alley for Mom's Cadillac.

Dad traded hers in every year, another dealership employee perk.

The building's windows sparkled in the morning sunlight. I'd splurged on the glass because it made such a bold statement—one that had taken me months to get approved by the town planners. Eventually they'd agreed to my *modern* touch and the day those windows had gone in, I'd nearly cried.

Both the studio and the loft apartment on the second floor were a far cry from what they'd been. Dark. Empty. Filthy. No one had occupied this particular downtown building in years, and scrubbing it clean had taken a lifetime supply of elbow grease.

Once upon a time, this had been Calamity's candy store. The words *Candy Shoppe* were barely visible in chipped white paint on the exterior brick wall.

The owners had gone bankrupt and closed the shop's doors when I was a kid. There'd been other occupants here but nothing that lasted. Maybe the building itself was cursed. Most of my financial problems had started when I'd added it to my list of projects.

Or maybe I'd been doomed after buying Widow Ashleigh's farmhouse.

No matter what, I was glad for the improvements I'd made. They were my small mark on this town. This building had rejoined the modern century and was no longer the sad, dilapidated eyesore on First.

Especially the windows. I'd never regret the windows or the small fortune they'd cost.

A fortune that hadn't been mine.

A fortune that I was supposed to pay back today.

The clock on the dash nagged that I needed to get on the road, so I reversed away from the gym and headed out of town. Nellie had emailed me directions to the cabin yesterday after I'd called and told her about my non-break-fast with Pierce.

The moment I'd agreed to join him, he'd slid out of the booth and disappeared. The man made no sense. He was ice cold and any rational woman would probably have written him off thirty days ago. But that kiss . . .

The sparks from that single kiss lingered on my lips.

That kiss portrayed an entirely different man, one I was sure could be found beneath that cold exterior, the man Gabriel had talked about over and over. That Pierce was in there somewhere. Because that Pierce was the man who'd kissed me senseless.

My phone rang as I reached the outskirts of town. "Hello."

"Hey," Nellie said. "Are you on your way?"

"Yep." My voice was shaky. I hoped that would stop

before I faced Pierce. I didn't want him to see me unsettled. "What can I expect today?"

"I don't know. He's not himself lately."

Nellie had said the same on more than one occasion. We'd developed a fast friendship and she'd been incredibly supportive, even though Pierce was her boss. It was also because of Nellie that Pierce seemed human.

The more she told me about his company and his clients, the more impossible it was not to feel singled out. Every interaction with Pierce felt . . . personal. The calls and emails that had gone unanswered. The letter and our argument on the sidewalk. It all felt personal, like I'd done something to offend him. But what?

I didn't have a damn clue. And neither did Nellie. I'd asked.

"Thanks for all your help, Nell."

"Always." There was a smile in her voice.

Nellie had been a godsend this past month. It had all started the day after the kiss, when Pierce had ordered me to deal with his assistant. I'd called her, per his instruction, to request a meeting. A sober, non-kissing meeting. We'd ended up talking for hours and since then, I'd spoken to her every day.

Nellie was the one who'd told me to just keep calling his personal line and emailing him directly.

Wear him down.

That had been her advice. And since I didn't have a lot of other options, I was taking it.

Maybe I could hire a lawyer and fight Pierce, but lawyers cost money and right now, the expense seemed silly. It was my word against the signed contract, and without Gabriel here to back me up, I'd lose.

"Stay tough," she said. "We'll figure this out. Don't forget, I'm your secret weapon."

I laughed. "What's *Mr. Sullivan* going to do when he finds out you're a double agent?"

"Ha! *Mr. Sullivan* can kiss my ass. What he's doing to you is wrong, and if he'd stop being such a stubborn mule, he'd realize it too."

"I don't want you to get in trouble over me."

"I won't."

"But—"

"Trust me," she said. "It will be fine."

"Okay." I blew out a long breath. "Thanks."

"You keep saying that."

"I mean it."

"I know you do. And I have to say thanks too."

"For what?"

"For going today. I'm glad he won't be there alone."

My heart twisted. "Any idea why Gabriel would want Pierce and me to do this together?"

"Probably because you were both important to him. But I didn't know Gabriel well. Mostly I knew him through Pierce, and their relationship was, um . . . strained."

Strained? I wanted to ask but bit my tongue. Talking to Nellie already felt like prying into Pierce's life. This was the man who'd likely crush my dreams in the next few hours.

"All right, I'm probably going to lose service soon," I said as I sped down the highway and the mountains drew closer.

"Talk soon?" Nellie asked.

"Definitely. Bye."

Nellie had been a wonderful surprise from this disaster. Our conversations were rarely about Pierce and we had a lot in common, like our love of wine and Netflix rom-coms, the cheesier the better. We were even into the same yoga gear and skin-care products.

Would it be awkward with her after my business with Pierce was over? Maybe. But that was tomorrow's worry, because I had plenty on today's plate.

Gabriel's cabin was located by one of the most popular ski resorts in Montana. As a kid, my parents had brought us here once or twice, but as I wound up the mountain road, following Nellie's directions, I realized much had changed since I'd visited last.

The place had boomed after a developer had come in with money and glamour. Homes and condos sprouted up where there'd once been open fields and thick forests. The only thing familiar was the ski hill itself and the swaths cut through the evergreens.

Next to a new, mammoth ski lodge was a towering hotel. There were signs for ziplining and gondola rides to the tallest peak. I doubted I could afford a lift ticket these days. Though I couldn't afford a latte, so that wasn't saying much.

I bypassed the turnoff for the ski area and continued on to the club. A black wrought-iron gate greeted me, and I punched in the code Nellie had sent with the directions.

Driving through the opening was like stepping beyond the veil into a world of money and opulence and power.

Every home I passed was larger than the next, though *home* wasn't the right word. These were mansions. The exteriors were all variations of the same, dark-stained wood or log to blend into nature.

"Whoa," I said as I reached the end of a private lane. "This is not a cabin."

It was a ski lodge of its own.

There was no need to check the address. The house screamed Gabriel.

It was lavish, but rustic. The architecture was complicated with varying roof slants and a covered expanse around the front door. The natural stone and heavy beams coordinated with the surrounding trees. Enormous windows faced the magnificent view at all angles. At the moment, they were all dark.

The clock showed I was thirty minutes early, but I parked in the space in front of the garage and climbed out, breathing in the scent of dirt and moss and mountain air.

I'd opted for black slacks today and a soft gray sweater. My patent wedge heels pinched at my toes but today, I'd wanted to look nice. For Gabriel.

And, though I'd never admit it out loud, for Pierce.

His handsome face unnerved me. Pierce oozed confidence and charisma. His strong body radiated power, and the clothes he wore screamed money.

Each time he'd come to Calamity, I'd been at work, wearing leggings and yoga tops while he'd been in three-piece suits. The navy jacket he'd worn yesterday had been perfectly tailored to his broad shoulders. The fabric had looked so soft and smooth that I'd had to clasp my hands together to keep from touching the sleeve.

Everything about him elicited a physical reaction. How unfair was that? There weren't many single men in Calamity. Why couldn't I be attracted to one of them? Why did I have to feel this desire for the man trying to ruin me?

Today, I wasn't going to let this chemistry or magnetism or whatever the hell it was fluster me. Today, I was here for Gabriel.

So I squared my shoulders and marched to the door,

hesitating only a second before pressing the bell. Then I stood and waited, shifting from foot to foot as I clasped my hands in front of me to keep them from fidgeting.

"Maybe this was a bad idea," I muttered as the moments passed and no one came to answer. Was he even here? This was the place, right?

I was seconds away from giving up and driving home when the door whipped open.

"You're early," Pierce snapped.

"Uh . . ." My mouth went dry.

Pierce was not wearing his signature three-piece suit. No, he was in a towel.

Nothing but a plush, white, terry-cloth towel wrapped around his narrow waist.

There were abs. A lot of abs. And the V at his hips. His arms were roped with muscle upon muscle and a few water droplets cascaded down his sculpted chest.

"I said ten."

I jerked, forcing my eyes up and away from all that skin. "Sorry."

He frowned and stepped away from the door, opening it for me to come inside. He closed it behind him and stalked away without a word through the entryway and toward a hall.

The rational part of my brain told me not to stare at his back as he walked but the irrational side won out and I stood, slack-jawed and gawking at the corded contours of his back and a towel that did nothing to hide the curve of his ass.

A low throb bloomed in my center.

"Damn it," I groaned when he disappeared around a corner. As if the mental image of him in a suit wasn't hard enough to erase.

Needing anything else to do but stand there and drool, I took a few steps deeper into the house and poked around the living room. My heels clicked with each step across the smooth hickory floor. I skimmed my fingertips over the textured wall painted a shade of tan. The furniture was rustic, a mix of patterned upholstery and cognac leather.

I'd spent a lot of time in recent years cultivating my own style. A budgeted style. There were paintings on the walls that likely cost more than my house. The live-edge coffee table was clearly custom built, and the slate stones for the floor-to-ceiling fireplace had probably been imported from Argentina.

The cabin was a dream, and given that I'd never be able to afford a single element from the home, let alone all of them combined, I lingered in the room, appreciating it entirely.

The room smelled like Gabriel, spice and expensive cologne. I heard his hearty laugh bouncing off the beams in the vaulted ceiling. I pictured him sitting on the couch, a fire crackling and roaring in the hearth.

There was a frame on the end table but it had been turned on its face. I checked the hallway—no sign of Pierce—and picked up the photo. The picture was of Gabriel and Pierce. When they stood side by side, their similarities were uncanny.

Both were tall, with Pierce standing slightly straighter than Gabriel. They had the same dark hair, though Pierce's lacked the streaks of gray. Gabriel had always been clean-shaven and Pierce's beard set them apart. But they had the same umber eyes and wide white smiles.

"Huh."

"Find something interesting?"

I jerked and looked up.

Pierce came striding my way, buttoning a cuff of his green button-down shirt. He was wearing jeans. His feet were bare. Add in the sexy beard and this was yet another version of the man I could not pin down.

"You're smiling in this picture," I said. There was no use pretending I hadn't been snooping.

"And?"

"And it makes you look like him." Handsome. Kind.

Pierce's gaze hardened. His jaw clenched.

Being compared to Gabriel Barlowe, of all the men in the world, should have been a compliment but clearly I was missing something.

Pierce stalked over as I returned the photo to the end table. I placed it up but the moment he was close enough, he turned it down.

Yeah, definitely missing something.

"Shall we?" Pierce motioned to the door.

I nodded and walked that way, weaving through the furniture and waiting in the entryway.

He came over and pulled on a pair of loafers. Then he picked up a plain white box from the console table, tucking it under his arm before stepping outside and marching across the patio.

I followed, rushing to keep up with his long strides. We rounded the house, and I realized my mistake. So busy appreciating the furnishings inside, I hadn't taken in the view beyond the windows.

The house sat on top of a hill, and forest disappeared down the slope for miles and miles. Peaks. Valleys. The ranges in the distance started green and faded to blue as they inched closer to the horizon.

"This is beautiful."

Pierce glanced over his shoulder as we passed by a large pool set into a concrete slab. The water was steaming. A hot tub, then, built beneath another roof overhang.

The scent of chlorine hit my nose and I drew it in, the smell always reminding me of summers playing with friends at the Calamity public pool.

Pierce stepped off the patio and onto a stone path that interrupted a manicured lawn. We followed it past a firepit surrounded by benches and chairs to the edge of the property, where the taller, native grasses swayed in the slight breeze.

Without a word, Pierce tore into the box and pulled out the plastic bag inside. Before I could even contemplate what was happening, he ripped open the sack, turned it upside down and then . . .

The wind caught Gabriel's ashes and carried them away.

My mouth fell open and I stood stunned, watching as the ashes floated away.

As Gabriel floated away.

Thrown out like trash.

Pierce abruptly turned, like he was done with this, but I shot out a hand and caught him by the elbow.

"That's it?"

"That's it," he rumbled.

"Don't you want to say anything?"

He glanced at my hand, still firm on his arm. "No."

This was not the man Gabriel had loved. This was not the man Nellie defended. This was not the man who'd kissed me. Pierce was being, well . . . an asshole.

I blinked. "Who *are* you?"

My question seemed to make him tired. The irritation on

his face vanished and his shoulders slumped. "I don't have anything to say."

"Maybe I do."

He sighed but turned back to face the view.

Gabriel's ashes had disappeared.

"Well?" Pierce prompted, standing with his shoulder beside mine.

"I've never met anyone like your grandpa before. He had this personality that drew you in." I wasn't sure where I was going with this, but the words came from my heart and if that was all I could give Gabriel today, then it was better than silence.

Pierce remained quiet. He kept his eyes trained forward, only giving me his handsome profile as I spoke.

"I will miss his belly laugh, the one I didn't hear often enough. I'll miss hearing him cuss under his breath whenever he ran a yellow light. I'll miss how he called me Kerri. No one really shortens my name."

Pierce stood so still, I wondered if hearing this hurt. "Sounds like you knew him well."

I shrugged. "Well enough. I cared for him a great deal."

"When did you meet?"

"I met him three weeks after I graduated from college. I was in Bozeman, working for this realtor as her bookkeeper-slash-receptionist-slash-general-lackey. She'd actually hired me before graduation as an unpaid intern and she gave me a job once I finished my degree. I was studying for my realtor license exam and sitting at the front desk in her office the first time I met Gabriel."

He'd told me over dinner once that it had been my name that had drawn him in. He'd had a college girlfriend—*in the dark ages*, as he'd teased—named Kerrigan. He'd called her Kerri too.

"I don't even know how it happened. My boss was running late so I sat and talked with him as he waited. We just . . . hit it off. He didn't buy a place from her that trip or the next, but each time he'd come into the office and chat with me."

For nearly two years, we'd have conversations in the lobby of that real estate office.

"He never did buy anything from her. My old boss." I smiled. "It irritated her to no end that Gabriel would come to talk with me before she'd show him properties. And when he bought this place—"

"He bought it straight from the club," Pierce said.

"Yeah." By that point, he'd stopped coming into the real estate office. Whenever he came to town, he'd call and invite me to dinner. "He believed in me. He believed in my dreams. I wish I could tell him thank you."

Thank you. I sent that silent whisper into the wind.

"There were times when I wavered," I said past the lump in my throat. "It was him who'd remind me of the end goal."

"Which is?"

"To live in Calamity. Raise a family here if I ever have one. Support myself and the community. A lot of small towns in Montana die off. There aren't enough businesses to compete with the larger towns like Bozeman or Missoula or Billings. Not a lot of people our age want to move to a town twenty years behind the times. It needs fresh ideas. It needs energy."

"And you're that energy?"

"No. I'm just one person. But there's potential in Calamity. For me and maybe others too."

Pierce didn't respond as he stared toward the mountains illuminated by the morning sun.

"Gabriel made my dreams possible. I think he did that for a lot of people with his company."

"My grandfather was ruthless."

"Maybe so. But I'll always be grateful that I had the chance to know him. I loved him. And I will miss him. Terribly."

Pierce faced me. "Are we done?"

"Why are there only two of us here?" I blurted, even though I wasn't sure I wanted the answer to my question. "Because he was ruthless?"

"No." He shook his head. "He didn't want a funeral. My parents have the other portion of his ashes and are taking them to Italy."

"Ah." I nodded, nearly crumbling with relief that Gabriel hadn't been so awful that no one would come to his funeral. "And you got stuck here. With me."

"Now are we done?"

"Not yet." Whether Pierce liked it or not, he could stand here and he could listen to me say a few nice things about Gabriel. "He was kind to me. He taught me a lot. He took me under his wing and gave me courage. Maybe I didn't know him as well as you, but the man I knew was a good friend. And I'm glad I can be here today to say goodbye. If no one else will talk about loving him, then I will."

Pierce stiffened beside me, his eyes cast to the distance.

"Thank you for inviting me today. I realize you didn't have to, but I appreciate it."

He gave me a single nod.

"I'll get out of your hair."

But before I could walk away, it was his turn to stop me. "Ms. Hale."

Ms. Hale. I didn't hide my eye roll. "*Mr. Sullivan.*"

The corner of his mouth twitched. "Your contract is due today."

"I'm aware. And I have no money for you."

I'd put the farmhouse on the market. I'd done the bare minimum with my duplex and listed it as well. I'd hoped either or both would sell, but duplexes weren't as popular as single-family homes and a woman had been murdered in that farmhouse. No local was going to buy it since everyone in the county knew the story. And the chance of an outsider moving to Calamity this time of year was slim.

"You're overextended," Pierce said.

"Yep. And broke." Brutal honesty had always been Gabriel's style. It normally worked for me too.

"Bankruptcy saves a lot of businesses," he said, and it might as well have been a knife to my heart.

"You won't get your money if I declare bankruptcy. And I would never do that to Gabriel."

"Gabriel is dead."

"Not in here." I pressed a hand to my heart. "I'll pay you back. Whatever it takes. You can either trust in that, like he did, or you can take what you have to take."

He didn't say a word. He just stood there and stared.

So I decided to take my leave.

"Kerrigan."

I froze at my name in that rugged, deep voice. "Yes?"

"Sixty days. Sell something. Consolidate. Get some renters. If you want to run your business, then run it smart. My grandfather would have told you the same thing."

Yes, he would have. "Thank you."

"Don't thank me." He nodded to the mountains. "Thank him."

"No, I'm thanking you."

His dark eyes softened. His gaze flicked to my mouth. Then he was gone, striding toward the house. "Good luck, Ms. Hale."

CHAPTER FIVE

PIERCE

TWO MONTHS LATER...

"Tell me this is the last one, Steve."

"This is the last one."

"Thank God." After this, there'd be no more of Grandpa's requests from the grave.

He chuckled and stood from his chair, picking up the wool coat he'd draped over the back. "Sure is cold out today."

"It is." I steepled my hands in front of my chin, my mind not on the weather. "It's been months since his death. He told you to wait this long?"

Steve nodded. "He was very clear in his wishes."

"What if I had already trashed everything in the cabin by now?"

He shrugged on his wool coat. "Did you?"

"No."

"Then I guess Gabriel assumed you wouldn't."

The bastard had probably known I'd avoid everything about that property. Which I had.

"May I ask . . . when did he do all of this? When did he

add in these demands? It had to have been recently." If it had been done years ago, he wouldn't have had to force me to the cabin. Because that was exactly what these requests were doing. The ashes. Now this. Even in death, Grandpa was still pulling my strings.

"About three months before he passed."

Three months.

A month after my divorce.

In a way, it was like he'd known he would die sooner rather than later. Though probably not in a plane crash. But the only reason he would have added this level of detail to his last requests was he'd known that I would never have spoken to him again.

Whether by accident or age, my relationship with him had ended the day he'd betrayed me. He'd been dead to me already.

Was this his way of punishing me after his death? His way of coercing me into doing what he damn well would have known I didn't want to do?

"I don't understand any of this." I sighed, then stood and walked around my desk, escorting Steve to the door.

"Your grandfather was a complicated man," he said. "But he always had his reasons."

"This must have been to torture me."

He grinned. "Spend a week up there. Clear out his things. You were going to sell it anyway, right?"

"As soon as the time limit has passed and I'm clear from the club's stipulations."

"Then you'd have to do it anyway."

"I was going to pay someone to clear it out."

"You still could. He's gone, Pierce. He can't *make* you do anything."

I frowned. We both knew that wasn't actually true. Just like I hadn't ignored his wishes to invite Kerrigan and scatter his ashes, I wouldn't ignore the letter Steve had delivered today either.

"Thanks." I shook his hand and opened the door as he nodded and headed down the hallway. Then I returned to my desk and picked up Grandpa's letter.

"What the hell are you doing, old man?" I touched the paper, taking in the familiar handwriting. I'd opened it and immediately recognized the tiny script. It was strange to see it again. Even stranger to feel so much from a few short sentences.

PIERCE,

As you know, the cabin is yours. I'd like you to be the one who clears out my personal belongings. Not your mother or a member of the staff. You.

Grandpa

READING those words was like a blow to the chest. In typical Gabriel Barlowe fashion, he'd skipped the sentiments. No hello. No sincerely. No emotion, just orders.

I hated that I missed him.

In the past two months, I'd done my best to not think of Grandpa and the destruction he'd brought to my life. Instead, I'd done everything in my power to erase him.

Merging Barlowe Capital with Grays Peak and incorporating his portfolio into mine was nearly complete. There were growing pains since my company had doubled overnight, but my executive team was ironing those out.

Every client had been notified. Employees had been moved under my umbrella. We were all working from a single letterhead.

With one exception.

Kerrigan Hale.

Hers was the only account from Barlowe's portfolio that hadn't been assigned to a member of my team. Instead, I'd kept her to myself.

It. I'd kept it to myself.

I'd been telling myself for two months that the reason was because she wasn't a long-term client. If Kerrigan didn't pay, I'd delegate and let an account manager seize the necessary assets.

Lies. Excuses. The real reason wasn't one I was going to admit, even to myself.

Every day, I waited for an email to appear in my inbox. Every day, I wondered if she'd call. In the past two months, Kerrigan had all but vanished.

Which should have made it easier to forget about her. Why couldn't I forget about her? Why was it her face that popped into my mind during my sleepless nights?

Her voice. Her smile. Her eyes, the color of the most exquisite chocolate. That chestnut hair and her slender body. Kerrigan Hale was the ghost who haunted my wet dreams.

My cell phone rang and I picked it up, hoping to see a familiar Montana phone number. Instead, the screen read *Cal Stark.*

"Hey," I answered with a smile. My best friend didn't call often during football season.

"I need to get out of Tennessee."

I chuckled. "You're a free agent after next season. Maybe the Broncos need a new quarterback. Move back to Denver."

He groaned. "They've got that hotshot kid they recruited from Michigan."

"Seattle? You crushed them on Sunday. They need some tenured talent."

"Maybe. But their GM is cheap, and I don't want to take a pay cut."

Cal's contract with Tennessee was for $39 million a year. He was the second-highest-paid quarterback in the league.

But a pay cut would not only bruise his ego, it would mess with Cal's retirement plans. Another couple of years and he'd walk away from football with money to last for generations if he was smart.

And though Cal had a reputation for being an asshole, he was very, very smart.

"I just want to be done with this season," he said. "We're only halfway through and I'm already tired."

"Maybe you should retire."

"Maybe. I don't know. Football has been my life for a long time. But damn I'm sick of Nashville. I went to the store today, popped in to get some steaks. Should have sent my assistant but he's about to get fired and I didn't want to talk to him. So I just went myself. Ten minutes. Fifteen, tops. Got mobbed with photographers and people wanting autographs. One guy came up to me, decked out head-to-toe in Packers gear, and told me exactly how I screwed up in the game they won against us in the preseason. People around us videoed the whole thing on their phones so I just had to stand there and listen."

"You really think that'll change if you move to a new city?"

"No," he muttered. "Maybe I should retire."

"You can come work for me. Nellie was telling me she needs an assistant."

He barked a laugh. "Not for every dollar to your name."

I laughed too.

Nellie and Cal had a hate-hate relationship. Putting them in the same room together always ended with a screaming fight.

This spring, I'd made the mistake of telling Cal that I was heading to Hawaii for a week. I'd needed to clear my head after the divorce. He'd decided to fly over as a surprise and join me. Except Nellie had come along too, both of them wanting to offer moral support.

The house I owned there was seven thousand square feet and the two of them could have easily avoided crossing paths. Instead, they'd woken me from a dead sleep and I'd had to break up a fight at three o'clock in the morning.

Cal had left early the next day. Nellie had informed me that if I ever let Cal sleep under the same roof as her, she'd never speak to me again. To this day, neither of them would tell me what that fight had been about.

Or why when I'd broken up the fight, Cal had been wearing only boxers and Nellie had been in a robe.

"What else is new?" he asked.

"Work. I've got to go to Montana again."

"More shit with Gabriel?"

I picked up the letter, scanning it once more. "He requested that I go through his belongings at the mountain house."

"He was a bastard, Pierce. Say fuck it, sell that place, and move on with your life. If you want a mountain house, build one in Colorado."

Cal wasn't wrong. But now my curiosity was in play and

damn it, Grandpa had probably counted on that too. What exactly had he left at the cabin?

"You've got a game tomorrow, right?" I asked.

"Yeah. We're at home so I can sleep in my own bed."

"Good luck."

"Thanks."

Nellie knocked on the door, then peeked her head inside. "Pierce? Oh, sorry."

I waved her in and held up a finger for her to wait. "I'd better let you go, Cal."

Nellie's lip curled as she came to the desk.

"Nellie's here," I said. "She says hello."

Nellie flipped me off.

"Gotta go." Cal hung up.

I grinned and set the phone down as Nellie took a chair across from my desk.

"Why are you friends with him?" she asked.

"Cal's not that bad."

She scoffed. "He's deplorable."

Cal was just . . . Cal. He was arrogant and bold. He was naturally talented and extremely competitive, which made him a star athlete. But he had a nasty temper that he occasionally let loose, especially after losing a game. More than once he'd blown a fuse on camera, so his reputation wasn't the best.

But the two of us had been friends since high school.

Cal worked hard and always had my back. He'd gone to Harvard with me for college, and though he'd been recruited to play football, he'd taken the opportunity to earn a world-class education in business.

He gave millions to charity. He loved his mother fiercely.

He was a good man, but Nellie, like the rest of the world, didn't see that version of Cal.

He didn't let people see that version.

"What's up?" I asked.

"Jasmine called. Again."

"Okay."

"Are you going to call her back?"

"I sent her a text last week."

Nellie scowled. "Pierce, we need to talk about this."

"Not yet. Please?" I sent her a pleading glance. I wasn't ready. Not yet.

"Soon," she warned.

"Soon." I had a little more time. "Anything else?"

"Your noon meeting needed to reschedule so you've got an hour free that I'm stealing so we can go through some contracts. I'll order us lunch. What do you feel like?"

"Whatever you want." I shrugged, then handed over the letter from Grandpa. "Read this first."

Her eyes were wide by the time she read the last line. "I don't understand this. It's been months, and this feels . . . cruel. I don't think you should go. Not after what happened. He's gone and doesn't get to order you around. Not anymore. My advice is to tear this up, sell that cabin and be done with him."

If only Nellie knew how much she and Cal had in common. They both usually gave me the same advice.

"No, I'm going to go."

"Why?"

"Steve said this was the last request. Maybe there's something important he stashed in his office up there. Something to do with Barlowe. I don't know. But if I don't go . . ."

"You'll feel guilty."

I nodded. "I don't want anything hanging over my head. Not where he's concerned."

"Understandable."

"I'll head to the cabin and sort through his things. There can't be much. And when I leave there, I'll be done with everything in Montana."

Nellie arched an eyebrow. "Even Kerrigan?"

I opened my mouth to say *yes* but the word wouldn't come off my tongue.

Nellie's expression was the definition of smug.

It was impossible to hide anything from her. She knew I hadn't handed Kerrigan's contract off to an account manager. She also knew that I'd been keeping an eye on real estate in Calamity—she'd caught an open browser window on my monitor weeks ago.

Kerrigan had put the farmhouse on the market. So far, she'd dropped the price twice, yet there didn't appear to be any movement. One half of her duplex had been rented but the other still appeared in the weekly classifieds along with the studio apartment above The Refinery.

I assumed Nellie was still talking to her on a regular basis but hadn't let myself ask. The number of times Kerrigan Hale crossed my mind each day was no one's problem but my own.

Yet she hadn't reached out. She also hadn't sent a payment. There'd been no emails begging for an audience. No calls asking for another extension. I'd stalked her social media accounts a week ago, curiosity besting me late one night.

In every photo of herself at the gym, Kerrigan wore a smile. A beautiful, sparkling smile I couldn't seem to get out of my head.

Maybe if she hadn't told me how she'd met Grandpa. Maybe if she hadn't spoken about him with such admiration and respect. Maybe if I hadn't felt a semblance of that affection myself, I would have been able to let her go.

It didn't really matter. Kerrigan's loan was coming due, and it was time to let it go. To let all of it go.

"How miserable is my calendar next week?"

Nellie winced. "Miserable."

"Clear it anyway." It would be a train wreck when I came back, but I wanted this done. "Let's get through as much as we can today. Then I'll head out tomorrow."

"Do you want to fly or drive?"

"Drive."

I'd take this one last trip.

And bid farewell to Montana.

———

"YOU'RE HERE for the week, correct?"

"Yes, just the week," I told the cabin's caretaker.

"Very good." He nodded. "I'm glad you made it before the storm. It's blowing in hard."

I glanced past him to the windows and the cloud-covered sky. It was nearly dark already and it was only four. "I'm glad I made it too."

When I'd hit a blizzard in Wyoming, I'd almost considered turning back.

"If the snow gets bad, the roads will be awful," he said. "I'd recommend staying close to home. But we've loaded the fridge and the pantry. I can always come over on the snowmobile if you need anything else. We keep plenty on hand for the whole club and there aren't many people here this week."

"Thank you."

"My pleasure, Mr. Sullivan. Please call me or the club office if you need anything at all."

"Appreciated." I escorted him to the door, then closed it as he headed out into the cold.

I shivered and walked to the fireplace, holding out my hands to the flames. A chill had burrowed under my skin and even though I'd been inside for thirty minutes, I couldn't seem to get warm.

The scent of wood, ash and furniture polish clung to the air. A cleaning crew had swept through the place after Nellie's call yesterday, alerting them I was headed up. I hoped that soup was part of the foodstuffs they'd left for me because I didn't have the energy to cook.

I didn't have the energy for much.

Last night, after a grueling day of work to prepare for a week I really couldn't afford to take off, I'd retreated to the penthouse around midnight to pack and sleep for a few hours. Then because of the weather report, I'd woken around three to hit the road.

Maybe it was just the lack of sleep, but I hadn't felt great all day. After thirteen hours on the road, a slow trip thanks to the storm in Wyoming, I felt more like roadkill than a road warrior.

There were emails and phone calls to return, but all I wanted was to sleep. But instead, I went to the state-of-the-art kitchen and made myself a cup of coffee. The sooner I got this trip over with, the better.

With a hot mug in hand, I forced myself up the stairs and down the hallway to the master bedroom. Grandpa's bedroom. I'd avoided this room the last time I'd come here, choosing to sleep in the guest suite. Of all the rooms, the master would be the worst to go through. And I might as well get it over with.

Not much could make this day worse.

The closet was empty except for a red ski coat he must have left behind. I tugged it from the hanger—it could be the start to my donate pile. The bathroom was empty except for some stocked toiletries that the club crew had brought over this morning. They had an outdated list because bottles of women's shampoo and conditioner were on the counter.

Dismissing them both, I went to the nightstand, where there was only one photo. I swiped it up and stalked out of the room, flipping off the lights. Then I took the photo to the garbage can in the kitchen and tossed it inside.

That photo should have been thrown out months ago. "Fucking bastard."

This whole trip was a mistake. It truly was his way of torturing me. Keeping that photo, forcing *me* to toss it out, was sadistic.

I pinched the bridge of my nose, my head beginning to throb at the temples. Then I took a long gulp of coffee, still feeling cold.

One room for today was enough. I dumped out the rest of my coffee and walked out of the kitchen for the living room, planning on sitting down and watching Cal's game. Then I was going to bed.

I was nearly at the couch when the doorbell rang.

"Ugh," I groaned and made my way to the door, not feeling like putting on a happy face for the club staff. I yanked the door open, a blast of cold wind hitting me in the face. I blinked and swatted at the snow blowing my way, only to find that it wasn't the caretaker on my stoop.

It was Kerrigan.

"Hi," she said.

Her cheeks were flushed. Her nose was rosy, and behind her, the storm raged over the mountains.

"What are you doing here?"

"Nellie said you'd be here."

Christ. These women were testing my sanity.

Another gust of wind blew Kerrigan's chestnut hair around her face and I stretched forward, taking her by the elbow and tugging her inside, shutting out the storm.

She stomped her boots on the rug. "I'm going to make this quick."

"Your loan is due tomorrow." Why was that the first thing out of my mouth? Maybe to remind myself that she was strictly a professional acquaintance so I wouldn't do something stupid like kiss her again.

"I have a check." She dove into her handbag, pulling out a folded piece of paper and thrusting it into my hand. "Here."

I opened it and looked at the amount. Forty thousand, six hundred twenty-three dollars.

"That's not everything," she said.

"Not even close." It came out sharper than I'd meant, and the look of sheer humiliation on Kerrigan's face was my punishment.

"That's what I have," she said. "It's a dent. A little dent, but a dent all the same. And I have a plan to discuss with you."

"And you couldn't have done it over the phone or email?"

"The last time I tried that tactic, you ignored me for thirty days. I'm sticking with what works."

"So you just show up at my house?"

"Desperate times, Mr. Sullivan." She raised her chin and put on a brave face. I'd seen the same the day I'd tossed Grandpa's ashes into the wind and she'd stood her ground, making me listen. I was glad I had.

Kerrigan opened her mouth to tell me whatever it was she was going to tell me.

But before she could speak, the power went out.

CHAPTER SIX

KERRIGAN

"UH . . ." A hum resonated through the dark house, then the lights flashed on. "Generator?"

Pierce nodded and tucked the check I'd given him into a jeans pocket. "Come in."

"Actually, I'd better get going."

Note to self: Never listen to Nellie again. Coming here had been a horrible idea. Why had I let her talk me into this? Was I really so desperate that I'd invade Pierce's life to get his attention? Apparently, yes.

Spinning for the door, I spoke over my shoulder. "Sorry to bother you."

"Wait." Pierce's hand shot out and landed on the door before I could yank it open and retreat into the blizzard. "You can't drive in this."

"Oh, I'll be fine. I'm a Montanan. Driving through snow-storms is practically an addendum to the driver's ed exam."

The roads had been awful on the way up here but not impassable. I'd probably make it home fine, right? It was already dark. That would make it, er . . . exciting? The trip would take me three times as long but if I made it before midnight, I'd call it a win.

I could do this. I had to do this. Staying here was not an option. I felt stupid enough as it was. Maybe I could drive down the street, park and sleep in my car to wait this one out. Well, Mom's car.

I'd sold my Explorer so I could write Pierce that check.

"Kerrigan," Pierce warned, shifting closer.

He was standing so close. His spicy cologne drifted to my nose and I drew in the expensive aroma. Rich sandalwood. Leather. Spice. Pierce smelled . . . oh God, he smelled good. That scent brought me right back to the night of the motel and the kiss.

"I can't let you drive in this weather." Pierce towered over me, his voice low and soothing.

I dragged my gaze up his hard chest and when I reached those dark eyes, I couldn't breathe. In the past two months, I'd forgotten just how handsome he was. I'd forgotten about that sharp jaw and sexy beard. The memory of his eyes, framed by dark lashes, had faded. Even his lips were softer than I'd remembered.

A rush of desire curled in my lower belly.

Oh, hell. I was entirely, irrationally attracted to the man out to ruin my life.

I most definitely could *not* stay here. This house was probably five thousand square feet, minimum, and it was much, much too small. Pierce needed to return to Colorado. I'd stay in Montana. Wyoming would be a lovely buffer.

"I should go." I tore my gaze from his and reached for the door's handle, yanking it open despite his hand still braced on the surface. The moment it was cracked, a blast of frigid air slapped me in the face and a flurry of snow rushed into the house.

The cold set me on my heels and when I shielded my face with a hand and looked out, I could barely see past the overhang of the porch.

Shit. This wasn't just a blizzard. This was a whiteout.

"You are a stubborn, stubborn woman." Pierce took my elbow and tugged me away from the door so he could shut out the storm. Then he leveled me with a scowl that—*damn it*—only made him look hotter. "Come inside."

Without waiting for me, he turned on his sock-covered heels and strode through the entryway, disappearing to the living room.

I tipped my head to the ceiling. "Why do I make such bad decisions?"

"Like I said, you're a stubborn woman. And probably because you let Nellie talk you into this particular bad decision."

I cringed. *Another note to self: Pierce has superhuman hearing.* "That was a rhetorical question to the universe."

"Are you coming in here or will you be hovering beside the door as we wait this storm out? That's not a rhetorical question, by the way."

I pursed my lips and pulled off my knee-high boots. Then I shrugged off my jacket and hung it on the rack in the entryway before following Pierce to the living room.

The scent of fire and warmth filled the room, chasing away the chill.

Pierce was sitting on the leather couch closest to the fire, his elbows on his knees as he leaned toward the blaze.

"I'm sorry for intruding." I chose the armchair farthest from him.

"Are you?" He smirked.

"Yes."

"What did Nellie tell you?"

"That you'd be here for a few days and if I wanted you to hear me out, the only way to do it was in person."

Her logic had made sense given that I'd spent my first thirty days calling and emailing him with no success. The only progress I'd made with Pierce had been the last time we were here. So her logic had clicked and once again, I was back in the camp of desperate times calling for desperate measures.

"I have a plan."

"And I have a headache." He sighed. "This storm is going to last for a while. Let's save the plan for another time."

I opened my mouth but clamped it shut when his shoulders slumped forward. "Okay."

"That's it?" He glanced my way, his eyes dropping to my legs before he turned his attention to the fire once more.

Was there something wrong with my clothes? I wore skinny jeans and a thick, oversized tan turtleneck that I'd stolen from Larke's closet because I'd sold all of my nice sweaters on eBay.

Cutting Pierce that check hadn't been easy, but dreams meant sacrifices, and thankfully, I had a younger sister who loved clothes and was my size.

Pierce wasn't dressed in a suit, but casually in a black quarter-zip sweater with a red and gray plaid shirt underneath. His jeans were a dark wash and I suspected that his ensemble was made entirely of designer labels. No closet-raided clothes for him.

"Can I get you anything?" he asked, sinking deeper into

the couch. He leaned heavily against an armrest like it was the only thing keeping him off the floor.

"No, thanks. Are you okay? Besides the headache."

"I'm just tired. Cold. The drive up was long." He blinked but it was more like closing his eyes for two seconds, then opening them again.

"I'm sorry." Idiot. I was an idiot. Nellie wasn't here so I was mentally shouldering her with half the blame.

She'd called me last night and told me that Pierce was coming to Montana. She knew how hard I'd been working and had promised that if I approached him, he'd listen. All I'd hoped for was a few minutes for him to hear me out. Nellie was certain that if he knew my plan, if he realized I'd sacrificed everything, he'd understand and give me more time.

I'd put everything possible on the market, including, as of today, my own home. So far, all that had sold were my clothes and my car.

Mom let me borrow her Cadillac today and whenever necessary for longer trips around town. Otherwise, I'd been walking around Calamity, even in the cold. My house was only ten blocks from the gym. I made daily trips to the grocery store to spread out purchases and limit myself to one or two bags a day. Ramen noodles had become a staple of my diet and instead of my nice shampoo, I'd switched to the generic bottles that cost ninety-nine cents.

All so I could write Pierce the check in his pocket.

I'd never forget the look on his face when he'd read the amount. God, I was a fool. Humiliation was becoming a constant companion.

I should have declared bankruptcy. I should have

admitted defeat, taken a job at the dealership with Dad and given up on running my own businesses.

That check I'd written Pierce was everything to my name.

And it wasn't enough.

A bone-deep disappointment became this black hole in my heart and my eyes flooded. *This* had never been the plan. What was I doing? I was thirty years old and living like a broke college student. Why? If Gabriel were here, he'd cheer me up. He'd tell me to keep fighting.

But he was gone. My dreams were crumbling to dust and I just . . . I didn't have a fight. Not anymore. And against Pierce, I'd never win.

I ducked my chin so he wouldn't see the tears swimming in my eyes. Maybe he'd beaten me. Maybe I'd failed. But I didn't want him to see me cry. I swallowed hard, willing the lump in my throat away. I blinked furiously and my nose was stinging but I refused to sniffle.

Breathe.

So what if I didn't own my own business? So what if I worked for my family? So what if my dreams had to change?

"Are you all right?" Pierce's voice cut through my turmoil.

"Yes," I lied.

"Kerrigan."

Why did he have to say my name like that? All soft and sweet and caring. It only made fighting the tears harder. He was the man with my future in the palm of his hand. Actually, in the front pocket of his jeans.

Maybe he'd cave if he realized I was seconds from crying, but I wasn't here to gain his pity.

I wanted his faith.

Gabriel had always told me I would do great things. Maybe he'd been wrong. But I'd believed because *he'd* believed.

Fight. Don't give up.

As the fire crackled and the storm raged beyond the windows, I grabbed my emotions with an iron fist. There would be no crying. If I gave up now, I'd regret it for the rest of my life.

I forced my chin up and steeled my expression. "I want you to *listen* to me. One more time. I want you to hear me out. Because I need you to take a chance. On me."

He shifted, kicking his feet up on the couch. He propped an arm behind his head, and though he still looked tired, his eyes stayed locked on mine. "Why?"

"Because I won't let myself fail. The truth is, I don't have a lot of tools in my arsenal. But I work hard. I am ambitious. And though my five-year plan isn't infallible, it's solid."

My goal wasn't to be the richest woman in the world. Hell, I didn't even want to be the richest woman in Calamity. I just wanted to be my own woman.

"You put a property on the market," he said.

"I did." I nodded. "Two, actually. My own home and the farmhouse. I take it Nellie told you about that."

He shook his head. "No, she didn't."

"Then how did you know?"

"I saw the farmhouse listed with the real estate agency in Calamity."

"You checked? Why?"

"I own an investment company."

"Like Gabriel's. He told me you started one of your own."

"I did," Pierce said. "And as much as I would like to

simply take my clients' information at face value, we follow up."

"We? Or you?"

He hesitated, shifting on the couch, and when he spoke, he turned his eyes to the fire. "Me."

Interesting. Why hadn't he assigned my loan to someone else? Even Nellie? I'd asked her about Grays Peak Investments. She'd told me that their account teams had been swamped since absorbing Gabriel's company. Was that why he'd kept track of what I was doing? Because I was an easy account to manage while his teams were working on others? Or was there something more?

He'd delivered that letter to me personally. I doubted he did that for other clients.

Gabriel had once boasted that Pierce's company would one day surpass Barlowe Capital. Pierce was busy running a huge corporation. Why would he care about my defunct business loan?

"I'm sure I'm small potatoes compared to most of your clients."

"Yes, you are." A grin tugged at the corner of his mouth. "Though you are the most persistent."

"Stubborn. Like you said."

"No wonder you've become friends with Nellie. She's stubborn too."

I smiled. "She's pretty fantastic."

"She is. Did she tell you how we met?"

"No."

Pierce swung off the couch, moving to the fire to add another log. Once it was crackling, he glanced out the windows, and like it could feel his stare, the wind screamed in the dark.

I shivered. Driving home would have been terrifying.

"Thanks for letting me stay, by the way. I'm sorry to do this to you."

"It's okay." He waved it off, returning to the couch. "I admire your persistence. And if our positions were reversed, I probably would have done the same."

"Did you just give me a compliment?"

He chuckled, stretching out on the couch again. "Lack of sleep. I must be getting delirious."

I brought my knees to my chest, relaxing into the chair and making myself comfortable. With the storm outside, there was nowhere for me to go until it calmed. Maybe in a few hours, the wind would calm and visibility would increase. Then I could attempt the trip down the mountain.

"What were we talking about?" he asked.

"Nellie and how you met."

"That's right. We've known each other since high school. We went to the same private school."

"In Denver?"

He hummed his agreement. "She was a scholarship student, which shouldn't have made a damn bit of difference, but it did. Kids can be mean. Rich kids can be cruel. But since you know Nellie, it won't surprise you that instead of keeping to herself like most of the other scholarship kids did, she threw it in our faces. She beat us at everything. And she loved to one-up me at every opportunity."

"Why is that? Were you mean to her?"

"No, just competitive. I like to be the best."

I laughed. "Why am I not surprised?"

"Nellie bested me for valedictorian, something she doesn't let me forget," he said. "After graduation, I lost touch with her for a while. Then I bumped into her at a restaurant about five years ago. She'd just moved back to Colorado from Charlotte and was looking for a job. I was desperate for a competent assistant and she agreed to work for me temporarily. She threatens to quit whenever I piss her off."

There was such fondness in his voice. And trust. Did he know that she spoke about him in the same way? "I doubt she'll ever quit."

"I hope not. She's one of my best friends. Work is a lot more fun when you can work with a friend. I'd miss her."

Where was the impatient, arrogant billionaire who hadn't been willing to spare me a moment? A knot in my stomach untwisted, a knot that had been there for months. For the first time, he sounded like the Pierce who Gabriel had spoken of so often. The beloved grandson of my friend.

"We went on a date once." Pierce chuckled. "What a disaster. It was our senior year. To this day, I'm not sure what came over me to ask her out."

"She's beautiful." Nellie and I FaceTimed on occasion and she was more than beautiful. She was stunning with silky, white-blond hair and sparkling green eyes.

"She is pretty, but to me, she's just . . . Nellie. Always has been. For our date, I picked her up and took her to the movie theater. We stood in the lobby arguing over which movie to watch and our debate lasted so long that we missed both of our choices."

"You couldn't agree on a movie but you can work together?"

"We grew up. Not that we still don't argue. Lately, our arguments seem to center around you."

"Me?" I knew Nellie was on my side, but to have her go to bat for me with Pierce was . . . Now I wanted to cry again.

His dark eyes met mine and the softness in them disappeared. "I hope you haven't kindled this friendship with her in hopes of getting ahead with me."

I flinched. Wait. What? Had he just accused me of using Nellie? I was out of my chair and on the way to the door faster than he could blink. "Just when I thought you weren't a complete and total asshole."

Screw this place. I'd sleep in the car. That was better than staying here with him.

"Kerrigan, wait." He rushed after me but I was already in the entryway and shrugging on my coat.

I bent to pick up a boot, my hair flying around my face as I put it on and then the other. "Nellie is a good person. So am I. You, on the other hand, have some major character flaws. I cannot believe you'd accuse me of using her. Or that you have so little confidence in her that you'd think she'd let anyone use her."

"That's not . . . where are you going?"

"Home." Eventually.

"You can't leave."

"Watch me." With both boots on my feet, I reached for the door. "Goodbye, Mr. Sullivan."

"Kerrigan." His hand whipped out, smacking against the door. "Just . . . stop. That's not what I meant."

"Of course it was."

"You're right," he admitted, rubbing at a temple with his free hand. "I'm sorry. I just . . . I'm not myself tonight. And Nellie doesn't have a lot of friends. She never has. I can tell that she really likes you."

"And I really like her."

He pulled his hand away from the door, holding them both up. "You can't leave. It's not safe out there. There's plenty of room in this house for us both if you'd like to avoid me until the weather blows over."

The wind chose that moment to let out another ear-splitting scream. *Son of a bitch.* I really didn't want to go out there. I might get buried in a snowdrift on the way to the car.

"Fine." I backed away from the door and without another word, wearing my coat and boots, stomped out of the entryway.

My pride wouldn't let me return to his living room. Instead, I marched in the opposite direction, unsure of what I'd find at the end of a short hallway. It was the kitchen.

The space was massive. Dark cabinets filled the U-shaped room and accentuated the rustic theme. A copper farmhouse sink gleamed under the lights and the range was larger than any I'd seen outside of a professional kitchen.

There was a bouquet of fresh flowers on the island. I walked closer to smell the roses and lilies. A note card tucked under the vase read *Welcome Home* and was signed from the club with a phone number.

"You've listed your home."

My head whipped away from the flowers as Pierce walked into the kitchen. "I thought you said we could avoid one another."

"I was thirsty." He walked to the cabinets, opening one after another until he found the glasses. "Water?"

"Please."

He took two glasses and filled them both with ice water from the fridge. After setting one beside me, he went to one of the stools at the island and took a seat. "Why did you list your home?"

"To pay you." *Duh.* "I'm selling anything necessary. My car. My clothes. My blood, if needed."

He took a long drink, his eyebrows furrowed. "You own seven properties. Why not one of the other properties?"

"Because they have tenants who pay rent. I'm not going to kick people out of their homes."

"You could sell them as occupied rentals."

"There aren't many people in Calamity who want to own and manage rentals. And I love my tenants. The last thing I want is to sell the place and then have them worry their lease won't be renewed. Besides, their rent is paying my mortgages with the bank."

The properties I'd bought with Gabriel's loans had been the farmhouse and the building downtown. If I had to sell one of my rentals, then I'd do it. But it would be my last resort.

"What about the gym?"

"It's covering utilities and my living expenses." Not that it was much.

"What happens if you sell your own home?" he asked.

"There's a vacant studio apartment above the gym. I'll move in there. If I find someone to rent that place, then luckily, I have a big family. I'll couch surf for a while." I'd hate every minute of it, but if I had to, I'd move home with my parents until I built up money for rent.

"And what about this farmhouse?"

"That's a long story."

He glanced to the windows and the gusts of snow hitting the glass. "We're not going anywhere. Not tonight."

Oh, how I hated that he was right. If this storm kept up, I wouldn't be able to leave for hours. Maybe not until morning.

But he was here, asking me questions. This was why I'd come here, right? To make him listen and understand. For some reason he was curious—maybe it was atonement for putting his foot in his mouth.

This was my opportunity and since I was stranded, I might as well make the most of my window.

I rounded the island and took a stool, keeping one between us. The distance was important, because even though I was irritated with him, the man was still too handsome for his own good. Or mine.

"Have you ever heard of Lucy Ross? The country singer?" I asked.

"Sounds familiar but I'm not really into country music."

"She's a friend of mine and lives in Calamity. She moved there two summers ago and rented my farmhouse."

It had been an interesting property, even before the drama from that summer. All my life I'd known it as Widow Ashleigh's farmhouse. I couldn't remember her husband, who'd died when I was a kid, but Mrs. Ashleigh had gone to our church.

When she'd died, the farmhouse had gone to her niece, who'd had no interest in owning a home in Montana. The niece had sold everything inside along with the house and its twenty acres.

The family who'd bought the property had been from Texas, and the year they'd moved in had been one of the coldest, snowiest years in decades. When they'd put the house back on the market the following spring, no one had been surprised.

They'd moved away but the house hadn't sold, probably because their price had been outrageous. Clearly they hadn't been desperate for the money—I couldn't relate, but Pierce probably could.

"Before I bought it, the property sat abandoned and

empty for years. There'd been squatters inside once. Another time, it had been vandalized by teens needing a place to have a keg party, so they'd used the land and the old barn. As you can probably guess, it was a mess, and I was able to get the place for a steal."

The Texans had finally dropped their ridiculous asking price when their realtor had texted them pictures of the interior and the county had sent a letter threatening a fine if they didn't clean it up.

The day they'd lowered the price, I'd jumped.

"I called Gabriel, so excited. When I told him about it, he immediately loaned me the money because I didn't have the capital on hand. The timing worked out because he'd already drafted our contract so I could buy two buildings on First. He just increased the loan amount."

"Two buildings." He cocked his head. "I thought you just had the gym."

"I sold the other. It was at the end of the street with the most room to expand. I bought it without plans for exactly what to do with it, but the price was right. A friend of mine runs a construction company. He outgrew his office and was looking for a new spot. I sold it to him and paid Gabriel some of the money I'd owed."

At one point, I'd owed him nearly a half million dollars. Apparently, my payment history didn't count for much in Pierce's book.

"I put a lot of money into the farmhouse," I told him. "Maybe too much. But it needed it and I was planning on renting it to vacationers coming through. When Lucy called and inquired about the place, she didn't bat an eye at my price. She wanted a longer-term lease, and I was ecstatic. It was better than I could have hoped for. But . . ."

How was I supposed to predict death? It was hard for me to go to the farmhouse now. I used to walk into the kitchen and see the new cabinets and the walls I'd painted myself. Now, I simply saw the blood.

"But what?" Pierce asked.

"Lucy had a stalker. She was living in Nashville and came to Montana, hoping the stalker would leave her alone. But it didn't work out that way. The stalker found her. Tried to kill her in that house. If not for the sheriff, Lucy would probably be dead—along with my other friend Everly and two teenaged kids who happened to be there that day. Duke saved their lives. But to do it, he had to shoot the stalker. She died in my house."

Pierce blinked. "Oh."

"Exactly. *Oh.*" I took a drink of my water. "I'm surprised you didn't come across the story."

"I checked for listings with the real estate office but that was about the extent of my research."

"Well, you didn't know about the incident, but every person in Calamity does. No surprise, nobody wants to buy the farmhouse. Especially in the winter. And now that it's on the market, I can't exactly set up vacation rentals."

The house was sitting empty, costing me money for utilities each month. I wasn't sure how I'd pay December's bill, which was coming in a few weeks. I'd barely managed November's. Hopefully when they asked what I wanted for Christmas, my parents wouldn't make too many comments when I requested cash.

"Do you think it will sell?"

"Not unless I slash the price." It was listed at $220,000, which was less than it was worth given its acreage and my updates. But because of the terms of my loan, I couldn't go much lower. If I could sell the farmhouse at that price, after the fees and such, I'd be close to paying off Pierce.

"Hmm," Pierce hummed, raising his glass to his lips.

Silence stretched between us. Without the noise from the fire, the wind seemed louder. Angrier. A nasty gust slammed against the windows and even though the house was solid, it was like a blast of cold snaked through the kitchen.

"How about a payment plan?"

I was midsip and nearly choked on my water. Had I heard him right? "What?"

"A payment plan. Ten years. Interest-only annual payments. Balloon payment of the principle at the ten-year mark or sooner. No prepayment penalty. Ten percent interest rate."

I waited for the catch. There had to be a catch, right? Those terms were almost as good as the ones Gabriel had given me. The interest rate was steep but I was in no position to argue.

"Why are you looking at me like that?" he asked.

"That's it?"

"Should there be more?"

"Uh . . . no?"

He chuckled and slid off his stool, coming closer and holding out a hand. "Do we have a deal?"

"Deal." I slid my hand into his and an electric jolt raced up to my elbow.

Pierce must have felt it too because his eyes flared, his gaze dropping to my mouth. He leaned in, just an inch, but what a difference it made. He was so close that his body chased away the room's chill. His eyes ensnared me and my lips parted.

Did I want him to kiss me again? *Yes.* But before I could get my wish, he let go of my hand and took a step back. "Come on. It's cold in here. Let's wait out this storm in the living room."

The living room. Where we could put more space between us. An excellent idea.

Because now that we'd come to an agreement on my loan, the last thing I needed was to screw it up by doing something stupid.

Like kissing Pierce Sullivan again.

CHAPTER SEVEN

PIERCE

THE BLACK of night seemed only to provoke the storm. As Kerrigan and I sat in the living room, the minutes ticked by at an agonizing pace. There was no way I'd let her leave but every minute she stayed was one where I needed her to leave.

What the hell was wrong with me? I'd almost kissed her. Again.

There was no alcohol to blame tonight. Maybe it was delirium—these chills wouldn't stop and my headache was blooming through my entire skull. Or maybe it was simply . . . her. She was as desirable as she was persistent.

With her knees tucked beneath her in the chair, she stared at the fire. It had been an hour since we'd retreated from the kitchen to the living room, waiting for the snow and wind to subside. It wasn't going to stop, was it?

"You'd better plan to stay tonight," I said.

The look on Kerrigan's face was pained but she forced a smile. "That would be great. Sorry."

"Don't apologize." Her presence had been a fantastic

distraction from the reason I was here. There'd be no sifting through Grandpa's belongings with Kerrigan under the roof and I'd rather sit in agonizing silence than face my task at hand.

Besides, we'd come to an agreement. My decision to extend her loan might be one I regretted in a month or a year. As far as loans went, hers was small potatoes—to steal her words—compared to the other investments and licensing deals in my portfolio. But I wasn't cruel and wouldn't kick her when her luck was down. The story she'd told me about the farmhouse was unreal. No wonder it hadn't moved. That sort of event would have made the news in Denver and I suspected it would live exponentially longer in the minds of Calamity's residents.

So I was cutting her a break.

Grandpa would have loved that.

I shuddered at the image of them together. I bet he'd had her here, sitting on this very couch before this very fire. He would have been in those silk pajama pants he'd always favored. Her hair would have been down, catching the light from the flames as she cuddled beside him wearing whatever skimpy piece of lingerie he'd bought her from La Perla.

The pounding in my head tripled as something in the room growled.

"What—" It was her stomach. "You're hungry."

"I'll be fine."

Returning to the kitchen was dangerous, but now that I'd conjured an image of her and Grandpa together on this couch, I was ready for a new room. Besides, I didn't trust myself with her in any space, so we might as well eat. "I'm not sure what the club caretakers stocked for me but let's take a look."

She waited until I was off the couch and already on my way to the kitchen before she peeled herself out of the chair. As she followed, the distance she kept between us seemed deliberate.

It probably was.

There'd been no mistaking the hitch of her breath earlier. The parting of those luscious lips. Either she was worried I'd kiss her again, or she was worried that she'd kiss me back.

The refrigerator was full of prepared meals when I opened the door. I chuckled.

"What?" Kerrigan asked, settling on the same stool she'd been on earlier.

I stepped aside so she could see the fridge. "Nellie called the club and arranged for meals. She knows I'm hopeless in the kitchen so it's all reheatable."

"You don't cook?"

"Rarely. I have a chef who prepares my meals for me at home, and I live in downtown Denver, so many of the restaurants will deliver."

She opened her mouth but closed it before speaking.

"What?" The more she spoke, the more I found myself hanging on her every word. I didn't want to miss one.

"We just . . . we lead very different lives." There was sadness in her voice. Resolution. Like she was drawing a visible line between us. We were in the same room, but we'd always be a world apart.

"We do." And it was just another reason to keep myself away from Kerrigan Hale.

My life was as complicated as it had ever been. If she actually knew the details, well . . . I doubted she'd look at me the same.

Turning for the fridge, I poked around until I found a glass bowl that looked appealing. "How about homemade chicken noodle soup?"

"That sounds great."

Maybe soup would help knock this bug out of my system. I pulled it out and began poking around the kitchen. "I've never, uh . . ." Where were the pans?

After I found them in the second to last cabinet I opened, my next search was for a spoon. Finally, with the soup poured into the pan and heating, I found a loaf of sourdough bread on the counter. Where were the knives? And a cutting board?

"May I help?" Kerrigan asked.

"Would you mind picking out a wine?" I nodded to the wine fridge on the other side of the room, hoping that I wouldn't feel like such a fool if she wasn't watching me fumble around the kitchen.

She slid off her stool and walked to the wet bar, bending to peruse Grandpa's selection. Her sweater rode up on her hips, giving me the perfect view of her ass.

Damn, but she had a great body. My cock swelled. Fuck my life. I might not feel one hundred percent, but my dick didn't care when Kerrigan was in the vicinity.

This was not what I needed tonight. I tore my eyes away from her curves and focused on the meal, yet the image of her bent before me was running rampant in my mind, doing nothing to help the problem behind my zipper.

How long had it been since I'd been with a woman? Months. On one of my work trips not long after my divorce had been finalized, I'd met a woman at the hotel bar and let her drag me to her room. But otherwise, it had been my fist in the shower.

And for the past three months, when I'd closed my eyes, the woman in my head was the woman stuck with me under this very roof.

By the time this meal was over, I'd be in dire need of a cold shower.

"Red or white?" Kerrigan asked.

"Either."

She picked out a red and while I stirred the soup over the gas range, she opened the bottle and found two glasses, giving them each a healthy pour.

"I'd better try and call home," she said after bringing me my glass.

I took a long gulp as she left the kitchen, then breathed. "What the hell have I gotten myself into?"

I swore I could hear my grandfather laughing. He'd love this, the prick. He'd love that I was into Kerrigan. He'd love that I'd caved and made a special arrangement for her business. He'd loved that I was trapped here with her, in his house.

He'd love that I was infatuated with a woman who'd been his.

I grimaced, taking another long gulp of wine. I hated that he'd had her. That he'd cupped her perfect ass in his palms. That he'd had those lips I wanted as my own.

"Fuck," I muttered.

"Something wrong?" Kerrigan asked, causing me to whirl around as she returned to the kitchen.

"Uh, no. Just not great at this," I lied.

"I'm happy to help. The only chef who cooks for me is me."

"That's all right. I can handle this. Enjoy your wine. Grandpa prided himself on his collection."

She hopped on her stool again, a smile on her mouth. God, I really had to stop looking at her mouth. "He made me try my first glass of wine. It was one of his trips to Montana, when he'd invited me out to dinner."

"You'd never had wine before?"

"Not unless you count Boone's Farm." She feigned a gag. "Up until that point, I mostly drank vodka or beer in college. The occasional red Solo cup of jungle juice if I went to a frat party. Gabriel ordered the best bottle of wine at the restaurant, and I remember taking a drink and doing my best not to cringe."

I chuckled, retrieving two bowls from the cupboard. "You didn't like it?"

"At twenty-one? No. But I do now." She swirled the deep red liquid in her glass. "I haven't had a drink in a while."

Oh, shit. She wasn't on some sort of rehab or recovery plan, was she?

"I can see what you're thinking." She laughed and the sound echoed in the room, suddenly making it brighter. "I've just been saving money and wine is expensive."

"Except for Boone's Farm."

She smiled. "I'm afraid Gabriel's good taste in wine was contagious."

"Yes, it was." Grandpa wasn't the only one in our family who had an impressive wine collection. "My mom's collection dwarfs his. She'll travel all over the world for wine."

"What about you?"

"Mom buys my wine too." I poured us each a bowl of soup and set them on the island. Then I plated our bread, finding some garlic butter in the fridge before joining her. "She says I'm hard to shop for, though I think she just likes buying wine. She'll gift me bottles that she finds on her vacations."

"Gabriel talked about her a lot. He talked about you too. So much so that I felt like I already knew you when we met."

"He, um . . . spoke of you as well." Except it wasn't until years later that I'd realized she was closer to my age than his. I'd always suspected he had a thing for her, the way he talked with such adoration. I'd wondered if he'd actually bring her to Colorado one day and introduce her to the family.

That would have shocked the hell out of everyone. Mom had been under the impression Kerrigan was older too.

"This is probably a rude question, but how old are you?" I asked.

"Thirty." Over four decades his junior. "Why do you ask?"

"Just curious."

She nodded, not pressing for a better explanation, and the rest of our meal was in silence other than the clinking of spoons to bowls. By the time they were empty, so were our wine glasses.

"Would you like more soup?" I asked.

"No, thank you. It was delicious."

I stood to clear the island, but she beat me to it, swiping up my bowl. Then she moved around the kitchen, putting dishes in the dishwasher and stowing leftovers like she'd been here countless times.

"Did you come up here often?" I asked.

"No. My first time was when we scattered Gabriel's ashes," she answered, wiping down the countertops.

"Huh." Well, that was a pleasant surprise for a change. At least now I could go back to the living room and not think about Grandpa and her on the couch. "You move around the kitchen like you've been here a lot."

"It's the layout." She gestured to the cabinets. "It's not all that different than how I would organize. When you were opening and closing the cupboards, I paid attention."

"Ah. I just . . . I wasn't sure if you and Grandpa had come here for a weekend away or something." I found the bottle of wine and refilled our glasses.

"A weekend away?" Her forehead furrowed as she took a sip.

"Couples often take weekend vacations together, don't they?"

Wine sprayed from her mouth into my face.

"A couple?" Her jaw dropped as wine dripped down my nose. "You think I was in a romantic relationship with Gabriel?"

"Weren't you?" I swiped the hand towel from the counter and dried my face.

"Oh my God." Kerrigan blinked, set down her wine and began pacing the kitchen, her hands to her cheeks. "Oh my God. This whole time you thought I'd been sleeping with Gabriel. Oh my God!"

I blinked. "You weren't?"

"No! Eww." She scrunched up her nose. "He was like my grandfather."

"He often dated younger women."

"Not this one!" She pointed to her chest.

Well . . . fuck. "Are you sure?"

"Of course, I'm sure."

She hadn't been his girlfriend or mistress or fuck buddy. She hadn't slept with him for his money. She hadn't slept with him period.

Oh my God.

The relief that coursed through my body nearly sent me to my knees. "Wow. I, uh . . ."

"Yeah. Wow." Kerrigan shook her head. Her pacing stopped and her shoulders fell. "You really don't think much of me, do you?"

"On the contrary, Ms. Hale. I think about you far too much."

Her eyes widened.

Before I could say something more that would only get me in trouble, I grabbed my glass and the bottle of wine and carried them both to the living room.

Kitchens were dangerous places.

I sat on the couch again, wondering if she'd avoid me for the rest of the night. I wouldn't blame her if she did. But a few moments later, she slipped into the room, once more taking her chair while I stayed at the far corner of the couch.

"Did you get ahold of your family?" I asked.

"No. There's no service. I think the cell towers must have been disrupted by the storm."

"The Wi-Fi password is Barlowe with a *three* instead of an *e* at the end. You're welcome to use it for your call. Or send an email. From experience, you excel at both."

She smiled and pulled out her phone, her fingers flying over the screen. When she was done, the silence returned, awkward and as heavy as the snow flying outside.

I busied myself by keeping the fire going, but mostly, I drank and let the wine soak into my blood. It wasn't doing anything to temper my headache and the soup hadn't chased away my chills, but maybe if I got drunk, the pain would go away.

Kerrigan relaxed deeper and deeper into her chair as the

time passed and her glass drained. She was intoxicating in her beauty. Her long hair looked thick and soft, her body trim yet curved in the wonderful places where a woman was supple. The sweet, honeysuckle scent of her skin drifted through the room.

She really hadn't been his lover. My attraction to her didn't have a damn thing to do with one-upping my grandfather. As the mental images I'd dreamed up of them together vanished, a knot loosened in my gut. What. A. Relief.

I'd made an unfair assumption, and though the blame for that was mostly mine, I was giving some to Grandpa too.

He'd jaded me. And I'd taken it out on Kerrigan.

Fuck, but I was an asshole.

I caught myself staring at her, but I couldn't tear my eyes away.

There was a foundation to her beauty that came from her soul. She was honest. True. A sharp contrast to most of the women Grandpa had kept in his life. Especially the last.

"I still can't believe you thought I was intimate with Gabriel." Kerrigan shuddered.

"He liked younger women. They were a challenge for him. And they liked him in return. His billions too."

"I hope . . . oh, never mind."

"What?"

She hesitated but when she looked up, her eyes were full of fear. "Do you think that was why he helped me? Why he'd take me to dinner and why he'd spend time with me? Because I was a challenge?"

God, I wanted to tell her no. I wanted to ease the vulnerability in her voice.

"I truly admired Gabriel," she said. "He was so dear to my heart. But if he . . . I don't want to think that of him."

"Then don't. He only ever spoke about you with respect. I don't think he viewed you in that way."

Her shoulders fell. "Good."

It wasn't for Grandpa's sake I lied.

It was for Kerrigan's.

Yes, he'd always spoken about her with respect. He'd never explicitly told me that he'd been out to fuck her.

Maybe his relationship with her had been innocent. Maybe he truly had taken her under his wing and cared for her the way he'd cared for me.

Except I knew Gabriel Barlowe.

His true talent was hiding the truth.

"Would you like more wine?" I asked.

"No, thank you."

Leaving the glasses on the coffee table—I'd wash them in the morning—I stood and headed out of the living room. "I'll show you to a room."

"Oh, I can just stay here."

"In the chair?" I gestured for her to follow. "Come on. There are plenty of bedrooms. You might as well claim one."

She unfolded from her seat and followed, once again maintaining her distance. We walked deeper into the house where I hadn't turned on many lights, so I flipped them on as we went, casting the halls in a golden glow.

"I'm sorry about this," she said.

"If you apologize one more time, I'm adding two percent to your interest rate."

She laughed. "Okay."

"How's this?" I stopped at the first guest room.

"It's beautiful."

The heavy quilts, blankets and curtains were all in shades

of earthy browns, burnt oranges and rusty reds to coordinate with the rest of the house. "The bathroom across the hallway is stocked with toiletries. Help yourself to whatever you'd like."

"Thank you."

I nodded and backed away, giving her plenty of space. "I'll see if I can find you some sweats."

"Oh, I don't need anything."

"Are you on a mission to turn down everything I offer tonight?"

Her cheeks flushed. "I guess so."

"Be right back."

I hurried down the hallway, past the theater room and two other guest suites to the bedroom I'd chosen for myself. My travel bag rested on the tufted leather bench in the middle of the room's walk-in closet. I opened it and pulled out my extra pair of sweats and the hoodie.

Maybe it was stupid to give her my own clothes, but the idea of her sleeping in only underwear—or naked—might make my already throbbing head explode. Not that her in my sweats was much better.

When I returned to her room, I found her standing by the bed, her fingers skimming over the thick throw by the footboard.

"Here." I handed over the gray sweats.

"Thank you." She took them, her hands brushing mine.

A current snaked up my skin. The need to take her was so consuming that I used every ounce of willpower I had to take a step back.

My cold shower was waiting.

Except two steps to the door, I spotted her purse resting against the wall. She must have grabbed it while I'd been getting her sweats. The purse reminded me of the check in my pocket.

I dug it out and held it between us. "You scraped together every penny to write this check, didn't you?"

"I did," she admitted.

Of all the people I'd judged in my life, I wasn't sure I'd ever been as wrong about a person as I had been Kerrigan. "Take it."

She gave me a sideways glance.

"Please." I chuckled. "We have our new terms. This is unnecessary."

"All right." Her sigh of relief was louder than the storm outside.

"Good night."

"Good night, Mr. Sullivan."

Christ. I really was an asshole. "Pierce."

"Pierce," she repeated.

I put the length of the house between us, and as I locked myself in my bedroom, I willed her face out of my head.

It was no use. When I dreamt, it was of her.

And my name on her lips.

CHAPTER EIGHT

KERRIGAN

I POKED my head out of the bedroom door, listening for any sound from Pierce, but the house was quiet. The only noise came from the gusting wind beyond the house's walls.

It was still dark outside. Maybe another woman would have capitalized on this mountain lodge escape and slept in. Except my curse seemed to be the inability to sleep past six.

Tiptoeing down the hall, dressed in yesterday's clothes, I searched for Pierce in the living room but it was empty. So I went to the kitchen and poked around until I found coffee grounds and brewed a pot.

"Oh, lord." My first sip was pure bliss. This was better than any coffee I'd had in months.

My phone rang in my pocket and I plucked it out before the sound could wake up my host. "Morning, Mom."

"Hi. Are you all right?"

"Yes, I'm okay." I took my steaming mug to one of the enormous windows and looked out into a world of white. The snow covered everything and was coming down hard. "But it is still snowing like crazy up here."

"I don't want you on the roads in these conditions."

I sighed. "The gym—"

"I'll take care of it."

"Are you sure?" She didn't even have a car to get around town because hers was currently buried outside.

"I'm sure."

"We can always put up a sign and just close." It wouldn't be the best customer experience, but I was running out of options.

"Pfft. That's silly. I have nothing else to do today. Your dad is going to drop me off on his way to the dealership and your aunt will come down later to keep me company. Plus I have a book."

"Thanks, Mom."

"Sure. Say, I ran into Jacob last night."

I stifled a groan. "Good for you."

"He asked about you. Again."

"That's, uh, nice."

Mom had been trying to set me up with Jacob for years. He was one of the only nonfamily members who worked at the dealership and had graduated with Zach. Maybe I'd consider a date with him, but he never actually asked me. He'd just ask Mom about me whenever she visited Dad at work.

"If you went to work at the dealership, you two could have a little office romance."

I shook my head. "Thanks again for watching the gym."

"Of course," she said. "Now don't hang up, your dad wants to talk to you too."

"Okay." I waited as they shuffled the phone around.

"Hey, kiddo."

"Hi, Dad."

"Some storm."

"Yeah. Sorry about this."

"It's no big deal. You just stay safe. There are plenty of us in town to help cover the gym. Zach is going to feed Clementine. I'd rather you not risk a drive home in this weather. It's going to take the road crews some time to get everything plowed."

And the highway to a ritzy mountain resort area wasn't going to be a priority over the interstates.

"Are you safe?" Dad asked.

"Yes."

"I'm not loving the fact that you're trapped in a house with a strange man."

"He's not a strange man."

"Keep your pepper spray close."

I fought a laugh. "I don't need my pepper spray."

"You might."

"Dad, he's not going to attack me."

"Just . . . be guarded."

"Okay," I drawled. "I love you."

"Love you too. Keep in touch so we know what's going on. And when you get home, I want to talk to you about something."

Something either meant a job at the dealership or getting a car. He wasn't happy that I'd been hoofing it around Calamity. But I didn't want him to buy me a vehicle like I was sixteen again.

Neither Mom nor Dad knew I'd put my house on the market. They were going to love that little surprise.

"Bye, Dad."

He blew me a kiss and hung up.

"Morning." Pierce's voice startled me, and I gasped, spinning from the window as he came into the kitchen. He held up his hands. "No need for the pepper spray."

I giggled. "My dad worries about his daughters." Me in particular.

"How did you sleep?" Pierce asked, going for the coffee pot.

"Surprisingly well considering I was in a strange bed."

He filled a mug, then walked over, joining me at the window. A crease formed between his eyebrows as he took in the storm. "That doesn't look good."

"I'm sure in an hour or two it will clear, and I can get out of your hair."

"There's no rush. I'd rather you stick around until the roads are safe."

That might take days, and as much as I didn't like driving on snow-packed roads, it might be more dangerous to stay here alone with Pierce.

He looked insanely handsome this morning. His hair was mussed and he was dressed in a pair of black sweatpants that hung loose on his narrow hips. The hoodie he'd pulled on was the same brand and style as the gray one he'd given me to wear last night.

They'd smelled like him. Maybe that was why I'd slept so soundly.

He raised his mug to his mouth, and it was impossible not to stare as he took a drink. That jaw. Those lips.

Memory was a cruel companion to temptation.

Would he taste the same as he had that night at the motel? Would the kiss be as powerful? Or had I exaggerated it in my drunken state?

Maybe he wasn't that good of a kisser. Maybe we had no chemistry. Or maybe . . .

I wasn't going to let myself dwell on that maybe. He was a business associate, nothing more. This pull between us was something we just had to fight until the snowstorm was over.

A few hours. One day, tops.

"Would you like breakfast?" he asked.

"Only if you let me make it."

"Was watching me fumble around last night that painful?"

"Not at all." On the contrary, it had been oddly endearing to see him bested by a kitchen, to watch his composure break, just a bit. "But I might as well make myself useful."

I hurried to the fridge, putting twenty feet and the island between us. Then I busied myself with scrambling eggs and chopping vegetables for an omelet.

Pierce took a seat at the island, finishing his coffee before pulling out his phone. "The road report is not looking good. It says emergency travel only."

"Ugh." Next time I decided to stalk a man to his home, I'd check the forecast first. "Sorry."

"Didn't we cover this last night?"

"I'm going to keep apologizing. It's who I am. I don't like being a burden or a nuisance."

"I'd say you are neither."

I gave him a small smile over my shoulder and went back to work, setting out plates and silverware. "I'll make a deal with you. I'll attempt to stop apologizing if you let me take over meals. If I feel like I'm contributing, I won't feel so guilty for invading. Besides, this kitchen is a dream."

"Done." He spoke the word with such authority, it was like he'd brokered a million-dollar deal, not meal assignments.

After breakfast was ready, we took our places at the island and dug in.

"This is delicious," he said.

"It's only eggs." I shrugged. "Why are you back in Montana? Are you just here for vacation?" Nellie hadn't told me why he was here, just that he'd be here all week.

"No, not vacation. Grandpa asked that I be the one to go through his belongings here."

"Oh." So I'd interrupted a personal week. This just kept getting better. Truly, my timing was epic. "I'll stay out of your way."

"Nah. I don't really want to go through his stuff. Now that you're here, I can procrastinate a bit longer."

"If there's anything I can do, I'm happy to help." It wasn't like he had anything else to keep me occupied.

"Hopefully there isn't much. His office will be the worst and I'll tackle that later." He dabbed his mouth with a napkin and stood to collect our empty plates.

"How's your headache today?"

He shrugged. "Still there but not as bad as last night. I'm sure I'll be fine. What do you feel like doing today?"

"Whatever. You don't need to entertain me."

"Maybe I am hoping you'll entertain me."

The way he said *entertain* conjured images of lips and skin, and I ducked my chin to hide my blushing cheeks. If he took off those sweats, it would be entertaining for us both.

What was wrong with me? Would I have these thoughts about him if he hadn't kissed me once? *Yes.* Pierce was the most handsome man I'd seen in my life. His appeal was undeniable and each time we touched, the electricity was palpable.

"Feel like watching a movie?" he asked as he did the dishes. "I haven't sat down to watch a movie in ages."

"Neither have I."

"Work is my reason. What's your excuse?"

"Same. I work a lot."

"At the gym?"

"As of late, yes. I haven't wanted to hire an employee to cover the day shift when I can be there myself." That, and I couldn't afford an employee at the moment. "Before we opened, I did a lot of remodeling work."

"Yourself?"

"If possible. The friend of mine who bought my other building on First is a contractor. Whatever jobs I couldn't manage on my own, he helped." Kase was a good guy who did quality work, but he wasn't exactly cheap, so unless it required more skill, able bodies or specialty tools than I had stashed at my house, I'd learned to do a lot myself.

"Impressive. Do you like it?"

"I do." I nodded. "It's very satisfying, working with your hands. Seeing a space transform because of your work. I've been exploring more and more ways to capitalize on it. There are quite a few influencers on social media who make a good living at remodels. I'm thinking of trying it."

My phone was full of before and after photos I'd taken of various projects. The gym would have been a great one to start with, but I hadn't really considered how I could leverage social media from small-town Montana.

"One of my vice presidents has a wife who started her own blog," Pierce said. "She mostly does cooking videos and posts. Whole foods and vegan recipes. But she's making quite a business of it."

"It's a lot of work, but it's worth a shot. And in a way, I have you to thank for pushing me in that direction."

"Me?" He grabbed a towel to dry his hands.

"You were honest the last time you were here. Brutally so."

He winced.

"You were right." I smiled. "I need to be in a better liquidity position. I don't want to sell my properties when times are tough. And eventually, there won't be any place to expand in a town the size of Calamity. There are only so many people. But there's a whole world online and maybe I'll have a message and platform that might ring true to others. And it could be a way to monetize what I'm doing already."

He studied me, his gaze serious.

"What?" Oh, God, did I sound like an idiot?

"I don't think you should give me any credit. I think it's brilliant and you should own it."

My chest swelled with pride. "Thank you."

Pierce Sullivan was worth billions. Not millions, billions. That kind of money was unfathomable. For a man my age, he was by far the most successful person I'd met.

Yes, he'd probably had a leg up from his family's wealth, but from what Gabriel had boasted, Pierce's company and his success were not hand-me-downs. He was wealthy because of his own intelligence and work ethic.

"What will you do first?" he asked.

"I've spent the last few weeks getting my social media accounts established and picking the aesthetic I want. I've done a lot of research into affiliate programs and how to apply. I'm hoping to use my own place as the baseline."

"Your own house that's on the market?"

I touched the tip of my nose. "It's coming off the market the second I get home."

"And the farmhouse?"

"That one . . . I don't know." I sighed. "What would you do?" If I was stranded with Pierce, I might as well get his input.

"I don't fully understand the Calamity dynamic the way you do." He leaned against the counter and he looked so sexy, so relaxed, that a throb bloomed in my core.

I crossed my legs, willing it to go away. It didn't.

"Do you think anyone who knows about the incident there will buy that house?" he asked.

"It's unlikely. And anyone new to town and looking to buy it will inevitably hear the story. Gossip is Calamity's favorite sport."

He chuckled. "Then I'd use it as a vacation rental and a start for your blog."

"Even though it's done?"

"Is anything really done? Take an empty room and paint the walls. Stage it with different furniture. It doesn't have to be a wreck to show an improvement. Content is content."

"True." I hadn't thought about doing anything with the farmhouse, but it wouldn't be hard to have some fun. Maybe I'd give it a modern cottage vibe by adding some bold colors to the walls or a unique wallpaper.

Now that I wasn't trying to come up with a quarter of a million dollars, I could afford a few gallons of paint. Plus I had hundreds of before photos. Maybe I could work those into my feed too.

"I can practically see the gears turning," he teased.

"I'm fighting the urge to whip out my phone and start jotting down ideas."

"Do it." He grinned and refilled his coffee mug.

"What about the movie?"

He jerked his chin to the windows and the snow that just kept piling up. "I think we'll have all day. Besides, I'd better check in with Nellie."

Pierce left the kitchen first, and the moment he was gone, I let the smile I'd been holding back stretch wide.

I loved my rental properties. And the gym, though taxing, had so much potential. But the last few years had drained me. For the first time in a long time, I was truly excited about a new adventure.

With my phone in hand, I made list after list, brain-storming ideas and blog post topics. An hour and two cups of coffee later, I left the kitchen and found Pierce in the living room. He'd built a fire and was once again lounging on the couch.

"Hey."

He looked up from his phone. "Hey. I was just about to come and find you."

My God, he was gorgeous. I swallowed hard and took my chair. "For what?"

"Nellie told me I wasn't allowed to work all day. That it would be rude to ignore a guest."

"I'm not really a guest."

"Try telling that to Nellie. Besides, she's right. Did you make your notes?"

"I did." I held up my phone. "I'll be busy when I get home."

"And I bet you prefer it that way."

"Most definitely. Ever since college."

He set his phone on the coffee table and tossed an arm over the back of the couch. "Where did you go to school?"

"Montana State in Bozeman. You?"

"Harvard."

We spent the next few hours talking about nothing and everything. Some facts I knew from what Gabriel had told me, but mostly, it was new. Discovering Pierce was like an adventure of its own.

The day passed without the awkwardness I'd feared. We ate lunch. We watched two movies. And after dinner, we retreated once more to the living room, where we talked in front of the fire and sipped a bottle of red wine that probably cost more than the most expensive car at my father's dealership.

When Pierce had stoked the fire last, he'd also lit a candle on the coffee table. It and one small table lamp joined the yellow glow from the hearth. The scent of balsam fir filled the room.

"This candle smells exactly like this house should."

He hummed his agreement.

The light from the fire flickered across his handsome features as he lay on the couch, his feet crossed at the ankle.

Not staring had been my biggest feat today.

Pierce groaned, shifting as a wash of pain crossed his face.

"Headache still?"

"Yeah. I'm just not feeling great. Started yesterday. Thought it was just from the drive and most of the day I felt a little better but..."

In the muted light, I hadn't noticed the pallor of his face or the sheen of sweat on his brow.

I stood from the chair and walked over, putting my palm on his forehead. "You're burning up."

He shivered and crossed his arms over his chest. "I'm sure I'll be fine."

There was a first aid kit under the sink in my bathroom. I'd spotted it last night in my search for towels. I rushed down the hall and grabbed it, cracking it open and digging for a thermometer.

"Hold still," I told Pierce when I came back to the couch, sitting at his side. Then I held it to his forehead, waiting for the beep and reading. No surprise, it was high.

"You've got a fever." I stood and held out a hand to help him up. "Come on. You need rest."

He didn't argue. He simply took my hand and got to his feet. Pierce shuffled more than walked down the hallway and I kept pace, wanting to make sure he didn't need anything.

We reached the door to his room and I hovered at the threshold.

He went straight to the bed and collapsed on the mattress.

"I'll get you a glass of water." When I returned, his face was buried in his pillows and he was already asleep.

I set the glass on the nightstand and tiptoed out of the room, turning off the lights. Then I returned to the kitchen for another glass of wine. My pour drained the bottle and I took it to the trash, tossing it in, but as it landed, there was a crack of broken glass.

"Uh-oh." There was a frame in the mix. I reached in carefully and pulled it out, shaking the glass away from the photo.

It was of a woman with sleek brown hair and a wide white smile. She was laughing at whoever was holding the camera. In the background, trees towered overhead and the chair she sat in matched those around the firepit out back.

She was gorgeous. Carefree.

"Huh."

Who was she? And why was this photo in the trash?

"Not my business," I muttered, then returned the frame to the garbage, giving the can one last glance.

Putting the photo out of my mind, I went to the living room to kill some time on my phone. When midnight hit, I yawned and decided to check on Pierce.

I opened his door and inched toward the bed. He'd kicked off his covers and his forehead was furrowed. His water glass was empty too.

I reached for it just as he shifted, cracking his eyes open. "Sorry."

"I was awake." The man looked miserable.

I put my hands to his cheeks, finding them clammy. "Shit."

We'd never make it to a hospital. Fevers broke, right?

"Why can't I stop thinking about you?"

I froze and met his gaze. "I don't know. But it's probably the same reason I can't stop thinking about you."

My confession came effortlessly. Too effortlessly. Tomorrow I'd probably regret it. With any luck, Pierce wouldn't remember.

"Why did you kiss me at the motel?" I whispered.

He lifted a hand and skimmed his fingers across my mouth. "You have the most perfect lips I've ever seen."

Had he not been delirious, I might have questioned the sincerity behind that compliment, but it was so candid, all I could do was smile. No man had ever praised my lips before.

"It was the best kiss," he murmured, his eyelids fighting a losing battle.

"It was."

His dark lashes fluttered shut and I waited a heartbeat, thinking he'd passed out again. I eased away from the bed, but before I could leave, his hand reached out and caught me.

"Kerrigan?"

"Yeah."

"Stay."

I sat by his side and brushed his hair off his forehead. "For a little while."

CHAPTER NINE

PIERCE

I SHOVED off my pillow and peeled my eyes open. Waking up felt like crawling out of a black hole. When was the last time I'd slept that hard? There was a dull throb at my temples but nothing like the pounding headache I'd had last night on the couch. Whatever I'd caught had hit hard but hopefully a long night's sleep had knocked it out of me.

It took me a few moments to summon the strength to climb out of bed, and after a few dizzy steps, I made my way to the bathroom.

A steaming shower chased away most of the fog and the stench of a hard, sweaty sleep. My forehead didn't feel hot, so my fever must have broken. And finally, I didn't feel like there was a jackhammer in my skull.

Dressed in my last pair of clean sweats, I headed downstairs to find Kerrigan. The glare from the windows made me squint. Beyond the glass, the world was nothing but white. Snow was piled up against the house nearly three feet tall, but the storm had passed. The sky was a cheerful blue and the sun was blinding.

Kerrigan was in the kitchen, standing in front of the stove wearing my gray sweats. Her back was to me and her hair was piled into a messy bun. A few tendrils tickled the long line of her neck.

She was beautiful.

I rocked on my heels as she moved with such grace and elegance, she could have been dancing, not cooking. And like I had too many times, I let myself drink her in. Last night, had she not been on the other end of the living room and had I not felt like complete shit, I would have kissed her again. I would have kissed her and never stopped.

She moved, half turning my way, and I tore my feet from the floor before she could catch me staring.

"Morning."

Kerrigan spun away from the stove where a pot was steaming. The scent of spices filled the room. "Afternoon."

"Uh . . ." The clock on the microwave showed it was nearly two. Grandpa hadn't had an alarm clock in the master because when he'd come here, he'd refused to be on a schedule.

I, on the other hand, couldn't afford to sleep an entire morning away.

"I didn't realize I'd slept so long. I don't even remember going to bed last night."

"It's actually Tuesday." She turned down the stove's burner and faced me. "You slept Monday away."

My jaw dropped. "Seriously?"

She nodded. "You were in bad shape."

"Hell." I shuffled to a stool at the island and sat down. My phone was on the counter, plugged into a charger. I picked it up and scrolled through a mass of unread emails.

"How are you feeling?" Kerrigan braced her hands on the island.

"Not that bad, actually. I guess I just needed to sleep." For almost two days.

"I talked to Nellie yesterday and told her you were sick. She said she'd run interference on your calendar and clear it for the rest of the week."

I raked a hand through the damp strands of my hair. "Thanks. I'll have to check in with her."

"Go ahead. I was just making some soup in case you woke up."

"Give me five." I slid off the stool but paused. "You stayed."

The storm had passed. The roads were probably being cleared. It was Tuesday yet she was still here.

"You, um . . . asked me to stay."

"I did?"

"It was no big deal." She lifted a shoulder. "The roads are still closed, and I didn't want to leave you alone. When your fever didn't break yesterday, I was worried that I'd have to load you on a sled and pull you to a hospital. But it broke this morning."

She'd checked on me. Often, it seemed. When was the last time someone had taken care of me? Not since I was a kid, and even then, it had been a nanny.

Something twisted in my chest. It was a feeling I hadn't had in a long, long time.

"Thank you. For staying."

"Of course."

"And for cooking."

"Don't thank me yet. It's sort of an experiment given the ingredients in the fridge so I hope it tastes all right."

There were emails waiting. I needed to talk to Nellie. But I set my phone aside because the woman in this kitchen had my complete attention.

"Are you going to call Nellie?" she asked.

I shook my head. "It can wait. I'd rather try your experimental soup."

She smiled, then went about ladling her creation into two bowls, setting them out. Then she poured me a huge glass of orange juice before taking a seat at my side.

I moaned at the first spoonful. "You're giving my chef a run for his money."

"I'm an amateur compared to my mom. She's the real cook in the family. There were always lots of mouths to feed at our house."

"Oh? Do you have a lot of siblings?"

"An older brother and a younger sister. But my entire family is from Calamity. Aunts and uncles on both sides. Our house always seemed to be the center of the action. Mom would cook for us and whichever cousins were over to play."

"That sounds entirely different than my childhood."

"You're an only child, right?"

I nodded. "Yes, and though they'd never call me an accident, I don't think my parents had ever intended to have kids. I was the result of a week in Paris and a lot of wine. My mom couldn't make soup from scratch to save her life. Not that she'd try. I love her dearly, but she's always known her limitations."

"Gabriel told me she traveled a lot."

"If she's home for two weeks out of the month, it's a lot. Mom is accustomed to a lifestyle of ultimate freedom—from work and money. Grandpa would have given her a job if she'd wanted one, but she doesn't need to work. Dad is the same. His family comes from money too."

"And what did you do while they traveled the world? Did you go with them?" she asked.

"Sometimes. Mostly, I stayed home in the hands of their capable staff. And I spent a lot of time with Grandpa. He'd come and rescue me. Take me to dinner. Invite me to his place to spend the night. On the weekends when he went into his office, he'd bring me along. I'd sit at his desk and he'd give me projects, so it felt like I was working too."

She smiled. "Is that why you followed in his footsteps instead of your parents'?"

"I suppose. I went to Harvard because that was his alma mater. I went to work for his company after I graduated."

He'd been my hero.

Once.

"How are you feeling?" I asked, changing the subject. "Are you sick?"

"I feel fine." Her gaze darted past me to the windows. "A little guilty for being trapped here and leaving the gym to my mom to run. Plus I stole her car. But it's not like I've got options. I've never seen this much snow. According to the news, it's a record."

"When did it stop?"

"Not that long ago. A few hours. And we're supposed to get more tonight. When I talked to Mom this morning, she said that the plows are having a hard time keeping up."

Their misfortune was my luck because the idea of being trapped with her for a few more days was the best I'd heard in weeks.

"Since you're stuck with me, you might as well put me to

work," she said. "I'm happy to help you clean out Gabriel's things."

"What if I wanted to avoid it for another day?"

"That would be fine too."

"Feel like another movie?"

Work was waiting and while I couldn't unbury myself from the snow, I should tackle a hundred emails. But at the moment, all I wanted to do was curl up on a couch beside Kerrigan and relax.

Which was exactly what we did. The two of us finished our soup and retreated to the theater room. We watched a movie until dark, then retreated to the kitchen for a dinner of pasta shells and salad that had been provided by the club.

"How are you feeling?" I asked as we stood side by side at the sink, doing dishes.

She smirked. "I should be asking you that question."

"I'm good." Spending the day with her had been rejuvenating. Unplugging, just being in her company . . . it was like I hadn't been sick at all. "I was thinking about jumping in the hot tub. What do you think?"

"Oh, I don't have a suit."

Naked. Naked was definitely an option.

"But you go ahead," she said.

There was probably a suit around here, but only one woman would have left a bikini behind, and I didn't want Kerrigan in her clothes.

"Or . . . you could just wear your underwear," I suggested.

Her eyes snapped up to mine and the swirl of lust was unmistakable. Those beautiful brown eyes drifted to my mouth, and I was done.

I captured her lips, wrapping my arms around her and pulling her into my chest.

Kerrigan gasped and her hands came to my shoulders, holding on as I dragged my tongue over that goddamn perfect mouth. She parted for me and I dove inside, my tongue tangling with hers.

God, she tasted good. Better than I remembered.

We melted into each other. She clung to me as I tightened my hold. Whatever I recalled from the kiss I'd given her at the motel was insignificant compared to this.

This kiss was the best of my damn life. Until the next. And the next. Something about this woman made me feel that it would only get better. Kiss after kiss, she'd put the past to shame.

She sank into my arms as I nipped at her full lower lip, taking it between my teeth. A whimper escaped her throat and that sound shot straight to my groin.

With a tilt of my hips, I pressed my arousal into her belly, earning another startled, sexy gasp.

"Pierce," she whispered, pulling back a fraction of an inch.

"Don't say stop." My chest heaved as I brought my hands to her hair, threading my fingers into those silky locks. Then I met those eyes of hers, the enchanting brown orbs that had drawn me into her spell.

She swallowed hard. "You're sick."

"Were." One afternoon and evening with her and I felt like a new man.

"Maybe we should just . . . slow down."

I groaned and dropped my forehead to hers. She was right. If we kept going, I'd fuck her on the kitchen island and that was not what I wanted. Not with her.

"How about that hot tub?" she asked, sliding free of my hold.

I nodded. "I'll meet you out there."

First, I needed a moment to get myself under control.

Her eyes flicked to my sweats and the corner of her mouth turned up when she saw the obvious bulge. The smirk widened as she slipped past me, her cheeks a beautiful shade of pink that matched her swollen lips. Then she disappeared from the kitchen and I closed my eyes, dragging a hand over my face.

God, this was stupid. This was probably the most foolish thing to do tonight. I wasn't in a position to have any sort of relationship, but Kerrigan was so damn tempting.

And tonight, I wasn't strong enough to resist.

We had no future.

I'd have to explain that to her.

Later.

I left the kitchen and strode down the hallway to my room, where I traded out my sweats for a pair of board shorts. Then I hurried to the patio door. One blast of the winter air and goose bumps pebbled my skin.

I clenched my jaw, swiped the shovel that was propped up against an exterior wall and went to work clearing a footpath to the hot tub. Thankfully, the overhang of the roof protected most of this area from the storm but the wind had still blown in a fair amount of snow.

The hot tub itself was sunken into the concrete slab. I brushed off some of the snow on its cover, then hit the button on the wall to open it up and start the jets. The warm water was nearly too hot for my frozen feet.

The moment my shoulders dipped below the steaming surface, the sliding door to the house opened and Kerrigan stepped outside, her arms wrapped around her waist. Her arms only accentuated the delicious swell of her breasts.

Oh, fuck me. "Those are your underwear?"

Her bra was a nude lace that gave the illusion she wasn't wearing a thing. Her matching panties barely covered her ass. I'd seen her in skintight leggings before but they'd hidden the smooth, toned skin of her long legs. One look and I was hard.

She smiled as she stepped into the tub, sinking beneath the water. "What were you expecting? Granny panties?"

"I think you'd best stay on that side of the tub," I said, moving to the corner farthest from hers.

She giggled. "Probably a good idea."

The conversation I'd planned to have later—much later—couldn't wait. I didn't trust myself around her in those panties and bra. If she gave me even the slightest opening, I'd take it.

And before that happened, she needed to know there was a line in the sand I couldn't cross.

"About earlier, Kerr. The kiss."

She relaxed against the wall of the tub. Steam snaked around her face, and for a moment I forgot what I was supposed to say. "The kiss?"

Right. "I'm not in a place to have a relationship. Probably something I should have told you before I kissed you."

There was a flash of disappointment in her eyes but she forced a smile. "It's okay. Now that we'll have a business relationship, it's better to keep this professional."

I fucking hated professional.

But she was right.

I also fucking hated that she was right.

Kerrigan turned her attention beyond the patio's overhang. Snow began to fall in tiny specks, dotting the black night.

I sank deeper into the water, enjoying the contrast of its warmth on my body to the frigid air that nipped at my ears.

"It's peaceful here," Kerrigan said.

"It is." I tore my eyes away from her and into the darkness beyond the house. "I was thinking of getting a place like this in the mountains outside Denver."

"You don't want to keep this place?"

I shook my head. "This cabin was his. Maybe he'd hoped that I'd keep it. Maybe that's the reason he had these requests in his will. But Montana isn't mine. It was his."

"It's a big state, Pierce."

I loved hearing my name in her sweet voice. "I used to spend time here."

"At this house?"

I nodded. "Grandpa loved it here because it was separate from Colorado. All of his friends have mansions in Aspen and the pretentious ski resorts within driving distance of Denver. But he chose Montana and loved having us come to visit."

"Us?"

"Me and my wife."

Her eyes widened. "I, um . . . you're married?"

"Ex-wife."

A flash of relief crossed her expression. "I didn't realize you were married. Gabriel never told me."

I huffed. He'd told her how many things, but he'd left Heidi out of the equation? "We divorced in March. She was from Montana."

"There was a photo in the garbage can." She scrunched up her nose. "I didn't mean to snoop, but I saw it the other night and thought it might have been tossed out on accident."

"Not an accident. I threw it out."

"That was her? Your ex?"

I nodded. "After he bought this place, she spent a lot of time up here. She'd come here because, for her, it was like coming home."

And I'd been the idiot to believe her. To trust her.

"Heidi grew up in Bozeman and we met at Harvard. She talked about growing up here often."

"Is that why Gabriel chose to buy here? Because of her stories?"

"Maybe. I don't know." I sighed. "It's hard for me to guess what exactly he was thinking. I've spent months and months analyzing the past. Trying to make sense of him. Why he did the things he did. Now that he's gone, I doubt I'll ever understand."

I cast my eyes to the water. The turmoil of the surface was a mirror of how I'd felt all these months.

"Understand what?" Kerrigan asked.

All this time, I'd protected Grandpa's image by keeping his secret. Not for him. For her. "I don't want to tell you."

"Why?"

"Because I don't want to ruin his memory for you."

"Will it?"

I nodded.

She took a moment, thinking it over. Then she whispered, "Tell me anyway."

"Grandpa used to bring Heidi here. Often."

Maybe it had started off as an innocent vacation. Maybe he'd wanted Heidi from the beginning. Maybe he'd loved her, like he'd promised.

Maybe he'd just wanted something and he'd taken it, even if that had meant taking it from me.

When I met Kerrigan's gaze, she was already putting the pieces together. But I wouldn't make her guess. "They were having an affair."

CHAPTER TEN

KERRIGAN

MY JAW DROPPED SO low that a splash of hot tub water landed in my mouth. "He had an affair. With. Your. Wife?"

Pierce nodded. "Yes."

"But . . ." I couldn't even put this together. I couldn't even fathom Gabriel doing this.

He'd loved Pierce. There was no mistaking it. For years he'd told me about his incredible and bright grandson. How could he have slept with Pierce's wife? That type of betrayal was simply . . . impossible.

No. There had to be a mistake.

"He wasn't the saint you made him out to be," Pierce said. "Or . . . he wasn't the man he made you see."

"I just . . . I'm sorry." Oh my God. "I'm so sorry. I-I had no idea."

"No one did."

Gabriel, how could you?

I didn't doubt Pierce. There was too much raw emotion etched on his handsome face. Confiding this in me hadn't

145

been easy. For a man like him, confident and in control, it was probably like admitting weakness.

Except this was on Gabriel.

For the second time since I'd come here, I thought back to the moments I'd had with Pierce. I replayed them and saw them in an entirely new light. No wonder he'd been so harsh with me. He'd thought I was sleeping with Gabriel, just like his wife. No wonder he'd been so angry at his grandfather.

"How long?" I asked but before he could answer, I held up a hand. "No, wait. You don't owe me any answers. It's not my business."

Pierce's eyes softened. "If I didn't want to tell you, I wouldn't have. I'm not exactly sure. According to Heidi, it had only been going on for six months."

"But you don't believe her."

"No." He sighed. "She'd been coming to Montana for a few years. Most trips alone. Most trips I learned later had been timed when he'd been here too. Maybe it really was nothing. I never pressed for details."

I wouldn't have either. Some people might want every tidbit of information to ease the sting or make sense of it, but in that position, I wouldn't want to know a damn thing.

The affair was enough.

Opening my mouth, I was ready to release a string of questions, but I stopped myself.

"What?" Pierce asked.

"It's nothing."

"Go ahead, Kerr."

I really liked that he'd started calling me Kerr. Couldn't we rewind the last hour? Go back to the kiss in the kitchen and forget this madness with Gabriel and Heidi? Except it was out there now and I couldn't think about anything else.

I mean . . . what the hell? This was daytime soap opera material.

Pierce shifted, leaning deeper into the side of the hot tub. Then he stretched those roped and sculpted arms along the back as he reclined in the water, tipping his head to the ceiling. "I haven't talked about it much."

"I don't blame you for that."

"But maybe I should."

I sat perfectly still, waiting. If he wanted to talk about it, I'd listen. If he didn't, that was okay too. Even though it felt like I'd known him for years, we were just getting to know one another.

"He always kept in shape," Pierce said. "He was always with younger women. I didn't think anything of it. That was how he was my entire life. Why would I ever worry that my own grandpa would be a threat?"

"Or that your wife would cheat on you." At this point, I was livid with them both.

Pierce scoffed. "Exactly."

"Can I ask . . . how old is she?"

"Thirty-one." The same age as he was.

"So that's . . ." I started doing the math in my head. Gabriel had been in his sixties when we'd met and that had been nearly ten years ago.

"He had my mom young. My mom had me young. He was seventy-five when he died."

Seventy-five and thirty-one. My head was spinning.

Gabriel had always been a handsome man, the definition of a silver fox. He'd looked much younger than a typical seventy-five-year-old man. But a forty-something-year age difference? It would have bothered me even if the woman involved hadn't been his grandson's *wife*.

How could Gabriel do this? That was not the man I knew. He'd always acted with such integrity, but maybe Pierce was right. Maybe I'd put him on a pedestal. Or maybe he'd let me.

Maybe both.

"I caught them," Pierce said.

There went my jaw dropping again. "No."

"In my own house, if you believe it. The cliches in this twisted scenario are endless. But I came home early from work one day. Heidi and I . . . we'd been having problems."

"Like the fact that she was sleeping with your grandfather?"

"To name one of many." Pierce chuckled. "We'd been talking about a divorce. It wasn't like our marriage was perfect, and that was on us both. But I never would have cheated."

"So you caught them."

"In my own fucking bed." He shook his head. "Took me a minute to even realize what I was seeing."

No wonder he hated Gabriel. Coming home to talk to your estranged wife only to find your grandfather in your bed . . .

"She says she didn't mean to fall in love with him. Whatever the hell that means."

"Do you think she loved him?"

Pierce ran a palm over his beard as he considered my question. "At first, I thought she was just saying it. Making an excuse."

"And now?"

"I think maybe she did love him. After the divorce, they stayed together."

Had that picture I'd found been taken by Gabriel? Heidi

had looked so happy. A woman at ease with her companion, enjoying a vacation. "Do you think he loved her?"

"I don't know." He shrugged. "He never loved his girl-friends. Told me that with each one it was casual. He'd admit that he liked having a pretty face in his bed. But after I caught them, he didn't call it off. He knew I was furious. He knew I wouldn't speak to him again. But he stayed with her regardless. That doesn't say *casual* to me."

Me neither.

The pain in Pierce's voice was hard to hear.

Gabriel had fallen in love with his grandson's wife.

"Did you talk to him?" I asked.

He shook his head. "He tried to call and visit. I refused him."

And now Gabriel was gone. Whatever questions he had would go forever unanswered, whatever grudge wouldn't be settled.

"After Heidi and I divorced, she moved into his home in Denver. We sold our place and I moved into the penthouse at my building. She was with him . . . in the plane crash."

I gasped. "W-what?"

"They died together."

My hand came to my mouth. "Pierce, I'm . . ."

Oh, God. He'd lost his grandfather and his ex-wife. Even if he had hard feelings for Heidi, they'd been married. He'd loved her. Maybe he still did. And she was gone too.

"I'm sorry," I whispered.

He turned to the darkness, giving me his profile. "So am I."

The only sound for minutes and minutes was the gentle hum of the hot tub and the whirl of the jets.

Finally, Pierce tore his eyes away from the night and gave

me a sad smile. "I don't tell you this so you'll hate him. I just want you to have the truth."

"I know."

Gabriel's image had tarnished but I didn't hate him. I was angry at him, on Pierce's behalf. But I still loved the man who'd believed in me.

"I just want to get on with my life," he said.

"Is that why you're selling this place?"

He nodded. "This is a fantastic house. I still love it. But it's strange to be here and know they were here together."

"Uh, yeah. I'm guessing that's why you're sleeping in the guest suite."

"I need to clean out his things from the master. I went in there when I first got here. That's where I found Heidi's picture. Other than tossing it out, I haven't been able to do more."

I gave him a sad smile. "I can help. It's not like I have much else to do."

"You know . . . I think I might take you up on it." His shoulders sagged. "It's been months since I found out. Months since the divorce. You'd think that should be plenty of time for me to get my head around it and walk into a room."

"Sometimes it's not as easy as just having time. You had no closure. And now they're both gone."

He studied my face for a moment, then closed his eyes. "I've been avoiding it. I've been avoiding everything where they are concerned. Other than his demands in his will, I haven't really spoken about their affair."

"Does your mom know?"

"She does." Pierce huffed a laugh. "When I told my parents, they shared this look, like they weren't surprised."

"Do you think they knew about it?"

"No. They would have told me. But I think they saw the signs that I missed. I can see them now. The looks. The laughs. The inside jokes. I always thought Heidi just loved him because he was, well . . ."

"Gabriel," I finished.

"People loved him. Fiercely. They hated him too, just as passionately. But when he was in the room, he commanded attention simply by being."

"You have that about you too. I don't know if anyone has ever told you that, but you're rather commanding yourself."

He chuckled. "You say that like a compliment. Nellie has said the same thing but it's not quite as endearing."

I giggled. "It's a compliment."

"Then I thank you." He dipped his chin, then locked his gaze with mine, holding it so long that it became hard to breathe.

It was like staring at an entirely new person. These past few months, Nellie had made comments about Pierce not being himself. How many times had she told me to give him a chance? To wear him down? She knew what he'd been dealing with and how devastating it must have been.

"Have you ever been married?" he asked.

I shook my head. "Engaged. But it fell apart."

"Mind if I pry?"

"I've been poking into your personal life, so it only seems fair."

"What happened?"

I lifted a hand out of the water and traced a fingertip over the rippled surface. "He called it off five days before the wedding. Went out for his bachelor party, got drunk and hooked up with a woman from a bar."

Pierce hissed. "Son of a bitch."

"I was pregnant."

The air stilled at my admission. The steam stopped swirling. The snow stopped falling.

I wished I could swallow up my words and bury them again.

"I've never told anyone that," I confessed.

"Why?"

"Because the same day the wedding was called off, I had a miscarriage."

"Fuck. Kerrigan, I'm sorry."

"It was for the best." I kept drawing circles on the water, unable to look at him.

Why had I told Pierce? Why? My mother, my father, my sister, not even my friends knew about the pregnancy. Literally no one knew because the day I'd found out, three hours after a positive pregnancy test, my ex-fiancé had come to my apartment and told me about his bachelor party. Later that night when I'd started bleeding, I'd gone to the emergency room alone.

"My ex had a long list of excuses," I said. "I'm not sure which, if any, I believe. He wasn't ready to settle down after all. He hadn't explored the world yet. He didn't want to move to Calamity."

The entire experience had been humiliating. My only saving grace was that the wedding had been in Bozeman. Word had definitely gotten around Calamity that my engagement had been called off, but at least the event hadn't been planned in my hometown. In a way, it had removed me some from the gossip circle.

And I hadn't had to worry about getting a pitiful look from a nurse or doctor after the miscarriage.

"How long ago?" Pierce asked.

"Eight years. We got engaged my senior year of college and were going to get married the summer after graduation."

I'd mourned my lost pregnancy more than I'd mourned my broken engagement. That day had been the single worst day of my life. On my bad days, I always reminded myself that I'd survived much worse.

"Does it still hurt?" Pierce asked. The raw edge to his voice made me want to swim across the hot tub and pull him into my arms.

I clasped the bench seat under the water and stayed put. "Yes and no. The miscarriage, yes. The wedding, not really. It was embarrassing. Any time I think about the phone calls I had to make and the money my parents spent for a wedding that didn't happen and the dress I still have in my closet, then it stings. But that's my pride, not my heart. Besides, it wouldn't have been a happy marriage."

Content, but not happy. I wasn't settling for contentment. I wanted love. I wanted passion. I wanted a man who stole my breath when he walked into the kitchen. Who kissed me and made the world melt away. Who would make every day an adventure.

"He wasn't the man for me. I see that now. But that's a realization eight years in the making. We all heal at our own pace."

Pierce looked at me so intensely that the heat from his gaze made the water feel cold. "You're a wonder, Ms. Hale."

"I'm just me, Mr. Sullivan."

He grinned and shook his head. "How about a lighter subject?"

"Please." I laughed.

"Tell me more about Calamity. I'm intrigued."

"What do you want to know?"

"Anything."

"Nearly my entire family lives there," I said. "If you ever meet my grandfather, he'll tell you all about how the Hales have been in Calamity since Calamity was Panner City."

"Panner City. A gold rush town?"

"It was. At its peak, there were almost three thousand miners living in the area. Then came the calamities."

"Hence the name. What happened?"

"The mine collapsed in Anders Gulch and killed a bunch of the miners. There was a flood from a heavy spring storm that washed out most of the smaller claims and panning sites. According to the records, it dried out hot and fast and a fire spread through the town and camp. And then that same summer, there was a lightning storm that caused a herd on the range to stampede. The mining was fairly nonexistent after that. Not to mention there wasn't enough gold in the area to rebuild. Most of the miners moved on. But some stayed, including Andrew Hale, who had seven sons, one of whom was my great, great, great grandfather."

"Very interesting."

"I probably have the *greats* mixed up." I always added one too many or was one too short. "My dad could tell you exactly how I'm related and the lineage." It was impossible to keep track. There were aunts and uncles and cousins—first, second and third. Dating was a struggle, not only because there were so few single men in Calamity, but because some of the few available men were also relatives.

"What does your family do?" he asked.

"My dad runs the car dealership in town. A bunch of family members work there, unlike me, much to his dismay."

"You don't want to sell cars for a living?"

I smirked. "No, thank you. I'll stick to my properties, The Refinery and maybe a new blog."

"I have no doubt you'll be successful." His voice held ten times the confidence I felt.

"Really?"

"Really," he said. "I owe you an apology."

"For what?"

"For being an ass. I should have heard you out. But I was angry about my grandfather. I assumed you two—"

I held up a hand and cringed. "Don't say it."

Pierce laughed and the smile that stretched across his mouth was breathtaking. I hadn't seen him smile enough. Before I left this cabin, I wanted to earn at least one more. "I'm excited to see what you do."

"Thank you." My toes bounced in the water at the rush of nerves and excitement. Becoming a successful influencer was a long shot. Most likely, I'd fail and end up selling a property to pay Pierce back. But it would be thrilling to try.

Pierce raised a hand and inspected his fingertips. "I'm becoming a raisin."

I mimicked him, checking my own skin. "Me too."

He surged across the hot tub and for a moment, I held my breath, hoping he'd invade my space and press that hard body against mine. But he shifted at the last minute, stepping onto the bench seat and shoving out of the water.

I swallowed a groan, then turned and stepped out. The winter air rushed over my heated skin and the snow around the pool nipped at the soles of my feet. I tiptoed to the door, leaving Pierce to hit the button to close the cover on the hot tub.

The moment I was inside, I swiped up one of the towels I'd brought out from the bathroom, wrapping myself in the plush, white sheet. I covered my body in time to watch Pierce walk through the door and grab the other towel, bringing it to his face.

Water cascaded down the broad plane of his chest. Drops trickled over the sinewed muscles of his arms. I wanted to trace them all with my tongue. In all my life, I'd never seen a man in real life with a body that belonged on magazine covers or in Hollywood movies.

He toweled off his torso, then wrapped the sheet around his waist.

It instantly brought back the image of him the day I'd come up to scatter Gabriel's ashes. Him in a towel, his abs on display and that V of his hips.

I tore my gaze away before it could drift any lower—and found his eyes locked on my breasts.

His Adam's apple bobbed as he stared, unabashedly.

Pierce didn't want a relationship. There was no fault in that. It was too soon after his divorce and the drama that had come with it. In his place, I wouldn't want a relationship either, especially not one where business was involved.

And *I* wasn't looking for a relationship either, right? Well, maybe. But not with Pierce. He lived two states away.

Did that mean we couldn't have fun? That we couldn't explore this chemistry between us?

How long had it been since a man had stared at me with such lust? Such hunger? Pierce looked at me like he wanted to devour me whole.

I'd let him.

He jerked out of his trance, forcing his eyes across the room. He raised a hand and rubbed the back of his neck. "How about some wine?"

I managed a nod.

Clothing would be better. Lots and lots of clothing. My only bra was soaked. So were my panties, and not just from the water.

But did I take my leave to get dressed? Nope. I followed him into the kitchen and didn't make myself keep three stools between us.

Pierce walked to the wine fridge and chose a bottle. Then he uncorked it, poured us each a glass and handed one over.

"Cheers."

I clinked the rim of my glass to his. "Cheers."

The wine was dry and rich and smooth. The flavor burst on my tongue, except all I could think about was Pierce's taste. How his tongue had tangled with mine in this very room.

I met his dark gaze and nearly came undone with the desire in those endless pools.

He raised his glass to his lips, taking a long drink. Then he set the glass aside and closed his eyes. "Damn, I want to kiss you."

Oh, how I wanted to be kissed.

He opened his eyes and the restraint was there, as obvious as his bare skin on display.

Pierce inched closer, raising a hand to tuck a lock of hair behind my ear. His fingertips left a trail of tingles in their wake. Then he leaned forward, just an inch.

I held my breath, tilting up my chin. Waiting.

But he didn't kiss me. At least, not on the mouth. He pressed his lips to my forehead, then took a step past me, padding out of the kitchen. "Good night, Kerrigan."

No. "Wait."

I cringed at the desperation in my voice. But if I left this cabin, if I left this man without at least one more kiss, I'd regret it for years.

Pierce stopped, his hands fisting at his sides as he turned. "I am hanging on by a thread here, babe."

"What if I wanted you to kiss me? What if you did? What if you let go of that thread for as long as we're stranded together? What if—"

I didn't get to finish. In a flash, Pierce closed the distance between us.

And answered my questions with a kiss.

CHAPTER ELEVEN

PIERCE

KISSING HER WAS RECKLESS. It went against my better judgment, but the moment my lips found hers again, nothing else mattered. Not the past. Not the future. Nothing but Kerrigan.

I slid my tongue against hers in a lazy swirl. The move earned me one of her sultry mewls. Threading my fingers into the hair at her temples, I tugged the strands free from their loose knot. I let myself drown in her for a moment, savoring her taste before moving my lips away from her mouth and down the column of her throat.

"Pierce," she whispered as her fingertips skimmed my abs.

I found her pulse and sucked, then pulled myself away to search those sparkling eyes. They brimmed with the same desperation that coursed through my veins, filling my blood. It was like being drunk on the most exquisite wine.

"God, how I want you. From the moment I saw you, all I could think about was your mouth."

She smiled, lifting her hand to my face and letting her

palm scrape against my beard. "I wanted to slap you that day on the sidewalk."

I chuckled. "I deserved it."

Her other hand rose and with both palms on my jaw, she dragged my mouth to hers. Any hope of keeping control was lost.

I dove into her mouth, finding her tongue ready for a duel. We twisted and tangled together until the kiss wasn't enough. Wrapping my arms around her, I hauled her flush against my body. Beneath the towel and my board shorts, my cock was painfully hard and I pressed my arousal into her belly.

"More," she panted against my lips, her hands roving my shoulders. Her fingertips dug into my skin as they moved, trailing up and down and up again, like she was trying to touch every inch of me.

With a fast swoop, I hoisted her up and off her toes. The towel wrapped around her chest came apart and I ripped it away, letting it drop to the floor with a muted thud.

Kerrigan's legs wrapped around my hips, dislodging my towel too. We left both in a heap as I pivoted and set her on the island before dotting a trail of nips across the soft, taut skin of her collarbone. Her whimper echoed in the kitchen, the sexiest sound I'd heard in my damn life. It was enough to make me pull away because otherwise I'd be coming in these drenched board shorts.

Sitting on a counter, dressed only in a soaking-wet lingerie set, Kerrigan was temptation personified.

Taking her might be the most selfish thing I'd ever done. There was so much happening in my life, things that I'd been avoiding that would soon be unavoidable. Things I couldn't explain to her, not now.

I should stop. But I wouldn't.

I wanted Kerrigan while I still had the ability to want for myself.

"You are beautiful beyond words."

Her breath hitched. "Pierce."

"It's selfish of me to have you."

"Not if I want you too." She crooked her finger, beckoning me forward.

Instead, I held out my hand.

She placed her palm in mine without any hesitation and hopped off the counter. Then I hauled her out of the kitchen, heading for the bedroom. Except when her hand ran up my spine as we walked, I didn't make it past the couch.

The moment my feet hit the plush rug in the living room I spun and slammed my lips on hers. I gave myself one kiss before I started stripping the straps of her bra off her shoulders.

She reached behind her back, freeing the clasp. My hands were on her breasts before the lace could land on the floor by our feet.

"Yes," she hissed when I kneaded the curves, my fingers finding her pebbled nipples. I'd thought her lips were her most perfect feature, but now that I had my hands on her bare skin, I realized I'd been wrong.

Kerrigan arched her back, pressing into my touch. Then her hands dove for the drawstring on my shorts, tugging it free. But I didn't let her drag them off, not yet. I captured her wrists, holding them back as I dropped to my knees.

Her eyes flared. "What are you doing?"

I answered by pressing my mouth to her navel, letting my tongue dart out for a slow lick of her belly.

"Pierce." Her hands came to my hair.

I glanced up and gave her a wicked smile. "Hold still."

"With you on your knees? No chance."

I chuckled and kissed her again, right above the line where her panties were hiding my treasure. My fingertips slipped into the lace and, inch by inch, I removed them from her hips. The entire time, I kept my eyes glued to hers. Only after she stepped out of her panties, did I take in her bare mound. "You are perfect."

My hands went to her thighs, spanning her creamy skin and forcing her legs apart. Her chest was rising and falling in quick, short gasps. Her nipples, peaked above me, begged for a suck, but instead, I dove into the apex of her thighs.

One stroke of my tongue and she swayed, her hands clenching my hair to keep her balance.

"Oh, God," she moaned, her head lolling to the side.

I shifted my grip to her hips, holding her tight, as I went in for another stroke through her glistening folds.

She trembled beneath my tongue and I ached to watch her come undone.

Lick after lick of my tongue, she rocked into my mouth as I sucked and nipped and savored her taste. I avoided her clit, waiting until she was soaked and trembling. Then I finally found the little bud and drew it into my mouth.

"Pierce," she hissed. My name on her tongue was as erotic as her taste.

"Get on the couch."

She swallowed hard but obeyed, perching on the edge.

"Lie back," I ordered, taking one of her ankles to spread her wide.

She opened for me, with one leg draped over the couch and the other dangling toward the rug. Thank fuck she was flexible because that was going to make this a lot of fun.

Bare and wet and ready, the sight of her pussy made my cock throb. I leaned in, flattening my tongue and dragging it along her slit until I reached her clit, then I latched on and sucked. Hard.

"Ah," she cried, her hips coming off the couch.

I held her in place and feasted on the woman who'd ensnared me from the moment she'd cursed my name on a sidewalk in Calamity.

I devoured her, shamelessly loving her juices on my face. Each lick made me want another. And as she trembled and writhed, I brought one hand to her center and pushed a finger into her hot channel.

She moaned, her neck arching. "I'm going to come."

I added a finger. "Come, babe."

Flicking my tongue over her clit, I kept at her until the flutter of her inner walls warned of her orgasm.

On a cry of my name, her body pulsed, quake after quake as she broke. As it rang through her body, I closed my eyes and memorized her taste. The sound of her coming. The silk of her skin and the warmth of her heat.

Someday, I hoped she'd remember this night and smile. I hoped she'd think of me as often as I'd think of her.

I already longed for her and she hadn't even left yet.

As her first orgasm eased, I planted a kiss on her inner thigh, then shifted to take in her face.

There was a gorgeous flush to her cheeks and her chest. She panted, trying to regain her breath. Then her eyes cracked open and sheer pleasure swam in those chocolate pools.

"That was the best orgasm of my life." A flash of shock hit her face and then she smiled, slapping a hand over her eyes. "That was supposed to stay inside my head."

I chuckled and moved on top of her, pulling her hand away. "Don't hide your confessions."

Her gaze softened and she lifted, pressing her lips to mine, tasting herself on my lips. Then she reached between us for my shorts.

I caught her hand. "I don't have a condom."

"Oh." She froze. "I don't either. But I'm on birth control. And I haven't been with anyone in a long time."

I gulped at the idea of sliding inside of her bare. "I'm clean."

She bit her bottom lip and tugged her hand out of my grip. Her palm came to my erection, dragging along the length. "Then fuck me, Pierce."

"Jesus." I couldn't get naked fast enough.

Kerrigan kept her legs spread wide, waving at me to hurry.

The moment the shorts joined her wet panties on the floor, I gripped my shaft and dragged the tip through her folds.

"Yes." She arched into me. "Pierce."

My name was all I needed to surge inside. "Oh, fuck."

She clamped around me and my God, she was tight and wet. I buried my face in her shoulder, taking a moment before I made a goddamn fool of myself.

Summoning every ounce of my control, I leaned back and pulled out, only to glide inside, burying myself to the hilt. "You feel . . ."

"So. Good." Her arms snaked around my ribs, her hands splaying on my back and holding me to her.

How could I have thought we'd only need tonight? It wouldn't be enough.

I shoved up on one arm so I could watch my cock disappear into her body as I thrust inside once more. Kerrigan's gaze was on us too. She fit me like the two of us had been meant for this.

That was not the thought I should be having. One night. Maybe two. That was all we had together. So I blocked out everything in my mind screaming to claim her, to make her mine, and focused on giving her another orgasm.

We moved together, her hips rising to meet mine, like practiced lovers. Her hands explored the contours of my back while mine traced the swell of her breasts and plucked at those rosy nipples.

Her breath hitched as I moved, faster and faster, until the sound of skin slapping skin chorused off the living room walls and the tremors in her limbs vibrated against mine.

Her mouth parted, her eyes flashed. Then she was coming, clenching around me so hard that it had to have shoved the orgasm I'd given her with my mouth to a distant second place.

I closed my eyes as she squeezed around me and let go of my own release on a roar. White stars broke across my vision as I poured into her, and the entire world ceased to exist. It was simply us and our bodies, reaching the highest peaks and tumbling into the oblivion.

It took minutes, hours, to return to the room. When I opened my eyes, I was splayed on top of Kerrigan, her hips cradling mine as her legs wound around my lower back.

"Damn." I planted a kiss on her neck, then lifted to an elbow.

Her hair was mussed and spread everywhere. A strand was caught in her mouth. I pulled it free as she opened her eyes and stared up at me.

Normally this would be the time to pull out and head for

the shower. But I stared at her, unsure of what to say, because everything I'd been thinking moments before coming inside her was written on her face.

It wasn't enough. There was something here, something deeper than either of us had expected. She was more potent than any drug. She was more addictive than any game. She was more powerful than money.

Tonight wasn't enough.

But it would have to be.

So I swept her off the couch and into my arms, carrying her to my bedroom. If I could never forget this night, neither would she.

———

LIGHT STREAMED through the windows and onto my pillow. I twisted and stretched an arm to the other side of the bed. Cold. I shot off my pillow. The room was empty and beyond the door, it was silent.

She left.

"No." My stomach plummeted, and I flung the covers free, swinging my legs to the floor. I sprinted for the closet, swiping up a pair of pants. I hopped into them as I moved toward the door.

"Kerrigan?" I called as I jogged down the hallway.

Nothing.

The house was silent.

Goddamn it. This was bound to happen. This is what *had* to happen. But I wasn't ready to let her go. Not after last night.

The kitchen was empty, but the coffee pot was full. I

passed the living room and stopped when I looked at the couch. How many times had I sat there?

Every single moment on that couch had been erased because when I stared at the leather, I only saw Kerrigan.

Damn it. Now she was gone.

It was probably easiest this way. The longer we were together, the harder it would be to hold back the truth. If she left, I didn't have to explain. I didn't have to tell her everything that was happening with Jasmine. I didn't have to say a word.

But she could have at least said goodbye.

"Fuck." I ran a hand through my hair just as a scraping noise came from outside.

My gaze whipped to the windows and the snow still piled against the glass. The tufts caught the sunshine and cast a blinding glow into the house. I moved for the entryway and the source of the noise.

A flash of a red coat. My grandfather's red coat I'd found in his closet.

There was only one person who could be wearing that coat.

A wave of relief hit me so hard I had to take a moment to steady my feet. She hadn't left. She was outside shoveling the damn sidewalk.

I shook my head and threw the door open.

Kerrigan whirled around, standing straight. Her cheeks were flushed and the tip of her nose was red. The woman was so stunning, wearing a too-big coat, that my heart skipped.

"What are you doing?"

She lifted the shovel. "Shoveling."

"Why are you shoveling?"

"Why not?"

"There's a maintenance crew who will do that."

She waved it off. "That's silly."

"Will you come inside?"

"I'm almost done."

"Kerrigan." I leaned against the door, crossing my arms over my bare chest. "Come inside."

Her gaze tracked to my arms and my naked torso. The desire in her eyes was as bright as the morning sun. "Okay."

As soon as she was close enough, I took the shovel from her hand and propped it beside the door, then I grabbed her arms and dragged her into mine, kicking the door closed as I crushed my lips to hers.

She moaned as my tongue swept inside her mouth. I kissed her long and slow like I'd planned to do in bed.

"Morning," I murmured when I pulled away.

"Morning."

"You snuck out of bed." I unzipped her coat.

She shrugged it off her shoulders, revealing my sweats beneath. "I can't sleep in."

"When I'm in bed with you, there's never a need to sleep."

"Noted." Her hand ran up my chest, then she leaned in and pressed a kiss to my heart. "Want some breakfast?"

"Not yet." I bent and, in one smooth motion, tossed her over my shoulder.

"Pierce." She giggled and swatted at me to put her down, but I carted her straight to bed, tossing her onto the mattress and diving for the waistband of the sweats.

"No panties." Goddamn, this woman. I was instantly hard.

She sat up and ripped the hoodie over her head. "They're drying in the laundry room."

My pants joined hers on the floor and then there was no more talking. We picked up exactly where we'd left off the night before, exploring and tasting and touching, until we both crashed into our pillows, totally spent.

There was a smile on her pretty lips as she stared at the ceiling.

"What are you thinking?" I traced a circle around one of her nipples.

"I haven't had this much sex in, well . . . a long time."

"Neither have I." I moved over her, taking in the line of her cheeks and the shape of her forehead. I touched the tip of her nose. "Don't go today."

"I should get back."

"Have you checked the road report?"

She shook her head. "Not yet."

"Then don't. Let's pretend we're still trapped here." One more day to be reckless. To live this dream. Then I'd go back to reality.

"Okay." She didn't hesitate. "Would you like me to help you clear Gabriel's things out today?"

I groaned and buried my face in her hair. "I don't want to."

"You can't avoid it forever."

"Why not?"

She laughed and brought her hands to the back of my head. "I'll help."

The two of us roused from bed and restarted the day with coffee and a late breakfast. Then we worked together, going room by room and sorting through Grandpa's cabin. Anything that I wanted to keep was put in a corner of the living room. I'd pay someone from the club to pack that pile and ship it to me in Colorado. Everything else was either put in trash bags or in a guest room where I'd instruct the caretaker to donate the items to charity.

In the end, the keep stack wasn't more than a cluster of framed photos and a few mementos. I'd found a carved wooden camel from Morocco. I had a matching one in my penthouse that he'd given me as a gift from the trip. There was a letter opener engraved with his father's initials. And his wedding ring from when he'd been married to my grandmother. Mom had looked for it at his Denver home but hadn't found it.

"That's it." I stared at the pile. "Should it be bigger?"

Kerrigan slid an arm around my waist, tucking herself into my side. "It's big enough."

"Why do you think he wanted me to go through this place?" There hadn't been anything shocking in his belongings. I'd feared I'd find a letter or note. But the only item that had been difficult to see had been Heidi's photo and I'd thrown that out days ago.

"Most of those photos are of you, Pierce." Kerrigan looked up and gave me a sad smile. "I think he wanted you to see that he loved you."

Nearly every shelf in his office had held a picture of the two of us amongst the books.

I leaned into her, dropping my chin to her hair. "He could have simply told me."

"Would you have listened?"

"No," I admitted.

I'd been so angry with him. I wouldn't have heard a word he had to say. The last words I'd spoken to him had been in a rage. I'd told him never to speak to me again. That he was dead to me.

And now he truly was.

All I had left of him were a pile of photos and unspoken regrets.

My chest tightened. "I don't know if I'll ever forgive him."

Kerrigan simply held me tighter.

We stood there together, unspeaking as the memory of Grandpa filled the room, until a pounding came at the front door. The knock was followed by the doorbell's chime.

I didn't let her go. I didn't move.

"Pierce."

"Don't," I pleaded.

There was no question who was at the door. It was likely a maintenance crew or the club's caretaker checking to make sure I was alive and had withstood the storm. And if they were here, then it meant the roads were beginning to clear.

The doorbell rang again.

"Stay the night." *One more night.*

Kerrigan loosened her hold, then she rose up on her toes to press her lips to mine. "Okay."

CHAPTER TWELVE

KERRIGAN

SHIT, I was going to cry. Why? This was crazy, right? I'd spent less than a week in total with Pierce, yet here I was, choking to death on the threat of tears.

I was definitely going to cry. In a minute. I'd save the tears for the trip home.

"Drive safe," Pierce said as we stood beside the open door.

I nodded and slung my purse over a shoulder. "You too."

He stepped in close, framing my face with his hands. There was restless urgency in his eyes. Like there were words inside his head clawing to be set free. It was much too soon for those kinds of words.

Still, there they were, swimming in his eyes. Swirling in mine too.

This. Us. There was something here worth exploring, but I couldn't bring myself to ask for more.

Because if Pierce rejected me, if he said no—and he would, his message about a relationship had been crystal clear—I wasn't sure I'd recover from it. I'd survived a broken engagement, but if Pierce turned me down, it might crush my heart.

He opened his mouth.

My breath caught. Maybe . . . *please*. Don't let this be the end. I hoped beyond reason, searching his eyes for a sign that I wasn't alone in this.

It was there in those dark brown irises. I wasn't alone in this.

Please.

Pierce closed his mouth. He shook his head and pulled me into his arms for one last hug.

Damn. My foolish hopes were swept through the door into the wind, like a snowflake vanishing into a drift.

"Take care of yourself." His voice was jagged. His arms tightened so hard it was like he was trying to brand my body against his.

Or maybe that was me clinging to him. I didn't want to forget the hard plane of his chest beneath my cheek. I wanted to remember for the rest of my days how it felt to be in his strong arms.

The tears were coming. They were scratching their way up my throat, but I refused to cry in front of him. This fling had been my idea. Whatever pain it caused was mine alone to bear.

So I peeled myself away and stepped back to force a smile. "Thank you. This was the best time I've had in a long time."

He reached out and tucked a lock of hair behind my ear. "Same here."

Moments passed as we stared, drinking each other in. My eyes roved over his face, committing every perfect piece to memory. The square line of his jaw. The beard that felt like sin against my skin. The sparkle in his eyes and the way he looked at me like I was the most beautiful woman in the world.

I'd seen that look before, on the faces of my friends' husbands as they gazed at their wives. It was wholly unsettling and powerful aimed my way. And it was heartbreaking to come from a man who wasn't mine to keep.

Pierce had made it clear . . . there was no future.

Without another word, I stepped through the door. The chill hit fast, and bless the cold, it gave me something else to think about as I took a step onto the snow-dusted sidewalk.

I made it three strides before a hand clamped over my elbow, spinning me around. Then Pierce's lips were there, moving over mine in a kiss that stole my breath and flooded my body with every sensation. One kiss and I came alive.

His arms banded around me as his tongue swept inside, dueling with my own. One last time. It hurt to kiss him because damn it, this man could kiss. He'd ruined me for anyone else.

For the rest of my days, I wouldn't forget Pierce Sullivan. Even if I had to let him go.

He broke away, dropping his forehead to mine.

He was barefoot.

I wouldn't say goodbye, so I simply stepped back, met those eyes of his once more before turning on a heel and striding away.

Don't look back. Oh, how I wanted to, but I didn't let myself. I didn't let myself see him go inside and close the door.

But I did let myself cry.

The moment I was out of the driveway and headed down the road in my mother's car, I let the tears fall. Mile after mile, they dripped down my cheeks. It wasn't until I was driving down First Street that I wiped the last one away.

I navigated the familiar roads, drawing comfort from home, as I headed to The Refinery.

The lights were on and Mom was there, sitting at the desk, reading a book. She'd see my splotchy face and know I'd been crying, but I didn't have the energy to hide from her today. To put on a false smile.

"Hi, Mom," I said, walking through the door.

"Hi!" She shot off her seat and rushed my way, blinking when she took in my face. "Honey, what is it?"

"Nothing." I waved it off and fell into her arms. Would there ever be a time when a hug from Mom didn't help? "It's just been one hell of a week."

"I'm sure you're exhausted after having to put up with that man." She stroked a hand up and down my back. "Was it awful?"

"No, it was fine." It had been wonderful. But I wasn't in the mood to tell her about Pierce or defend him when I doubted she'd understand.

Maybe he'd stay my secret forever. Like the pregnancy I'd lost. Maybe the only person who'd ever get my confessions was Pierce.

"You should go home," she said.

"No, I'll take over." I let her go. "You've been here all week."

"I don't mind. I actually like it here."

Did she have to sound so surprised? "That's great."

"I even did a yoga class yesterday."

I raised my eyebrows. Mom had shown exactly zero interest in this gym's offerings. "Really?"

She nodded. "It was fun. I invited your aunts down to do

it with me this afternoon. This studio is really something special."

I blinked. Had she just given me a compliment about my business? Since I'd opened The Refinery, the only family who'd come in were three of my cousins and Larke. "That's . . . great."

"See? There's really no need for you to be here today. Besides, you look wiped."

Because Pierce had kept me up all night long. "Are you sure?"

"Yes. Your dad is picking me up so you might as well drive my car home. We can pick it up here tomorrow."

"Okay." I should probably stay and do some work, but I could use some alone time at home. Some time to get my bearings, because everything seemed to have shifted. How did life change so quickly?

Days. That was all I'd had with Pierce. Days. But it was like I'd stepped off a cliff to return to reality.

"Are you sure you're okay?" Mom placed her hand on my arm and gave me her worried look. Furrowed forehead. Lips pursed.

"I'm good." I forced one last smile and hugged her again. "Like I said, it was just a weird week." Weird and wonderful and wild.

"Did something happen?"

I think I might have fallen a little bit in love. "No."

"Did he mistreat you?"

"Of course not."

"I don't trust that man." She huffed. "His grandfather either."

My family had never understood my relationship with Gabriel. Whenever I brought him up in conversation, I'd end up defending both Gabriel and my own choices. They thought taking his money was unnecessary since there were banks in town. Dad especially didn't like Gabriel—part of me wondered if it was jealousy.

After a few years, I'd stopped talking about Gabriel at all around my family. It was easier that way.

And since I was sure it would be the same with Pierce, I'd keep my mouth closed.

"Thanks again, Mom."

"Get some rest. I'll take care of everything here, and I'll see you tomorrow morning."

"Okay. Bye." With a wave, I returned to her car and drove home. The moment I stepped through the front door, a fresh batch of tears welled.

This home, a place I'd cherished, was so . . . lonely.

"What is wrong with me?" I asked the empty living room as I dumped my purse on the couch.

Days. It had only been days. Pierce and I didn't even know each other. He didn't know that I rarely painted my nails because I ended up picking off the polish within a day. He didn't know that I'd had an irrational fear of tornados ever since my third-grade teacher had made us study them for a class project. He didn't know my favorite color was green and that I preferred still water to sparkling.

He didn't know me, like I didn't know him. So why did it feel like I'd just lost someone? My someone.

"I'm crazy."

"For talking to yourself? Uh, yeah."

I screamed and whirled around as my brother came striding out of the kitchen with Clementine in his arms. I'd been so distracted that I hadn't noticed his car when I'd pulled up.

Zach wore a pair of black slacks and a blue button-down shirt. My brother was tall, like most of the men in our family. His hair was a shade lighter than mine, but otherwise, there was no mistaking us for siblings. And dressed in the dealership's unofficial uniform, he was the spitting image of our father.

The moment Clementine spotted me, she squirmed and jumped to the floor, trotting over to rub up against my legs.

"Oh, Clem. I missed you." I swept her up, pressing my cheek to the soft white fur on her head as she nuzzled against me. "Thanks for feeding her."

Zach was the only one she tolerated besides me. Probably because they both had attitudes.

"Her litter box is full," he said. "And now that you're here, I'm not going to clean it."

"A welcome home gift."

He chuckled and came over to pull me into a sideways hug. The scent of smoke and cigarettes clung to his clothes.

I squirmed away. "You said you quit smoking."

He frowned. "Well, I didn't."

"You promised."

"Let it go, Kerrigan. I've got things on my mind."

"Like what?" He had a good job. He had his own home. He wasn't married and didn't have kids.

"Like . . . it's none of your business. Don't you have enough of your own problems to worry about? You're going broke. You don't even have a car. This place is a wreck. Mom's running your fancy studio because you don't have any employees to cover while you're spending the week at a mountain resort. Maybe instead of worrying about me, you should tackle some of your own problems first."

I blinked.

Wow.

It stung every time he threw my failures in my face. Every. Single. Time. I should be used to it by now because Zach had taken it upon himself to act as the outspoken authority on all the ways I was messing up my life.

Once upon a time, I'd looked up to my big brother. I'd valued his opinion. When he'd been racing ahead, I'd just kept running to catch him.

But these days, I avoided his company unless it was Sunday dinner at Mom and Dad's.

I walked to the door and flung it open. "Well, it looks like you're working so don't let me keep you. Thanks again for feeding Clementine."

"Yeah." He scowled and stormed out.

I slammed the door behind him. "Ass."

Clementine flicked her tail in my face.

"Don't defend him."

I set her on her feet and went to my purse, digging out my phone. My heart sank at the empty screen.

Would I hear from Pierce again? Or had today really been goodbye? Now I regretted not saying the word.

Maybe Lucy or Everly would be up for a drink at Jane's. I went to type out a text only to delete it before hitting send. It would probably be best not to sit at home alone and dwell, but I didn't want to be around people. Tonight, all I wanted was to hang out with my cat and nurse the ache in my chest that shouldn't be there.

It shouldn't be there, right?

"But it is," I whispered.

Even though I didn't want to change my clothes because they still smelled like Pierce, I went to my bedroom and stripped off my jeans and sweater, trading them for a simple white tee and my paint-splattered overalls.

Tomorrow, I'd have to talk to my realtor about taking this place off the market. The farmhouse too. The term on my listing contract was three months but I doubted she'd hold me to it. In the meantime, I needed something to take my mind off Pierce.

So I went to work, first by taking pictures of the powder bathroom off the kitchen. I snapped photo after photo at varying angles. I'd already primed and prepped the walls a couple weeks ago so these were actually mid-progress shots but I had a few true *before* pictures saved in my camera roll. Then I went to the dining room table and plucked up the gallon of deep green paint I'd earmarked for the space.

The color was dark and bold, a reflection of my mood, and as I sat on the tiled floor and began to cut in around the trim, I found a center. The strokes of the brush helped ease some of the sting and as the hours passed, the room transformed.

How many women could say they had a romantic, exhilarating week filled with passion? How many women could say that a man like Pierce had treated them like a queen? How many women had literally been swept off their feet?

Yes, I should simply be grateful. To count myself lucky to be one of those women. But . . .

"I want more," I whispered.

For the first time in years, I wasn't okay looking into the future and seeing a solitary life.

The tears had dried up, shed for today, but the hole in my chest had doubled and this tiny room couldn't hold it all, so I shoved off my feet, slapped the lid back on the paint can and went to the kitchen.

I was putting my roller and paint brush into a plastic bag and stowing them in the fridge when the front door opened.

"Kerrigan," my sister called.

"I'm in here," I called back, going to the sink to wash the paint from my hands.

"Hey." She came into the room, shrugging off her coat. "I'm glad you're home. I was getting worried."

"All is well." I smiled over my shoulder.

"So? How'd it go?"

"It was, um . . . fine." Incredible. Life altering.

"Did you get it from him?"

"Uh." I froze as the water rushed over my hands. How did she know?

"The extension on your contract."

"Oh." I blushed and shook my head, turning off the faucet and swiping up a towel to dry my hands. "Yes. He agreed to a payment plan, so I won't have to sell everything."

"Yay! Then it was worth being stuck up there with the arrogant jerk. Ugh. I can't imagine. Did you have to deal with him much or did he at least leave you alone?"

"He was . . . nice."

"Nice?"

"Yeah. Nice."

"What did you even do up there?"

Each other. The admission nearly slipped out and I hid a smile. Maybe someday I'd share my story about Pierce with her, but for now, he was mine to keep for myself. "Mostly just hung out." *Naked.* "Anything exciting happen here while I was gone?"

She shrugged. "Nothing much. My students were driving me insane today and I was doubting everything about being a teacher. But then one of the girls came up to me at the last recess and told me that I was the prettiest teacher in the whole school, so it cheered me up."

I laughed. "She's not wrong."

Larke waved it off and went to the fridge. "What are you doing for dinner? This is empty."

Besides my paint tools, all I had was ketchup, mustard and jelly. The bread I'd bought before my trip to the mountains was probably stale and moldy.

"Now that I'm not trying to save every cent I can find, I might splurge on pizza," I said.

"I'll go in half with you."

"Deal." I found my phone and called in the order for delivery. Then I showed Larke the progress I'd made in the powder bath and told her about my idea to start blogging.

"What do you think?" I held my breath. She was the most supportive of any family members, but my sister was also the most honest of any family members.

"I like it."

"Yeah? It might flop."

"But it might not. And what do you have to lose? Try it. If you hate it or it goes nowhere in the next five years, you're not out much. Besides, you love the DIY stuff."

"I really do." I smiled, loving the smell of fresh paint coming from the powder room.

The doorbell rang.

"Pizza," Larke and I said in unison.

"I'll get it." She headed for the door while I took out plates and glasses. What I needed was wine, but tonight, we'd have to settle for water.

"Uh . . . Kerrigan?"

"Yeah?"

"Can you come out here?"

Not liking the uncertainty in her voice, I hurried from the kitchen. "What's—"

My feet stopped short at the man in the doorway. He didn't work for the Pizza Palace.

Pierce stood on my stoop, wearing jeans and a sweater. His frame seemed to fill the entire threshold.

Was he really here? Or had I fallen asleep and the paint fumes had conjured him in a dream?

"Hi." That voice, rich and deep, was most definitely real.

"Hi," I breathed.

As Larke looked back and forth between us, a smile stretched across her face. Then she left Pierce's side, walking past me for the kitchen and returning with her coat. "I'll expect more details later other than he was nice and you hung out. Have a good night."

"Bye," I murmured, not looking away from Pierce.

When Larke slipped past him, he stepped inside and closed the door.

The state of my house was a wreck of half-finished projects. The far wall in the living room was edged with a plum paint but I hadn't had time to roll the rest of the wall. The end table that I'd sanded down sat in a corner, unstained and raw. The couch was draped with Clementine's favorite blanket and it was long overdue for a dehairing.

Then there was me. My hair was a mess, twisted on top of my head. My overalls were splattered with every shade of paint, not just the powder room's green. And my tee was so threadbare that it was practically transparent.

"I'm a mess," I confessed.

"You're beautiful."

A flush crept into my cheeks. "What are you doing here?"

He crossed the room, his long legs and confident swagger sending a rush of desire to my core. Then he was there, towering over me like he had been just this morning. "I need one more night."

My knees nearly buckled.

"Give me one more night."

"Yes," I said in a rushed breath. He could have as many nights as he wanted.

Pierce's hand came to my cheek and his thumb brushed across my skin. He pulled it away and showed me a streak of green. "You've been busy."

I giggled. "I was trying to get my mind off of a certain tall and handsome billionaire."

"Did it work?" His fingertip returned to my face, tracing the line of my cheekbone.

"No."

He leaned down, grinning against my lips. "Good."

Then his mouth was on mine and my hands snaked up his chest to wrap around his shoulders. We kissed like we'd spent days apart, not hours. And when the doorbell rang again, I had to tear myself away.

"Who's that?"

"Pizza," I panted.

I rushed to answer on unsteady legs. "Hi," I told the delivery kid. "One sec."

My purse. Where was my purse? I spun in a circle, searching. I scrambled for it on the couch, but before I could dig out my wallet, Pierce strode past me, taking out some cash from his pocket and trading it for a medium, hand-tossed pepperoni pizza.

"Thanks. Keep the change," he told the kid, whose eyes widened at the hundred-dollar bill in his grip.

Pierce carried my dinner to the kitchen.

I unglued my feet and followed.

"Are you hungry?" he asked, the box hovering over the plates I'd set out for Larke and me.

"Not for pizza."

He smiled and stowed the box in the fridge.

Then it was my turn to lead, straight for the bedroom.

Hours later, we reheated the pizza and, barely clothed, ate it standing in the kitchen because my table was cluttered with paint cans and drop cloths and random tools I'd deposited in between. Then we returned to my bed and spent the rest of the night in each other's arms.

———

ONE MORE NIGHT together didn't make it easier when morning came. I fought the same tears as I stood in my doorway, watching Pierce drive away.

I made a wish as his taillights disappeared around a corner.

Come back to me.

CHAPTER THIRTEEN

PIERCE

"HI." I hated myself for being so damn weak when it came to this woman.

"Hi." There was a smile in Kerrigan's voice on the other end of the phone call. "I wasn't sure I'd hear from you. How was your trip home?"

"Long." By the time I'd made it home on Friday evening, I'd been exhausted. Saturday and Sunday had been spent in the office, mostly in an attempt to keep myself from calling Kerrigan.

I'd done well. With a hectic Monday calendar, it should have been easy to keep my thoughts on business. But as it turned out, letting her go was harder than I could have ever expected.

"How was your weekend?" I asked.

"Um . . . fine? I worked."

I miss you. I swallowed it down. Admitting that to her would only make this harder. "I wish . . ." I wished everything were different.

"You don't have to explain, Pierce. You said you weren't in a place for a relationship. I understand."

Of course she did. Because she was unlike any woman I'd ever met. "I have to say goodbye."

"Didn't we do that on Friday?"

"I don't remember saying the word." But I had given her a kiss I wouldn't forget. And hopefully . . . neither would she.

Eventually she'd move on with her life. I wasn't stupid enough to think otherwise, but the idea of her with another man made my stomach churn and my temper rage.

She was mine.

And I was in no position to keep her.

This phone call was a fucking horrible idea.

"I wanted to let you know I've given your information to my attorney. He'll pass along a new contract."

"Oh, okay."

"If you ever need anything, you know where to find me."

"Same to you."

"All right." End the call. Say goodbye. Be done with this.

Neither of us hung up.

"You're still there," I said.

"So are you."

"Can I call you again?" *Damn it, Sullivan.*

What the fuck was wrong with me today? Another phone call was as bad an idea as this one. It would only delay the inevitable.

Maybe she'd say no. I needed her to say no.

I needed her to break this off. To find the strength I lacked.

Instead, she said, "Yes." Relief beat out frustration. "But if you don't, I'll understand."

How? She had no idea what was happening in my life. I'd denied her the explanation she'd earned.

Kerrigan deserved to know the reason I couldn't pursue this with her. But I'd kept Jasmine a secret, probably because I wasn't ready to accept that everything in my life was about to change.

"Take care of yourself," I said.

"You too."

I opened my mouth to say goodbye. The word hung on the tip of my tongue, but rather than speak it, I took the coward's way and hung up the phone.

"Fuck," I muttered, dragging a hand through my hair.

Calling her had been a horrible idea. It should have ended at her house on Friday, but now I just wanted to call her again.

Nellie knocked on my office door, opening it a crack. "Pierce?"

"Come on in."

She smiled and strode inside with a stack of papers in one hand. "I need twenty minutes."

I checked my calendar. My meeting with our general counsel was in ten. He could wait five. "I've got fifteen."

Nellie took the chair across from my desk, spread out the papers and went through them, one by one. As she talked about the next executive team meeting agenda and finalizing the upcoming year's business plan, I studied my phone.

I needed to call Kerrigan again. I needed to explain or, at least, end things differently.

I had time.

Not much, but I had time. Maybe I could go to Calamity, just once more. Spend one more night in her bed.

Kerrigan's house had surprised me. There'd been

projects everywhere, some further along than others. I'd expected to see something clean, like The Refinery. But then again, she'd put her businesses first, saving her own home for last.

The image of her naked in her bed, her hair spread across her lavender pillows in the muted light, tiny specks of green paint on her forehead . . . I'd never get that image out of my head.

"Well?" Nellie asked.

I blinked and looked up. "Huh?"

She frowned. "You haven't listened to a word I've said, have you?"

I rubbed my face and sighed. "Sorry."

"What's going on with you? You've been distracted all day."

Distracted? Right now, I'd kill if distracted was my biggest problem. "Just a lot on my mind."

Nellie tossed her pen on the desk and leaned back in her chair, taking out her phone. Her fingers flew across the screen and when she was done, she set it aside. "I just canceled your next meeting. Talk."

I stood from my desk, not wanting to feel trapped in a seat, and walked to the windows. It was a beautiful winter day, the sun shining across the city. This view had been a sanctuary for me this past year. When everything had fallen apart with Heidi, I'd stared out the glass and silenced my thoughts.

Today, they screamed despite the view.

"Do you think it's possible to fall in love with someone in just days?"

Nellie's breath hitched. "Oh, Pierce."

"She's special. I wish the timing were different."

"You could tell her the truth. Kerrigan would understand."

Yes, she would. But I wouldn't put this burden on her. "I need to do this on my own."

"Why?"

"Because that's how it should be. Parents should put their children first."

"It doesn't have to be one way or the other. You could have both."

I shook my head. "She lives in Montana."

Kerrigan wanted a life in Calamity. That was where she was building her dreams. I wouldn't steal them from her.

"People have moved before," Nellie said.

"I won't ask her to do that."

"Not her. You. There's no reason you have to live in Denver."

"My company is here. My parents."

"Your parents are never here. They look for any excuse to travel. And since you've been driving everywhere lately, you must have forgotten that you own a plane."

I closed my eyes. "It would never work."

Why would a woman like Kerrigan want anything to do with the insanity that was going to be my life?

"Did you tell her about Heidi?" Nellie asked.

"Yeah."

"What did she say?"

I turned from the glass and returned to my chair. "It shocked her."

"Duh. It shocked everyone."

Nellie had adored Grandpa before his affair with Heidi had come to light. From that moment on, she'd loathed him.

Probably because she knew, though I was angry and hurt, I couldn't despise him myself.

Kerrigan had been right about what she'd said at the house. Those photos and the memories that accompanied them had made some of the pain go away. Not a lot, but some.

"Do you think he loved her?" I asked.

"Kerrigan?"

"No. Heidi."

Nellie gave me a sad smile. "Yes, I do. And I think she loved him."

"It just . . . it's so fucked up." I pinched the bridge of my nose. "I'd like an updated status report on the ventures we brought in from Barlowe."

Nellie's sideways look said she didn't approve of the change in subject but she went along with it. "I'll have it by the end of the day."

"Now let's go through this again." I motioned to the paperwork she'd brought in.

"Pierce—"

"What?"

"Never mind." She pursed her lips, then picked up a page and started where I'd zoned out earlier.

Twenty minutes hadn't been enough to make it through her list or mine. After an hour, she had more to do than when she'd walked through the door.

"Anything else?" she asked.

"I'm going to lean on you. Hard. I'm sorry for it."

Her expression softened. "Don't be. I'm here."

"Has Jasmine called?"

"Every day."

Damn it. She'd called me every day too. I hadn't returned those calls either. I wasn't ready. Not in the slightest.

"I want to fly to Montana tonight."

"What?" Nellie's jaw dropped.

I couldn't leave things with Kerrigan after that phone call. "Will you make arrangements with the pilot and airport? Just tonight. And . . . tomorrow night." I bit my tongue before I could add a third night.

"Are you going to tell her?"

"No."

"Then what are you doing?"

"Saying goodbye." How many goodbyes had I missed lately? My grandfather. My ex-wife. No one could have predicted that their plane would have gone down over the Rocky Mountains. The engine had failed on Grandpa's Cessna and they'd crashed in just minutes.

It would be hard as hell to step inside an airplane, especially since it was the same model as Grandpa's. But flying was safer, it should be safer, than driving in December. And I just . . . I had to get to Montana. I wanted one more night with Kerrigan.

One more before my life changed forever.

"I have time."

"You keep saying that." Nellie shook her head. "But you don't."

"I have time."

"Two nights?"

"Actually, you'd better make it just the one." Tonight. It would have to be enough.

"Okay." Nellie sighed and stood from her chair, disappearing to her own office where she'd make the necessary calls.

I had time.

One more night. I hurried upstairs to my penthouse and began packing the bag I'd just unpacked. The sweats that I'd lent Kerrigan were on a shelf. This morning they'd been in my hamper.

Damn. My housekeeper had already washed them. I picked up the hoodie and pressed it to my nose, wishing I could find Kerrigan's sweet scent.

It was gone.

One more night. Then I could let her go and get on with what was coming.

I picked up my phone, pulling up her name.

She answered on the second ring. "Hi."

"I'm flying up there tonight."

"Tonight? Um, okay."

"One more night. That's all I have."

"Then I'll take it."

My heart hammered. "It'll be late."

"I'll wait up."

Ending the call, I shoved my phone away and started grabbing clothes, not really caring what I picked because I didn't plan on wearing much.

Then with my overnight bag in hand, I strode through the penthouse toward the front door. I hit the button for the elevator and returned to my office, grabbing my laptop so I could work on the plane.

"Pierce." Nellie came into my office.

I scrambled to wrap up a power cord. "I should have time in the car for my last meeting of the day. Just have them call my cell."

"Pierce."

"Thanks for making this work." I took my wallet and keys from the top drawer of my desk. "I appreciate it."

"*Pierce.*" The urgency in her voice made me pause and look up.

The color had drained from her face. Her eyes were full of apology.

Nellie had looked the same the day that she'd come in to tell me that Grandpa and Heidi had died. Mom had tried to call me but I'd been busy, so she'd called Nellie and asked her to break the news.

I swallowed hard. "What?"

"It's Jasmine."

My heart dropped. "What happened?"

"She's at the hospital."

"Is she okay?"

Nellie nodded. "She's in labor."

The world shifted under my feet.

I was out of time.

"But it's early."

Nellie shook her head. "Not by much."

"Which hospital?" I asked.

"P/SL."

My gaze landed on the overnight bag I'd set on the desk. There would be no trip to Montana.

"I'll go with you," Nellie said.

I swallowed the lump in my throat, unable to tear my eyes from the bag. "Give me a minute."

"Of course." She turned to leave me alone.

Then I pulled the phone from my pocket and hit Kerrigan's name for the third time today.

"Hi." She laughed as she answered.

"Change of plan." My voice sounded hoarse and as

heavy as my heart. "I'm not going to make it up there tonight after all."

"Oh." The disappointment rang loud and clear.

"I'm sorry."

"Maybe another time."

I wanted to agree. I wanted to promise I'd come back. But the truth was, I had no idea what life would look like after today.

"Goodbye, Kerrigan."

The line went silent for a long moment, then she breathed, and my heart broke because there was pain in that sigh. Pain that was my doing.

"Goodbye, Pierce."

———

I JOGGED out of my office and found Nellie waiting in the foyer. We drove in silence across town, and when we reached Jasmine's room, Nellie hung back.

"I'm going to find a waiting room," she said. "But I'm here. Just call me if you need anything."

"Thanks." I squared my shoulders, knocked on the door and pushed inside the delivery room.

On the narrow hospital bed, Jasmine was propped up with a bunch of pillows. Her mousy brown hair was braided over one shoulder. Her pregnant belly protruded from the white hospital blanket draped over her legs.

The glare she sent me was as cold as the ice chips in her cup. "I'm shocked you actually showed up."

"I'm sorry." I sat on the edge of the bed. "I'm so sorry. But I'm here now."

Her jaw clenched. "Heidi would be so pissed at you."

"Yes." I chuckled. "And rightly so."

"You're an asshole."

"Pretty much."

The corner of her mouth turned up. "I'm not far along so this might take a while."

I stood and shrugged off my suit jacket, draping it over a chair in the corner. "I'm not going anywhere."

Not anymore.

CHAPTER FOURTEEN

KERRIGAN

FOUR MONTHS LATER...

"How's the new employee working out?" Lucy asked.

We were sitting on the couch in Everly's office at the art gallery, visiting while Lucy's son, Theo, played on the floor.

"So far so good." The woman I'd hired was sweet and bubbly. She worked five days a week, allowing me some flexibility in my schedule. I loved The Refinery but it was nice to have a break. Mostly, it was nice to afford an employee.

Two weeks ago, the sale on the farmhouse had closed. That property was now someone else's joy. Someone else's burden.

"Okay, I'd better go." I swallowed a groan. Jacob was meeting me at the White Oak for dinner at five thirty and I was already a few minutes late.

"You don't seem excited," Lucy said from the couch in Everly's office where the three of us were sitting.

I'm not. "Just not really in the mood for a date."

"So cancel," Everly said, placing her hands on her pregnant belly. "Hang out here with us. I haven't heard from Hux, so I'm sure he's zoned out in his studio painting."

"Duke is covering for one of his deputies for the evening shift so he's still at the station," Lucy said. "We haven't had a girls' night in ages."

"I want to, but I'm sure Jacob's already waiting for me, and I'd feel like an ass if I stood him up last minute."

After leaving the gym at four, I'd come down to meet them both and catch up with my friends. When they'd both moved here, we used to hit Jane's for a drink, but these days, we found ourselves either here at the gallery or at The Refinery.

It was easier with Theo to give him some space to explore. He'd just started crawling a couple of weeks ago.

He came up to my feet and I bent down to help him up, holding his hands as he swayed on his chubby legs. A drooly smile squeezed my heart.

Maybe someday.

Or maybe the chance to be a mother had passed me by.

Lucy and Everly had become good friends. Unlike most of Calamity's residents, they didn't even bat an eye at my business ideas. Maybe because they weren't from here. They'd moved here from Nashville and when I had an idea, they were completely supportive.

Lucy had been the first member of the gym, joining before I'd even opened its doors. Everly bragged that she was my first follower on Instagram *and* TikTok.

When the farmhouse had sold, they'd shown up at my house with champagne.

They were good friends and I adored them. But these past four months had been hard, for many reasons, and I found myself pulling away.

Theo squirmed and dropped to his knees, crawling over to his mom at my side.

"We should plan a movie date," Lucy said, picking him up and kissing his cheek. "How about tomorrow night? I think that new rom-com is at the theater this week."

We only got one or two movies at our local theater each week, and even then, oftentimes they'd already been released on a streaming platform. Thankfully, people around here usually went anyway for the popcorn, candy and atmosphere. The owners of the theater tried to plan fun events to keep the seats full. But one day, as the world changed, so would my town. Would the theater survive?

Probably not.

The past four months my head seemed to swim with grim thoughts. What was wrong with me? It was like a gray cloud had settled over my mind, tainting each thought with a depressing rain.

"I can't tomorrow," I said. "It's my grandma's birthday so we're having a big family celebration at the community center."

I did not want to go to a family event. But I didn't want to go to a movie either.

Except how did I tell my friends that their happy lives were hard to see? That while they were in love, I had never felt more inadequate and alone?

Everly was due in a couple of months with a baby girl. How did I tell my friend that just seeing her pregnant made the hole in my chest grow?

There was no way.

So I'd been tending to my businesses. My house. Every project on my list was nearly complete and for the first time, when I came home, there weren't paint cans and tools waiting on the dining room table.

"Then next week," Everly said. "Even if we just meet for lunch."

"Sounds good." I smiled and the three of us stood, making our way through the gallery to the front door.

"Have fun on your date." Lucy held up Theo's hand in a wave.

"Bye." I waved back, walking past the colorful paintings on the wall to step outside and onto the sidewalk.

Down the block, country music escaped Jane's front door. They had the live band playing tonight. Some Fridays, Lucy would join them and sing. The bar would be packed because how many towns could say they had a legitimate country music superstar as a local?

I turned the opposite direction and headed toward the White Oak, not far from my building. The scent of spring was on the breeze, but it hadn't warmed up yet and I was glad I'd worn a coat because there was a nip in the air.

Walking had become a type of therapy, a chance to think and reflect. I'd finally bought another car, another Explorer, but those months walking around town had made an impression. So I kept on walking, one step at a time, day after day.

"Hi, Kerrigan."

"Hi, Dan." I smiled at the owner of the hardware store as he passed me. He was always friendly, but every time I came in, he'd give me a look and say . . . *Another project?*

Yes, more projects. Lots and lots of projects. Because those projects were keeping me sane. And like my new employee, for the first time in months, I could afford them.

After Pierce had returned to Denver, I'd met with my realtor, fully intending to take both the farmhouse and my home off the market. But as we'd talked, I'd realized that I didn't want to own the farmhouse.

My two friends had nearly died there. It had been poisoned by a tragic event.

So I'd kept the listing at the market value, but decided to post photos about its remodel anyway. I'd gone through my archive and found the original pictures I'd taken after buying the place. Then I'd walked through each room, snapping new photos of the renovations I'd already done.

Somehow, a woman from Utah had stumbled across my Instagram feed. She'd been searching for listings in Montana because she and her husband had been planning a move. When she'd learned that the farmhouse was for sale, she'd called my realtor and offered the asking price. Not only had I recouped my tangible investments, but my sweat equity as well.

If all I accomplished with my blog was selling that property, I'd take it as a win.

At almost the same time, one of my renters had approached me about buying the home he and his wife had been renting from me. They loved the place and didn't want to move. So I'd sold it too.

With that, I'd paid off a mortgage. And the first thing I'd done when the funds from the farmhouse had hit my bank account was issue a check to Grays Peak Investments, paying off my entire debt.

With Pierce's payment plan, I wasn't required to pay him for years. But I'd made the decision to move on.

We'd said goodbye months ago, but it was time to actually let him go.

I found Jacob's white truck parked outside of the café as I crossed the street. My date was there, waiting for me. I slowed, hoping to feel a little blip of excitement. A tiny thrill at the thought of meeting a nice man for dinner.

But . . . nothing.

My feet carried me forward regardless. A green and white license plate caught my eye, causing me to do a double take. Parked three spaces away from Jacob's truck was a green Mercedes G-Class SUV with Colorado license plates.

As the daughter of a car salesman, I knew expensive cars. It was rare that Dad sold a vehicle with that price tag, especially a foreign model that would require specialty parts, but we had enough tourists in the area that he'd point out the fancy cars.

My feet slowed, my eyes glued to the Mercedes. It couldn't be him, right? Why would he come to Calamity? He wouldn't.

In four months, I hadn't heard a word from Pierce.

And I was a complete bitch for doing so, but I'd severed ties with Nellie too. I just . . . I couldn't talk to her. As sweet and kind as Nellie had been, I couldn't bring myself to call her because I knew the limitations of my self-control. If I talked to Nellie, I'd ask about Pierce. She'd tried me twice, around Christmas, but when I hadn't answered or called back, she'd given up.

Just like her boss.

There was no way that was Pierce's car. I shook myself out of that foolish dream, aimed my gaze and my feet to the White Oak and met my date.

"Hey." Jacob slid out of his chair, his arms wide open.

"Hi." I stepped into his embrace and prayed for the spark.

Again . . . *nothing*.

"Sorry I'm late," I said, wiggling free.

"No worries. Your brother was actually in here picking up a to-go order so I was talking to him."

"Did he leave already?" I scanned the room. Many familiar faces, but not my brother.

"Yeah, a few minutes ago. You just missed him."

"Darn," I lied.

Zach's latest criticism was that the woman I'd hired to work at the gym was a former girlfriend of his. How was I supposed to know who he dated? It wasn't like he'd ever brought her to a Sunday family dinner.

"How was work today?" I asked, taking the chair across from his.

"Good. Busy. How was your day?"

"Fine. Normal." I met his blue eyes and wished they were a dark brown.

Jacob and I had been dating for a month. Maybe after one more, I'd stop comparing him to Pierce.

But they couldn't be more different. Where Pierce had strong lines and sharp angles, Jacob was the exact opposite. His blond hair was cut short, making his face seem rounder than it already was. He was in shape, but he didn't have a cut, muscular frame like Pierce. I'd never seen Jacob in anything but a polo shirt. His nose turned up slightly at the end and his lips were thin.

Jacob wasn't bad looking. He just wasn't Pierce.

The waitress came over and took our orders, then the community came to my rescue. The great part about dating Jacob was that we both knew everyone in town, so as people left or came into the restaurant, they'd stop by our table and say hello.

It saved me from making small talk with my boyfriend.

Was he my boyfriend? I grimaced at the word.

"Are you okay?" Jacob asked as his cheeseburger and my chicken salad were delivered. "You seem off."

"I'm great," I lied, picking up my fork. Then I dove into my meal, making sure that my mouth was full to avoid conversation.

I was off. Off was definitely the word. Sure, I smiled. Everyone expected me to smile.

It was ironic that the only smiles that felt real these days were the ones I posted on social media. Weren't those supposed to be the fake ones? The highlight reel?

When I was working on a project at home, my hair would be a mess and I'd have paint on my fingers. But with a hammer or screwdriver in my hand, the smiles didn't seem so difficult.

"Then I called the guy and had to go through line by line on the invoice where they'd overcharged us." Jacob shook his head. "Took almost an hour. You'd think a large tire supplier would have a better system for billing."

"Yeah," I agreed, pretending that I'd been listening.

If there was ever motivation to make sure my blog and influencer plan took off, it was Jacob talking about work at the dealership. If we worked together, this was what our life would be. Cars. Parts. Tires. Mechanics.

Save me.

What was I doing here? Why was I dating him?

After so many years, I'd finally given in to Mom's pressuring. Probably because I'd been so hurt over Pierce's disappearance. And when I'd stopped by the dealership one afternoon last month to look at cars with Dad, Jacob had asked me out.

In a moment of weakness, I'd agreed.

The first few dates hadn't been bad. He hadn't talked

about the dealership as much. Mostly, we'd caught up on life since high school. But these last couple of dates had been . . . irritating.

Jacob was nice. He was smart and occasionally funny. So what was it about him that bugged me so much?

"How was the little gym today?" he asked, popping a fry into his mouth.

"Good." I studied him as he chewed. He had a normal chew. No strange sounds or weird chomps. I didn't have the overwhelming urge to devour his lips like I'd had with Pierce, but nothing with Jacob was like it had been with Pierce.

"And the little blog? Any new followers?"

A zing of annoyance skated up my spine. There. That was it.

Little.

How had I not noticed this before? I quickly replayed each of our dates, thinking back to the conversations we'd had about my rentals, the gym and my blog.

It had taken me months to get my website set up, and I'd shelled out a few thousand dollars to have a professional design it exactly the way I wanted because the standard cookie-cutter templates were not the aesthetic I was going for. That website was the reason I'd gone without a car for a couple of months in the new year.

But the end result had been worth the investment. Working on posts and photos was the highlight of my day.

My happiness wasn't *little.*

Yes, I only had 362 Instagram followers, most of whom were residents of Calamity or friends from college. Yes, my newsletter only had 102 subscribers. Yes, the only income I'd earned was thirty-six dollars and change from my Amazon affiliate sales.

Yes, it was little.

But the way he said that word diminished everything I'd been striving for. Like this was a hobby, not the start of what might become a career.

Well, this *little* relationship was over.

I finished my salad and drained the rest of my Diet Coke, then signaled for the waitress that we were ready for the check. "I'll buy dinner."

"No, I can't let you."

"I insist." I pulled out my wallet. "You've bought all of the others. It's only fair."

"But I have a job."

My body froze. Yep, we were done. So, so done. "I also have a job. I just happen to work for myself."

He didn't miss the sharpness in my tone and his eyes widened. "That's not what I meant."

"It's fine." I waved it off and plastered on a fake smile. "And I'm buying dinner."

"Okay." He wiped his mouth with a napkin and watched me hand over my credit card to the waitress.

When she brought it back over, I signed the receipt with an angry scribble, then shot out of my chair and yanked on my coat.

Jacob kept pace, hurrying with his own jacket.

I didn't wait for him when I turned and marched for the door. The moment I hit the sidewalk, I aimed my feet toward the gym.

"I was thinking." Jacob caught up, walking at my side. "Want to come over to my place tonight? We could have a drink. Watch a movie or . . . something."

Or something? No, thanks.

I came to a stop, whirling to face him so that I could

break this off now. But from the corner of my eye, I caught a tall figure on the other side of the street. Whatever words I'd had for Jacob died on my tongue.

My breath hitched.

Pierce.

He stood in front of the real estate office, his hands in his jeans pockets, staring my way.

"Kerrigan—"

"One second." I held up a hand, already walking away. I checked both ways, then jogged across First. My heart galloped faster and faster with every step.

Pierce stood there, watching with an unreadable expression on his face.

I slowed as I approached the curb, then stopped in front of him. His towering frame pivoted so he could stare down at me as I struggled to fill my lungs.

Why was he here? Why now?

He looked as devastating as always. His camel coat showcased his broad shoulders and his jeans molded to his strong thighs. His dark eyes looked as exhausted as I felt. But otherwise, his face was granite.

Pierce's jaw clenched and he tore his eyes away just as a hand came to the small of my back.

I jerked, surprised that I hadn't heard Jacob approach.

His hand moved up my spine and his arm came around my shoulders, pulling me into his side. Claiming me.

In our month together, I'd kissed him twice. Each time had been awkward and unfulfilling. This touch was nothing more than his way of puffing up his chest.

"Everything okay, baby?"

Baby? Where the hell had that come from? No. Just . . . no.

I shifted away, shaking loose of his arm, and gave him a smile. Jacob had pissed me off tonight, but I wasn't going to dump him in front of Pierce simply to be cruel. "This is Pierce Sullivan. My investor."

Pierce's body tensed at that designation as he held out a hand. "And you are?"

"Jacob Hanson. Kerrigan's boyfriend."

The men shook and when Jacob reached for me, trying to take my hand, I moved and tucked it into my coat pocket.

"I didn't realize you were in town," I told Pierce. Was that his Mercedes I'd seen earlier? It had to have been.

Something flashed in his eyes. Sadness. But it was gone in an instant, his expression once again unreadable. "I should have called."

Months ago. He should have called months ago.

I'd told Pierce I understood. I'd done my best not to be angry at him. He'd been clear about not wanting a relationship. But . . .

We'd had something, hadn't we? I hadn't imagined our connection. And it wasn't the sex.

Now he was standing here and damn it, I wanted an explanation.

Jacob inched my way. "We were just heading home—"

"Jacob, I'll call you later."

His eyes widened. "Oh, okay."

I smiled at him, holding it through the awkward silence as he stared between Pierce and me. Finally, he clued in and retreated to his truck on the other side of the street.

Pierce and I both watched him until he'd turned off First.

Then, when we were alone, I faced Pierce. "You're in Calamity."

"I am." He nodded, dragging his eyes up and down my body. They narrowed and I knew what he saw.

In the past four months, I'd lost weight. Weight I hadn't had to lose.

I was dressed in the leggings and long-sleeved top I'd worn at the gym today while training the new employee. My coat was baggier than it had ever been. But sleepless nights and heartache had ruined my appetite.

"I got your check." Most people wouldn't sound so disappointed about getting paid.

The check had cleared, but I wasn't sure if he'd known about it. When he'd left me behind, I'd assumed he'd handed my contract off to someone else. Though other than his lawyer, I hadn't heard from anyone at Grays Peak. "I sold a couple of properties. The farmhouse and a rental."

"You didn't need to do that."

"Yes, I did."

I'd needed to unburden myself. Life was easier now. For so long, I'd dreamed about having my own empire here in Calamity. I wasn't giving that up. Not yet. But it was time to slow down, to be methodical in my purchases and make sure I could weather any storm.

We locked eyes and my heart climbed into my throat. In a way, it was like no time at all had passed. He could kiss me right now and I'd melt into his arms. One touch and the past four months would evaporate.

I rooted my feet to the sidewalk, not trusting myself to move.

"You came back."

"I did."

"Why?"

He blew out a long breath. "For you."

CHAPTER FIFTEEN

PIERCE

SHE WAS one of the most beautiful sights I'd seen in months. Kerrigan had been a constant on my mind since December. Countless hours of picturing her face hadn't helped me let her go. And damn it, I'd tried.

Then that fucking check had shown up last week.

Nellie had brought me the payoff report and when I'd seen Kerrigan's name on it, paid in full, I'd immediately started making plans for this trip.

Fuck this distance. Fuck this decision of mine. It wasn't right. No woman had ever stuck with me like Kerrigan, and I wasn't going to let her check be the last thing between us.

So here I was in Calamity, hoping I could convince her to listen. Hoping that maybe she thought about me as much as I thought about her.

Apparently not, since she'd been on a goddamn date.

Talk about a knife to the heart.

That pissant she'd been with earlier had competition. I hadn't come all this way to walk away. I'd tried that once and it hadn't worked.

Now I was here until I won her back.

Or she asked me to leave.

"Can we talk?" I asked.

She nodded. "Sure. Where?"

"Your place?"

"Okay. I walked to work today."

"Then I'll drive." I turned and strode across the street to where my new Mercedes SUV was parked.

When I'd arrived in town, my first stop had been the gym. The receptionist at the counter had told me that Kerrigan had gone to the art gallery, so I'd trekked there next. The pregnant woman who'd greeted me at the gallery had given me a head-to-toe inspection before finally telling me that Kerrigan had gone to dinner at the café.

I'd been on my way there, ready to interrupt her meal, when I'd spotted her walking with the pissant.

She'd sent him away, and for now, I was taking that as a good sign.

We reached my SUV, and I opened her door for her, crowding her a bit and drawing in a long breath of her hair. God, she smelled good. I'd forgotten that sweet scent.

She hesitated, staring up at me, before taking her seat. But once she was in the vehicle, she kept her eyes down, her expression neutral.

Part of me wished she'd scream and yell, that I'd get some reaction from her, even if it was negative. Maybe she was saving it for her house. I'd find out soon enough. Rounding the hood, I climbed in behind the wheel and reversed out of my parking space.

"Do you remember where it is?" she asked.

"Yes." There wasn't a moment I'd spent in Calamity or with Kerrigan that I'd forgotten.

Even the moments when I hadn't physically been here, when I'd been states away, there was always that tie. Because she'd been with me. On my mind. In my heart.

The atmosphere in the car was thick as we drove. I clutched the wheel and bit my tongue, holding in everything I had to tell her until we were inside.

When I parked in front of her house, I took in the changes she'd made. Months ago, this home had been burgundy. But now, under the fading evening sunlight, the fresh white paint glowed.

Like the other projects she'd tackled and posted on Instagram, I'd kept track of them all. My chest swelled with pride whenever she gained a new follower. Her captions were witty and funny. Her photos were better than some designers who'd been doing this for decades. And her style was unique and impeccable. Maybe she'd done this as a whim or hobby, but her potential was endless.

It had been torture not sending her account to a famous designer I knew in Southern California. Except I suspected Kerrigan would want to do this on her own for a while.

Thank fuck, she hadn't posted any pictures of the boyfriend on social media.

Just the image of his hand on her back made my skin crawl. I wasn't a violent person but I'd been seconds away from ripping that son of a bitch's arm out of its socket.

She was mine.

"Are you, um . . . coming inside?" Kerrigan asked.

I loosened my grip on the steering wheel. I'd been sitting there, staring down the street and imagining a one-armed *Jacob.* "Yeah."

As she hopped out, I turned off the rig and drew in a long

breath. The nerves I'd been fighting had subsided thanks to jealousy. But they roared to new life now that we were here.

Now that the explanation I was terrified to give was only moments away.

I followed her inside, giving her space in the entryway to shrug off her coat. "You're too thin."

Her face whipped to mine. Her lovely cheeks were too hollow. Her eyes had dark circles and the shirt she wore with those skin-tight leggings showed the bones of her shoulders.

I reached out, unable to stop myself, and fit my palm to her cheek.

Kerrigan's eyes flared and for the briefest second, she leaned into my touch. Then she was gone, slipping from my grasp.

"Are you sick?" I asked, following her to the living room.

She shook her head and held up her chin. "No. It's just been . . . it was a hectic winter."

"There's that brave face I admire so much." I stepped in closer. "You wear it for everyone. You don't need to wear it for me."

Her lips parted.

Maybe shocking her wasn't the best way to handle this, but tonight, I wasn't holding a damn thing back. If it came to mind, it was coming out of my mouth. "You're beautiful."

She swallowed hard. "What do you want, Pierce?"

"To talk."

"Okay." She rounded the couch and took a seat on a chair.

I would have preferred we sit together, but her guard was up and space might be a good thing for what I was about to tell her.

"You've done an amazing job with this place."

"Thanks." A smile tugged at her mouth. "It's been fun."

Based on her photos from Instagram, I'd expected to find her happier. Lighter. It could just be the shock from seeing me, but on the street earlier, there'd been a hollowness to her expression. And it wasn't just from the weight she'd lost.

Yet as she glanced at the painted walls and the refinished fireplace, the happiness I'd expected shone through her eyes.

"I've been following you."

She blinked. "You have?"

"I have." I nodded. "It's fantastic. Truly. I've seen a lot of people pitch social media accounts over the years and yours is so real, so undeniably you, it's incredible, Kerr."

Her eyes turned glassy as she swallowed hard. "Thank you."

"Why didn't you keep the farmhouse?"

"It was time to let it go. I wasn't actually sure I'd even get an offer, but when it came, I knew in my heart that it was the right decision."

"You didn't need to pay off your loan."

"Yes, I did." She sighed. "You were right. I was overextended. And as much as I appreciate what you've done, I don't want to be tied."

"Tied to me."

She met my gaze and her barely-there nod slashed deep.

"You're dating."

"No." She scoffed. "Well, yes. But no. Jacob is an old family friend and we've gone out a bit over the past month."

"Is it serious?" I had no business asking but I was going to anyway.

"No."

The air rushed from my lungs. *Thank fuck.* "I'm sorry."

"You don't need to apologize. You were honest from the start that you weren't in a position for a relationship."

"That doesn't mean I don't want you all the same."

Her entire body stilled like she feared to breathe.

"I'd like to explain. If you'll let me."

"Okay."

I leaned forward on my elbows and started at the beginning. "Heidi and I met in college. We dated for a couple of years, and I proposed after graduation. A year later, we were married."

It was entirely predictable and what most of my friends had done too.

"I was working for Barlowe Capital at the time and determined to prove myself. That I was good enough to be an executive there, not just a token VP because I was Gabriel Barlowe's grandson."

Kerrigan sat deeper in her chair, pulling her knees into her chest. She looked like I was going to hurt her.

Because I had hurt her.

And for that, I'd always be sorry. This story might hurt too, but she deserved to know the truth. Even if I was four months too late.

"Heidi was dedicated to her own career," I said. "We both worked a lot. A few years into our marriage, she came to me and said we were drifting apart. That we needed more to our family and she wanted to try for a baby."

There were so many things I wished I had done differently with her. Mostly, I wished I had been honest. With Heidi. And myself.

A baby hadn't been the right decision, but I'd gone along with it. Neither of us had been happy. We'd gotten married because it had been convenient and the next logical step, not because we'd been passionately in love.

"There were complications. For years, we tried. Heidi didn't ovulate regularly so eventually we went to a specialist. The hormones. The doctor appointments. The shots. We got pregnant three times and had a miscarriage with each within weeks. It was hard for me. But it destroyed Heidi."

Kerrigan gasped, her hand coming to her mouth. "Oh, Pierce. I'm so sorry."

I'd never forget her confession at the mountain house. She knew that pain. And as she stared at me, her eyes full of tears, there was so much sympathy in her face for both Heidi and me that if I hadn't already fallen for her, I would have that very second.

"She decided on surrogacy," I said. "The first attempt was another miscarriage. After that . . . we totally fell apart. For the first time, we sat down and talked. She was unhappy. I was unhappy. I didn't know it at the time, but she'd been sleeping with my grandfather."

"When did you catch them together?"

"A couple of weeks later. We'd been dancing around the idea of separating, just hadn't pulled the trigger yet. Then I walked in on them together and divorce was the next discussion."

"I'm sorry."

"I think they'd planned to hide it from me, then maybe tell me after the divorce. I don't know." I raked a hand through my hair, taking a moment. "We had given our fertility specialist permission to try again with the surrogate. In all the drama with Grandpa and Heidi, I forgot about it. Crazy as it sounds, I just . . . forgot. There was so much more happening and I assumed that while we were negotiating the divorce, Heidi would shut that all down."

Kerrigan's eyes widened as she put it together. "The surrogate got pregnant."

"Two weeks after I found out about the affair, Heidi called and told me that Jasmine, she was our surrogate, was pregnant. My son was born the day I called you in December. The day I was going to fly here to see you again."

Her jaw dropped. "You . . . you have a baby?"

"Elias." I pulled my phone from my pocket and scrolled to the latest photo I'd taken yesterday before the drive to Montana. He was lying under a mobile, smiling a toothless grin as he played with his toes. I handed it to Kerrigan.

Her face softened as she took in the picture. "He's beautiful. He looks like you."

Elias had my dark eyes and a mat of dark hair. He'd been born with both and they hadn't changed. "Not exactly how I imagined having a family but he's the best, most incredible gift to come from that mess."

My only wish was that Heidi could have been here to meet him.

"I didn't handle the pregnancy well," I told her. "Actually, I didn't handle it at all. Heidi chose the name when we found out that the baby was a boy. Heidi went to all of Jasmine's doctor's appointments and ultrasounds. I just . . . avoided it. All of it. I was so furious with her and Grandpa. I was even angrier when they stayed together."

"Well, yeah. Who wouldn't be angry? You had every right." There was a fire in her now as she spoke. A fire for me.

"Heidi let me check out of the pregnancy. I always intended to be a part of my son's life, but I needed time to get my head around it all. How to parent with an ex-wife—an ex-wife sleeping with my grandfather. How to know that she'd betrayed me in every possible way. How to ever forgive her or Grandpa. Then . . ."

"The plane crash." Kerrigan pressed a hand to her heart.

"One day I was furious with them. The next, they were both gone and I was still angry." And sad.

Heidi would never get to meet the baby boy she'd loved before he'd ever taken his first breath.

"I was hurt. And instead of dealing with the pain or coming to terms with being a single dad, I focused on what I knew. Business. It was the one thing in my life that I could control. Grandpa left me his company and all I wanted was to erase it all. To consume it. I wanted every piece of him gone because it was easier to blame him than deal with how much I regretted that he'd died and the last words I'd ever spoken to him were in hate."

The lump in my throat started to choke me so I dropped my eyes, staring at the coffee table. "I didn't do a damn thing right."

"That's why you came here and gave me that letter."

"You were special to him. I hated that you were special. Then I got here and . . . I saw it. I saw why he'd loved you. And that just made me even angrier."

"I couldn't believe it." She huffed a laugh. "That day on the street, I just couldn't believe *you* were the Pierce I'd been told so much about. But it makes sense now."

"I'm so fucking grateful that you pushed and pushed. You were there, and without you, I would have had more regrets."

The ashes. Going through the lodge. I would have tossed the ashes and the photos and, later, despised myself for it.

"Why didn't you tell me any of this?" she asked.

I sighed. "Can you imagine how that conversation would have gone? I wasn't even sure how I was going to deal with any of it, let alone ask you to take it on."

There wasn't a doubt in my mind that she would have been there to support me. But I'd needed to take this on. I'd needed to come to terms with it.

"Elias had to be my focus."

"And I would have been what? A distraction?"

"No, a crutch," I admitted. "I would have leaned on you. Too much. I was afraid, Kerr. I was goddamn terrified. I couldn't fail. And the only way I knew I wouldn't fail him, fail you, was to put some blinders on and just focus."

It had been the same way with my business. It had been scary and intimidating to start my own company, to know that if I failed, it would be on my shoulders. So I'd put on blinders and worked my ass off. Those blinders had been the reason I hadn't seen my marriage crumbling around my feet. I'd been too busy staring at the stars.

"Why are you here now, Pierce?"

"Because I can't stop thinking about you. Because you sent me that check and the idea that I'd lost you sent me into a blind panic. So I came, as quickly as possible, because I had to see you. I made a mistake walking away. I don't plan to do it again."

"This is . . . crazy." She shook her head. "We don't even know each other."

"I disagree. We know each other." We knew what mattered. Maybe I didn't know everything but that was the fun part about spending your life with a person: learning something new, each and every day.

Kerrigan shifted, giving me her profile as she stared at the wall. "Where is your son?"

"At the motel."

Her face whipped back to mine. "He's here?"

I shrugged. "I wasn't going to leave him in Colorado. He's at the motel with the nanny."

"Oh." She picked at some invisible lint on the knee of her leggings. "I don't know what to do with all of this."

"That's fair." Fair, but I did not like the tone of her voice. It sounded a lot like I'd be leaving here with a hole in my chest.

"Thank you for telling me," she whispered.

I'd been in enough meetings to recognize the end of a discussion, but I couldn't bring myself to get off this couch. So I stared at her as she stared back.

All I wanted was to take her in my arms and hold her. To feel her lips against mine and show her that everything would be different this time around. It would be better.

No more secrets. No more hesitation.

My life was exponentially more complicated than it had been. A baby did that effortlessly. But we had a shot. This—us—was worth a second chance.

"You'd better get back to the motel." She untucked herself from her chair, then stood and walked to the door.

Fuck.

Following on leaden feet, I joined her beside the new coat rack she'd posted about last week.

She stood with her eyes cast to the floor, looking anywhere but at me.

I reached for the doorknob, ready to take my leave, but stopped.

This wasn't how I was leaving. Not tonight. She could be

pissed at me for pushing, but I didn't care. I needed to see that spark in her eyes. I needed her to remember just how good we'd been.

So I took her face in my hands, tilting it up. Then I smashed my lips against hers, swallowing a gasp as my tongue stroked across her lower lip. A jolt of electricity raced through my veins, spreading with a fire that was wholly Kerrigan's.

She clung to my forearms, holding me to her.

My knees nearly buckled when her tongue snaked out and the tip touched mine. Then I slanted my mouth over hers, taking a deeper taste, until I knew if I didn't pull back, I'd sweep her up and carry her to the bedroom.

I broke away and dropped my forehead to hers. "What do you want? Tell me what you want and I'll give it to you."

"I don't know," she breathed. "I don't know what to do with all of this."

Not that long ago, I'd felt exactly the same way. Time. We needed time. So I dropped a kiss to her temple, and without another word, I let her go and walked outside.

Kerrigan stood in the open doorway as I pulled away from the curb, her silhouette limned by the house's golden light. Her hand was pressed to her lips.

This wasn't over.

Not yet. Not ever.

Not by a long shot.

CHAPTER SIXTEEN

KERRIGAN

A BABY.

Pierce had a son.

It took about ten minutes after he'd left for that fact to sink in. Then the pieces began to click together like a brick of Legos. I replayed our days at the cabin. Our phone conversations, especially his last when he'd called to say goodbye.

He had a baby.

Once the shock wore off, blood-boiling anger took its place.

Oh, I wasn't just mad. I was enraged.

He could have told me. He could have explained it all when we'd been baring our souls to one another.

He *should* have told me.

After everything I'd confided in him, my broken engagement, my own miscarriage, how could he have stayed quiet on this? I'd split myself open for that man and he'd kept his child—*his child*—a secret.

Pierce hadn't trusted me with the truth.

Then he'd had the nerve to kiss me.

"Oh, that son of a bitch." I paced the living room, furious that I could still feel his lips on mine. Once again, I'd kissed him back when I should have smacked him across the jaw.

Damn him and that sexy beard. Damn him and that talented tongue.

Damn him for coming back.

All this time, I'd thought he'd forgotten about me, but he'd come back.

"How dare he?" I threw up my hands. "How *dare* he?"

Pierce had come into my home and dropped his confession like a gallon of paint, leaving me to clean it up. "No. Nope."

He'd had his chance to speak and now I had a few things to say too.

I flew into action, grabbing my coat and pulling it on. I yanked the front door open, only to run into a visitor on my stoop.

"Whoa." Larke held up her hands, shying away before I could slam into her. "In a rush?"

"What are you doing here?"

Zach's car was on the street. He sat behind the wheel, his focus on his phone.

"We're helping Mom decorate, remember? Seven thirty?"

"Oh, shit," I groaned. "No. I forgot."

"Good thing we came to pick you up." She turned and walked down the sidewalk.

I closed the door behind me and sighed, following her and getting into the back of my brother's car. It reeked of cigarettes. The same cigarettes he swore he didn't smoke in the car, just at home.

"Hi," I muttered.

"Hi." Zach didn't offer a smile or glance.

"I guess I just missed you at the White Oak earlier."

"Yeah, I stopped down to get dinner. Now we get to *decorate*." He popped open the console and pulled out a cigarette, placing it between his lips.

"Seriously?" Larke said. "You're not smoking that in here."

Zach found a lighter. "Why? The window's down."

"Because some of us don't feel like smelling like an ashtray," I snapped. "If you're going to smoke, I'll drive myself."

If Zach wanted to smoke, fine. But he needed to stop telling everyone he quit and subjecting us to his bad habit.

He glared at me through the rearview but put the cigarette and lighter away. Then he grumbled something under his breath before driving down the street.

The community center was the last place I wanted to be tonight—there was a billionaire at the motel I needed to strangle—but this birthday party was a big deal to Mom. I'd be there decorating until she dismissed us, and since we'd agreed to ride together, I was at the mercy of my family's schedule.

My trip to the motel would have to wait until tomorrow. Then, I'd give him a piece of my mind. If he was still here.

Would he really stick around? Or would he leave again without an explanation?

"Earth to Kerrigan," Zach said.

I tore my eyes away from my lap. "Huh?"

"We've been talking this whole time." He came to a stop outside the community center. "Want to grab a drink at Jane's after this?"

"Oh, um . . . maybe." Maybe not. If Zach and I had been

getting along, then yes. But suffering through party prep and the party tomorrow would be enough time with my brother for the week.

The three of us walked inside the community center. Our mother and aunts all rushed around in a flurry of crepe paper and plastic tablecloths and balloons.

"I want you to hang up the *Happy Birthday* banner between those two posts in front of the stage," Mom ordered the moment she spotted us.

"Hello to you too," Larke muttered as she went to search for the banner in the bags of party supplies in the middle of the room.

The center wasn't much more than a wide, open room. There was an industrial kitchen because most of the time, this hall was used for birthday parties and funerals. At the far side of the space, a stage ran nearly the length of the building. When I was in third grade, the gym at the high school had been getting its floors refinished so we'd had our Christmas program here instead.

The beige walls were sterile and dull. The linoleum floor had been freshly waxed and the reflection from the florescent lights hanging from the tall ceiling was glaring.

The storage room door opened, and my dad emerged with two plastic folding tables, one in each hand. "Zach, help me get these hauled out."

"I'll do it," I said, bypassing him for the storage room.

"Let your brother. These are heavy."

"I can do it." Christ. I worked out more than my brother. I didn't smoke a pack of cigarettes a day. Oh, and I owned a freaking gym.

Dad's hands were too full for him to stop me from marching into the storage room and hefting a table.

For the next hour, I ran circles around my dad and brother. Each time they tried to take a chair or table from me, I wrenched it free. Each time they told me to help my sister, aunts and mom with the decorations, I simply returned to the storage room for another armful of folding chairs.

It took nearly the entire time to get the room staged, even with three of my cousins showing up to help. I'd shed my coat and sweat beaded at my temples when Dad and I escaped to the kitchen for a glass of water.

"Are you all right?" he asked. "You seem upset."

"I'm great," I lied.

"Your mom's worried we won't have enough seats."

"We have two hundred seats. That's the center's occupancy."

The room had grown smaller as we'd filled it up, cramming tables and chairs in every available corner. We'd even shortened the buffet line because Mom had wanted *one more table* for seating.

"She's a bit stressed." Dad chuckled. "Thanks for coming to help."

"Sure."

"Come on." He threw an arm around my shoulders and steered me to the room. "Let's make your mother sit down for a few minutes."

It wasn't easy, but when every other person sat down, Mom finally huffed and joined us.

"What do you need for tomorrow?" I asked.

Because Mom was the oldest of her sisters, she'd been deemed chief organizer for this party. Or rather, she'd claimed the title before anyone could object.

"I think once we finish with the decorations, we'll be

set," she said. "The food and drinks are in the fridge. The cake is being delivered at noon."

"Zach is picking up Grandma from the home at twelve thirty and the party starts at one," Dad said. "If you'd like to come around noon to help with last-minute prep, that would be great."

"You invited Jacob, didn't you?" Mom asked. She was overjoyed that I'd been dating him. I'd wait until after this party before announcing that his ass was getting dumped.

"Yes." The invitation had already been extended. But there would be enough people here tomorrow that he'd be easy enough to avoid.

A silence settled over the room, all of us ready to escape. I made the move to stand, thinking it was my chance to disappear, but then my brother shot me a smirk.

"Are you going to take pictures of the party for your little Instagram?"

Little. There was that word again.

How had I not noticed that word until now? It wasn't the first time any of my ideas had been deemed little, but now it grated on me like sandpaper on smooth skin.

"I wasn't planning on it," I said with a fake smile.

"There's probably no point." Dad chuckled. "Everyone who sees those pictures will be here themselves."

That wasn't true. I had followers outside of Calamity. Not many, but some. And if I did take pictures and post them, it would be to showcase small-town life. It would be to share my grandmother's ninetieth birthday and a part of what made me, me.

Defending myself would only lead to an argument, so I clamped my mouth shut.

"I ran into Jessa Nickels at the coffee shop earlier," Larke said.

Shit. My stomach dropped and I widened my eyes at my sister, hoping she'd get the hint that this was not something I wanted to discuss. But she wasn't looking at me. She was toying with a piece of confetti.

"She said you met with her on Tuesday to look at a place across from the park."

All eyes at the table swung my direction.

Awesome. "Yes, I did."

So much for keeping this to myself for a while. I was going to have to find a new realtor. One who hadn't graduated from high school with my sister and one who would remember to keep my private business private.

"You're buying another place?" Dad asked.

"Oh, not this again," Mom groaned.

"You've done such an amazing job with your house," Dad said. "It turned out beautiful. Why not live in it for a while?"

"Because I like having a project."

"An expensive project." Zach scoffed. "You just went broke. Didn't you learn anything from that experience? I'm sure they taught you in *college* that you have to spend less than you make."

The tether on my tongue snapped. "Is there a reason why you throw that in my face all the time? It's my money. What I do with it is my choice."

"Until it becomes Mom's problem." He swung a hand out to our mother. "She's got to sit at the gym and cover for you while you take her car and disappear."

That was months ago. Months. But that was Zach. He

loved to store up my indiscretions and save them as ammunition for later arguments.

"Why does my business bother you so much?"

"It doesn't."

"Bullshit," I clipped.

"Hey." Dad held up his hands. "Let's take it down a notch. I think what your brother is trying to say is that we don't want you to fall into the same situation where you're overextended."

"I don't plan to get overextended."

"Well . . ." Dad sighed. "If you do decide to buy it, just take a loan out from a bank this time. At least they're local and we can trust them, unlike that other guy."

"I trusted Gabriel. He was a good man."

"We know you trusted him," Larke said, her eyes wide as she mouthed *sorry*.

"Do you really need another house?" Zach asked.

"It won't be another house. It will be my house." Now that my current place was finished, I wanted to buy a fixer-upper and start over again. Both for content and because without anything else to do, I needed the distraction.

"You're selling your house?" Dad's forehead furrowed. "But you just finished it."

"And I'll finish the next one."

"While you're living in a construction zone." Zach pursed his lips. "What does Jacob say about all of this?"

"I didn't realize I needed to run this by the guy I'd been dating *for a month*." I stood from my chair so fast its legs scraped against the floor. "I need to go."

Without another word, I turned and strode from the center, picking up my coat before I walked through the door.

Once outside, I blew out a frustrated huff, then aimed my feet down the sidewalk toward home. The blocks disappeared in fast, angry strides and when I walked through my front door, I was no less irritated than when I'd left the community center.

What was it going to take for them to support me?

"A miracle," I barked to the empty house.

The air in the living room held the faintest scent of Pierce's cologne. I drew in a long breath as I sat where he'd been on the couch.

My mood was his fault. And Jacob's. And Zach's. And Dad's.

Damn these men. Damn Pierce.

He'd come back just when I'd given up on him. He'd come back and kissed me.

He didn't get to kiss me.

A rush of déjà vu hit hard as I leapt from the couch and sprinted for the door. This time, my sister wasn't on the other side to stop me. I jogged to my car, climbing behind the wheel, and zoomed down my street to a quiet house six blocks over.

The home was dark except for the blueish light of a television coming from the front bay window. I parked, marched to the porch, raised my fist and knocked.

Jacob answered seconds later, the surprise on his face morphing to an arrogant grin—one I was about to wipe clean. "Hey, come on in."

"Oh, I can't stay. I just wanted to stop by and do this in person."

His eyes narrowed. "Do what?"

"It's been great hanging out with you this month. But I don't see us continuing this relationship."

He blinked, quickly covering up his shock with a neutral frown. "Yeah. I was thinking the same thing at dinner."

Sure, he was. "Have a good night, Jacob."

He didn't say a word as he stepped back and slammed the door. I was already retreating down the sidewalk to my car.

One man down.

One to go.

The motel's parking lot was nearly empty when I pulled in. The lights underneath the second floor's exterior hallway illuminated the walkway and the red-painted doors.

This place had been in Calamity for so many years that it had gone out of style and was now on the cusp of returning. The dark wooden exterior fit with the vibe of the town. Western. Rustic. There was an old wagon wheel beside the door to the lobby. Soon, the flower planters would come out and the owners would dazzle the rest of town.

Marcy, the owner of the motel, had the greenest thumb in Calamity. Each year, she hung overflowing baskets of flowers outside each room for the tourists visiting the area.

Pierce's green Mercedes stood out amongst the midsize sedans and half-ton trucks. It was parked outside room seven. The same room he'd been in last time. Probably because it was the room Marcy and her husband, Dave, had most recently renovated.

Parking beside his SUV, I marched his door and knocked, squaring my shoulders to deal with Pierce like I'd dealt with Jacob. Efficiently. There was a bottle of wine waiting for me at home.

A shuffling noise came from the room, then the chain slid free and there he was, filling the threshold exactly the way he had his first night in Calamity.

"Hi." He looked so handsome. So . . . relieved.

"You should have told me."

"I should have told you."

I narrowed my eyes.

I didn't want him to agree with me. I wanted him to fight back, to give me an outlet to get out all of this frustration. With him. With my family. With myself. "I trusted you with everything. All of it. And you left this out."

"I'm sorry."

"That's not good enough."

"I know." He sighed. "Will you come in? Please."

Against my better judgment, I stepped inside.

Pierce closed the door behind us, then walked toward the bed. He dragged a hand through his disheveled hair. His eyes were heavy like he'd been asleep.

While he stared at me, I was stuck staring around his room.

A portable crib had been set up in the corner. There was a small bouncy chair at its side. Next to his suitcase was a diaper bag. The TV was on but muted.

Because there was a sleeping baby on the bed.

I took one step, then another, until I was hovering at the foot of the mattress, staring down at the most precious face I'd ever seen.

The baby's eyes were closed. The long swoops of his eyelashes formed sooty, crescent moons above his rounded cheeks. His arms were raised above his head, his hands in loose fists. His lips formed a little pink bow. A tuft of dark hair rested on his forehead and my fingers itched to smooth it away.

The picture Pierce had shown me hadn't conveyed the perfection that was this baby boy.

"He's beautiful."

"Thank you." Pierce came to stand by my side and the love on his face twisted my heart. "I didn't love him. Before he was born. I hate even saying that out loud, but part of me . . . I didn't want to be a father."

"You needed to fall in love with him."

He nodded. "I was scared that if I was too busy falling in love with you, I wouldn't fall in love with my son."

The world tilted. The anger vanished.

He'd been falling in love with me.

I hadn't been alone in this. Somehow that was the realization that soothed the most.

Pierce had been my first real gamble on a man since my ex-fiancé. He'd been the one I'd given a chance. Maybe because he'd told me there was no chance. He'd been safe because I'd known he would walk away. There'd been no fear of commitment because Pierce had promised the opposite.

What I hadn't counted on was hurting so much when he delivered on that promise.

But he'd come back. He'd come back to me, just like I'd wished. And brought this little boy along too.

Elias rested on a white fleece blanket printed with safari animals. He was dressed in solid-blue footed pajamas.

It was impossible to blame Pierce for his choice. This tiny life had deserved his father's attention.

As if he could feel my stare, the baby stirred, squirming and screwing up his mouth in a pucker.

"He's probably hungry." Pierce flew into action, rushing to the bathroom, where a drying rack was full of bottles and plastic nipples. He mixed some formula with water, shaking it furiously. Then he came back and picked up his son, whose eyes and mouth flew open, ready for a snack.

Pierce rounded the side of the bed, sitting where some pillows had already been propped up. Then he shifted his son to cradle him in a strong arm.

"Stay, Kerr."

Goddamn it. The picture of them was irresistible.

I walked to the other side of the bed. "For a little while."

CHAPTER SEVENTEEN

PIERCE

"SO." Kerrigan's fingers fiddled in her lap.

"So." I studied her profile, doing my best to keep my heart from galloping out of my chest.

She'd stayed. After I'd left her place tonight, I was sure I'd have to be the one to hunt her down.

Silence stretched as she glanced around the small hotel room.

This was the same room I'd stayed in before, number seven. The white comforter was soft and smooth over the king-sized bed. I'd put the small blanket down for Elias because he tended to spit up and that smell was not easy to get out.

The floor was crowded with Elias's things. This was our first trip out of Denver and if there was a way to travel light with a baby, I'd failed spectacularly. A portable crib. Diapers. Clothes. Bottles. Formula. Blankets. We had a traveling nursery. I'd brought one suitcase for myself and the rest of the SUV had been packed for the bundle in my arms, who was inhaling his bottle.

"Does he sleep all night?" Kerrigan asked.

"If he goes four hours, it's a good night. He usually takes a bottle around one or two."

She hummed, her eyes darting to him before she stared straight ahead to the TV on the wide oak dresser. "Does your nanny help?"

"She does during the day while I'm at work. She helped in the beginning too. But now it's mostly me and my boy." I smiled down at him as he chugged.

It was too early to tell if he'd favor my features or Heidi's, but he had my brown eyes and my dark hair.

"Where is she? The nanny. Didn't she come along?"

"She did." I nodded. "But that was mostly just to help on the drive. Her husband followed us in their own car. They're using the trip as an excuse to visit Montana. They'll be going to Big Sky and then spending a week in the Bozeman area."

"And then you'll go back to Denver."

"They will. I won't."

She met my gaze. "You're staying here?"

"Not in this room, but Montana, yes. My plan is to stay at the cabin for a while." And if I was lucky, I'd convince Kerrigan to come along.

"Are you getting ready to sell it?"

"No. I might actually keep it." I'd had every intention of selling Grandpa's cabin. My time limit was nearly up and soon I'd be free to do so. But when the club had sent over the preliminary paperwork, I hadn't been able to sign it.

Maybe that would change one day. My feelings were jumbled about the house and my grandfather. But there were good memories there.

Like Kerrigan, I hadn't been able to let it go.

"How long will you stay?" she asked.

"I don't know." It depended on her.

"What about work?"

"There isn't much I can't do over video conferencing. It's how we interact with our clients. I don't need to be in the room to be effective. Having Elias, I've taken a step back already. This is simply a continuation of the same. And Nellie just got a promotion so she'll be helping when I can't be there in person."

Her eyes softened. "How is Nellie?"

"She's good. Living to give me a hard time about my life's decisions."

"I feel awful. We talked so often and then I ghosted her. Does she hate me?"

"Never." I leaned over to brush my shoulder against hers. "She knows why you didn't call her back."

Kerrigan blew out a long breath, then looked at the baby and smiled. "He's out."

Elias's mouth was hanging open, the bottle empty. I shifted him to my shoulder to pat his back. Usually he had a burp or two to work out and if I didn't give his stomach a chance to settle, we'd be in for a long night.

"I've spent more time in a rocking chair than I ever expected. We sit like this, him asleep and me just rocking, over and over. I listen to your voicemails on the nights it's hard for me to go back to sleep."

"What voicemails?"

"The ones from this fall. In the dead of night, I'll pull out my phone and press it to my ear. Just to hear you call me Mr. Sullivan."

The corner of her mouth turned up. "You were such an ass."

"I love those voicemails." I chuckled. "The emails too. I

love that you didn't give up. Even when I ignored you."

"I feel like such an idiot." She covered her face with her hands. "Me and my little business and I called you every single day."

"Your business isn't little."

Defeat clouded her expression as her frame slumped. "No, it is little."

"Not to you. Not to me." Her heart was involved and that meant the world.

"Thank you," she whispered, her voice hoarse.

"What did I say?"

"Nothing." She waved it off. "And you're right. My business isn't little, not to me."

In all my years of meeting with entrepreneurs, it was the ones like Kerrigan who always made the long shots worth it. Her heart was in it. Her passion. I'd bet on someone like her ten times over a person who might have perfect financials but a disconnected heart.

"I've been following you," I said.

"You told me."

"What you're doing on TikTok is brilliant. A woman who's not afraid to pull out the nail gun and lay some tile is going to take off. Just watch."

"It hasn't yet."

"It will," I promised because I believed in her to the depths of my soul. "My favorite post of yours is the one of you on First. Your hair is in a bun and you're wearing that long-sleeved top with *The Refinery* on the chest. Behind you is the street and you can see down the sidewalk."

"That's your favorite? Why?"

"Because it reminds me of the day I met you." A day I'd

never forget. The day my eyes had landed on her perfect lips and she'd captured my attention.

She leaned her head against the headboard, her gaze flicking to the door. "Why did you kiss me? That first night?"

"When you were yelling at me on the street, I couldn't stop staring at your mouth. It had been a long time since I'd wanted to kiss a woman so badly. It unnerved me. And when you showed up here, I'd had enough to drink that I just decided *fuck it*."

"Better watch the language, Dad." She jerked her chin to Elias.

"There's no hope he goes into kindergarten without dropping the f-word a time or two."

She giggled. "My sister is a teacher. She always talks about her first year teaching. She was subbing because full-time positions don't come open very often here, but when another teacher got divorced and moved away, Larke was able to pick up a spot for fifth grade. She started midyear and this kid walks into the room and asks, 'Who the fuck are you?' To this day, he is her favorite student. He's in middle school now but stops by to see her once a week."

I laughed, then swung my legs off the bed and stood, carrying Elias to his crib. The moment I laid him down, his hands, like always, went straight above his head. With him settled, I returned to the bed and stretched out on my side, propping up on an elbow. "Tell me more."

Kerrigan shifted, turning sideways to face me. "About what?"

"Anything." I'd listen to her tell me stories all night, every night. "What's next for your business?"

She blew out a deep breath, sinking deeper into the pillows. "I am thinking about selling my house and buying another one to remodel. If I live there for two years, I won't have to pay taxes on any capital gains."

"Smart plan. And it gives you so much opportunity to post content."

"Exactly." Her eyes lit up. "I looked at a place on Tuesday. The exterior is in pretty good shape so I could probably get away with just some fresh paint and new shutters. The interior is a mess though."

"Tell me about it."

We spent the next hour talking about the three-bedroom, one-bathroom house. She talked about what she'd need to remodel and how much work she could do on her own versus what she'd have to hire out. The place needed two bathrooms to compete as a single-family home and though I didn't doubt she could do it on her own, she wasn't comfortable tackling an addition without professional help.

"I don't want to get myself in a financial bind again," she said. "But I think I'll make enough profit on my house to pay for the remodel work on something new."

"Then go for it. As long as you don't mind living in a construction zone, it doesn't sound like there's much downside."

She thought about it for a moment, then she gave me a sure nod. The look of determination on her face was one I'd seen before. "I will. I'm going to do it, no matter what my family thinks."

"Your family doesn't approve?"

"Not really." She sighed. "They're supportive in their own way. If I ever fall, they'll be there with a safety net. But their idea of success is working for the family business."

"The car dealership, right?"

She nodded. "It's so strange because my granddad built

that business on his own. And then my dad was the one who pushed to expand it. People told him that Calamity wasn't big enough for a dealership of that size, but he proved them wrong. He's built so much, all without a college degree. You'd think my parents would be all for me doing the same. But they don't support me like . . ."

"*My* grandfather," I said as she trailed off.

"Yes," Kerrigan said. "I don't know if I should talk about him or not."

"You should." Because he'd been important to her. And to me.

"Gabriel never doubted me. My family does."

"Have you talked to them about it?"

"Yes and no. It falls on deaf ears and sometimes it's just easier to tune them out. My family is huge. If there's a fight, it becomes this big thing. The argument gets totally blown out of proportion. Privacy is nonexistent. Everyone is expected to choose a side."

"And you're worried that no one will pick yours."

"Yes," she confessed. "I consider myself to be a confident person."

"I would agree." It was that confidence that had made her call me each and every day. That confidence was what had made her fight.

"When it comes to my family, I'm not as tenacious. With so many feelings involved, it's too exhausting to fight. Which totally messes with my mind because you'd think it would be the opposite."

"I get it. They feel comfortable questioning you, so they do. And then you question yourself."

"Yes." She touched the tip of her nose. "Exactly."

"Grandpa was that way with me."

"But it didn't mess with your head."

"Of course it did. Why do you think I had to leave his company? I needed to prove to myself and to him that I could stand on my own two feet. The minute I shut out his voice, I learned to rely on my own instincts."

"My brother is the worst. Zach is the oldest. He acts more like a parent than a sibling. We got into an argument earlier tonight. It's happening more and more these days, and I just don't know what his problem is."

"Family is hard."

"It is." Her eyes drifted to Elias's crib. "He's beautiful, Pierce. Truly."

"I didn't know that I needed him. But I did. He put everything into perspective."

Hate. Anger. Resentment.

Joy. Hope. Love.

With him, it was easier to let go of the bitter emotions and focus on the good.

"When I got that check, I thought I'd lost you," I said, holding her mesmerizing gaze. "I don't want to lose you, Kerr."

Her eyes searched mine. If she was looking for raw honesty, it was there.

"That guy from earlier."

"I broke it off."

I blinked. "When?"

"Before I came here."

"Why?"

"I'd planned to before you showed up. He wasn't the guy for me."

"And who is?"

She didn't admit it was me. She didn't have to because I saw it on her face.

Surging across the bed, I crossed the invisible line that separated us. Then my mouth was on hers and the rest of the world melted away.

Her lips parted and I slid my tongue inside, savoring her sweet taste. A moan came from deep in my chest, like that knot that had been there for months was finally unraveling.

Her hands came around my ribs, holding me to her as she leaned in, giving as much as she took. We kissed like kids in the backseat of a car, rushing to get it in before curfew.

My cock swelled as she shifted, taking more of my weight. God, what I wouldn't give to sink inside her body. To feel her grip me as we came together.

I slid my hand under her top, feeling the silky skin over her stomach. She arched into my touch, breaking her mouth away to kiss at the underside of my jaw.

Diving under her bra, I cupped her breast. She moaned as I rolled her nipple with the pad of my thumb, then her hands were between us, going for my zipper.

A squawk came from the crib.

I froze.

Kerrigan froze.

Don't be awake. Please, don't be awake.

When no other sound came, I breathed, ready to keep going, but when I met Kerrigan's gaze, the moment was gone.

"We should probably slow down," she whispered.

Fuck. Cockblocked by my own kid.

"Yeah." I swallowed hard, rolling to my side of the bed and staring up at the ceiling. My breaths came in pants and the bulge behind my zipper was painful. "Want a glass of water?"

"Sure." She sat up against the headboard and brushed the hair out of her face.

I jackknifed off the bed and walked to the bathroom, checking on Elias as I passed. He was sleeping, his eyes fluttering behind his lids. With the door eased closed behind me, I braced my hands on the counter and took a breath.

Screwing Kerrigan in a hotel room with my son just feet away was not a great idea. My dick didn't agree but . . .

I'd kissed her twice tonight.

Both times, she'd kissed me back.

That was a damn good sign this might be moving in the right direction. If I could just have more time with her, we might get back to the place where we'd been, the place where the two of us had been so in sync that it was like we'd known each other for years, not days or weeks.

Another cry echoed from the main room and I hurried to fill two of the hotel's glasses with some tap water. I opened the door, glasses in hand, ready to deliver one to Kerrigan and then collect my son. But as I stepped into the room, she was settling on the bed with Elias in her arms.

"Shh." She cooed. "You're all right."

He squirmed and puckered up his face. I opened my mouth, ready to tell her that he probably needed to let out the burp he hadn't after falling asleep with the bottle in his mouth, but there was no need.

Kerrigan hefted him up against her shoulder, patting his back like she'd done it a hundred times.

I stood there, my mouth agape, as she rocked back and forth. If I'd thought there was a sight more beautiful than her naked, then I'd been wrong. Totally fucking wrong. Because this, her sitting cross-legged on a motel bed with my son in her arms, was the most breathtaking sight I'd ever seen.

Her eyes met mine. "You're staring."

"I am."

"Why?"

"Because I can." Because I'd gone too long without her face.

Her cheeks flushed and she continued to rock Elias.

I moved to her side of the bed, setting down a glass, then bent to kiss her forehead before retreating to my side. The invisible boundary had returned, so I reached for the TV remote to take it off mute. "Want to watch something?"

"Sure."

"Want me to take him?"

"No, I've got him."

I grinned and hit the volume.

An hour into a movie on HBO, I got up to shut off the lights. As the credits rolled, Kerrigan shifted and laid Elias on the safari blanket still on the bed, keeping him between us.

And when she didn't make a move to leave, I chose another movie.

———

A SUNBEAM STREAMING through the motel's window warmed my face. I jolted awake, frantically scanning the room for my son as my heart raced. It should be dark, not light. He was overdue for a bottle. Something had to be wrong.

Except Elias was exactly where Kerrigan had laid him earlier, my son still asleep.

"He slept through the night," Kerrigan whispered. Her hands were folded under her cheek on the pillow.

I breathed and pressed a hand to my racing heart. Then I glanced at the clock. It was past six. "He's never slept this long."

It had to be the sound of my voice because one moment he was out, the next his mouth turned down in a pout and his eyes blinked open.

I bolted off the bed for the bathroom to mix him a bottle. By the time I was shaking it up, he was crying, a sound that broke my heart every damn time.

"Here you go, pal." I walked into the room, and like last night, Kerrigan had Elias in her arms.

She murmured to him, holding out one hand for the bottle.

When I handed it over, she gave it to him and my boy chugged.

"Easy." She laughed.

His eyes were open wide now, his gaze fixed on her. Already under her spell.

Yeah, kid. Me too.

"He's got such expressive eyes," she said.

"He does. My mom said mine were the same way at that age."

Kerrigan took in such a long breath, it was like she was filling every piece of her lungs. Then it came out in a rush, and she breathed, "Okay."

"Okay, what?"

"Okay, I'm not mad at you anymore."

"Were you mad at me when I kissed you last night?"

"Yes."

"And through the movies?"

"Yep."

"But not anymore."

She shook her head. "No, but you're on thin ice."

"Then I'll be on my best behavior." I smiled so wide it pinched at my cheeks. "Go on a date with me. Today."

"I can't. Today is my grandma's ninetieth birthday party. We're having a big celebration at the community center. It'll be exhausting and emotionally draining."

"Then tonight."

"I doubt I'll be very good company."

I sat on the edge of the bed. "Then what if I came to the party with you as your buffer?"

Her eyes widened. "Really? You'd go?"

"Sure. We have no plans today." Other than chasing her.

"It'll be awkward, that I can promise. My parents and sister and brother know about you. Actually, the entire town knows about you. Our argument on First was the favored headline with the rumor mill for nearly a month."

I frowned. "Does your family know about the cabin? About us?"

She shook her head. "Only my sister and that's just because she was there when you came to my place. But she never asked and I never shared. I doubt she mentioned anything to anyone else."

So it was likely that her family simply knew me as the guy who'd nearly bankrupted her. *Fuck.*

But eventually, I had to meet them. A party might be better if there was a crowd. Why not get it over with?

"Okay. We're in."

CHAPTER EIGHTEEN

PIERCE

YEAH, this party was probably a bad idea.

I stepped into the community center with the car seat in one hand and my other on the small of Kerrigan's back.

There weren't many people here yet, but the moment the door closed behind us, all eyes swung our way.

A tall man with dark hair and gray at his temples spotted us first. The smile he'd had for Kerrigan flattened when he noticed my hand and how closely we were standing together.

A woman with Kerrigan's chestnut hair did a double take, then tore across the room.

"Okay, maybe this was a bad idea." Kerrigan voiced my own thought. Then she stood straighter and put on that brave face of hers. "Hi, Mom."

"Hi." Her mother looked me up and down, but when she saw Elias in his car seat, she froze. This was not a happy mother.

"This is Pierce Sullivan and his son, Elias," Kerrigan said. "Pierce, this is my mom, Madeline Hale."

I held out my free hand. "It's a pleasure to meet you."

Madeline didn't shake my hand. She continued to stare between the three of us until a scowl replaced the shock on her face. "You're the man who tried to ruin my daughter."

Madeline must be out for blood today.

I cleared my throat. "I am."

"Mom," Kerrigan hissed. "Can we not do this?"

"You." Madeline shook a finger in her daughter's face. "I'll have words for you later. Bringing *him* to your grandmother's ninetieth birthday party. What are you thinking?"

"Pierce is important to me. He's here as my friend."

A friend? We'd be discussing that classification tonight.

Not one to be discouraged, Kerrigan glanced around the room. "What would you like us to do before the party starts?"

Before Madeline could answer Kerrigan's question, the man who'd seen us first joined the huddle.

"Hi, Dad." Kerrigan waved my way. "This is Pierce. Pierce, this is my dad, Colton Hale."

"Nice to meet you." I held out a hand.

Colton, unlike his wife, actually shook it, his grip tight enough to make a point.

"So is the cake here? I'd love to see it," Kerrigan said, and before we could suffer through more of this introduction, she grabbed my hand and dragged me across the room.

We passed table after table covered with bright plastic cloths. Confetti was strewn on each and small bouquets of spring flowers made up the centerpieces. Toward the stage was a round table with a small chalkboard, the word *GIFTS* hand drawn in white. Next to it, the cake.

I expected Kerrigan to lead us there but instead, she veered directions, her hand never loosening over mine. She pulled me past more wide-eyed people and into the industrial kitchen.

"Hi, Aunt Jenn," she said to a woman stirring an enormous bowl of macaroni salad.

"Hi, Kerrig—" Aunt Jenn's greeting died when she spotted me.

Kerrigan kept on pulling.

Through the kitchen. Down a short hallway. Past one door. Then another. Finally through a third that opened to a sitting room with one navy tweed couch and two tan leather chairs.

Kerrigan stopped in the center of the room and breathed. "Not great. But not bad."

"Are you planning on us hiding out here the entire party?"

"No. Maybe? I was hoping there would be more people here already." Her shoulders fell. "I'm sorry my parents were rude."

"I expected as much." If she hadn't told them about us, then their surprise was justified. But I wasn't going anywhere. If their rudeness was what I needed to endure to be here for Kerrigan, so be it.

Everyone important in my life knew about Kerrigan. Granted, that list was small. My parents. Nellie. They knew what she meant to me and what I was hoping to have happen by returning to Montana. In time, her family would know too.

"It'll be fine." I put my hand on her cheek, my thumb gently stroking her soft skin. Then I leaned down and brushed my lips to hers.

The door to the room opened. "Ker—oh. Uh, sorry to interrupt."

Kerrigan pulled away. "Hey, it's okay."

I turned and faced the woman I'd seen once months ago. It had to be Kerrigan's sister. They had the same hair, the same pretty eyes.

"Larke, this is Pierce. Pierce, this is my sister."

Larke held out her hand. "You're—"

"Kerrigan's."

Might as well clear it all up right now. I wasn't the investor. I wasn't the friend.

I was hers.

Kerrigan's gaze was on the floor but there was a smile tugging at her lips.

"This should be interesting." Larke laughed. "Welcome to the madness, Pierce."

I chuckled. "Thanks."

"Are you guys hiding out in here?" Larke asked. "If so, I'm joining you."

We sat down and I unbuckled Elias from his car seat.

Kerrigan instantly stole him away, propping him on her knees. "Hey, buddy."

He reached for a lock of her hair, wrapping it in a fist.

She laughed and his eyes whipped to her face.

Then my entire world stopped.

Elias gave her his wide, toothless grin and let out a string of baby babbles like he was telling her that he was going to keep her forever.

With any luck, he'd get his wish.

"Oh, he is cute." Larke squeezed in on the couch beside Kerrigan and tickled the baby's side.

I stretched back in the couch, relaxing as they talked to him. Mostly, I stared at Kerrigan. These months apart had been too long.

She looked gorgeous today, even after a night of limited sleep. Still too thin, but beautiful. Her hair was curled into waves and they draped over her shoulders, thick and silky. Her dark jeans and heeled boots made her legs look a mile long. The chunky gray sweater she'd pulled on draped wide at the neck, showcasing a hint of her flawless skin over one shoulder.

My hand moved of its own volition, landing on that bare skin.

She glanced over and smiled, then focused on my son.

"What if we hid out here all day?" she asked Elias.

He garbled some incoherent string of sounds.

"That sounded like a yes," Larke said. "But if we don't come out of this room, Mom will come searching."

"Ugh," Kerrigan groaned. "I hate these parties."

"Look at it this way," Larke said. "The entire family is here so you only have to suffer through today and then everyone will know about you and Pierce."

"This is true." Kerrigan sighed, then looked over at me. "Ready for this?"

"It'll be fine." I sat up straighter. "This was going to have to happen eventually. Might as well be today."

She leaned into my side, then steeled her spine and stood with Elias.

"Want me to take him?" I asked.

"No." She kissed his cheek. "I've got him."

We followed Larke and returned to the party, where I spent the next hour meeting what must have been the entire town of Calamity. Everyone knew or was related to Kerrigan. She smiled politely, laughed when necessary and introduced me as we wandered around the room.

But with every sideways look or whisper behind our

backs, she clutched my hand tighter. Every time I offered to take Elias so she wasn't hefting him around, she'd kiss his cheek again and tell me she wanted to hold him.

He seemed perfectly content to let her.

Elias hadn't taken to anyone this quickly. Not the nanny. Not Nellie. Not even my mother. Maybe Elias sensed Kerrigan's unease. Or maybe he just loved playing with her hair.

"Ah. There you are." A man who resembled Colton approached Kerrigan. Next to him was the guy from last night. *Jacob.*

"Hi, Zach," Kerrigan said. "This is Pierce Sullivan. Pierce, this is my brother. And you remember Jacob."

Neither of the men extended a hand as she did the introductions. Neither returned her greeting, which pissed me right the fuck off. Other than a glance at Elias, they focused on me and ignored Kerrigan completely.

I'd been sized up many times in my life, normally by older clients who didn't believe someone younger could possess their level of business acumen. Those meetings never went well . . . for the clients.

Jacob could go fuck himself. Zach could too, but given that he was Kerrigan's brother, I'd bite my tongue.

"So you're the guy," Zach said.

"I am." I slid close to Kerrigan, putting an arm around her shoulders.

Jacob's eyes flared as she leaned into my side and held up her chin. "I'm going to take off," he told Zach, then disappeared through the crush of people.

Zach's eyes alternated between us both. "You're together?"

"Yes," I answered. "Is that a problem?"

"Yeah. You don't belong here." He reached into his

pocket and pulled out a box of cigarettes, shaking one loose. Then he left, striding for the door.

What an asshole.

"Sorry," Kerrigan whispered.

"Don't apologize."

"We're leaving as soon as the cake is cut."

"No arguments here."

We'd ridden together to the party. I'd dropped her off this morning, giving her some space to shower and change during Elias's morning nap. Then I'd picked her up to come here. Maybe once the party was done, we could skip town and head to the cabin.

Elias made a noise, then his little body lurched, and a glob of white spit-up landed on Kerrigan's sweater. Another on my son's hoodie.

"Oh, hell." I scanned the tables, finding a pink napkin on one. I wiped but the damage had been done. Regurgitated formula had a unique sour smell. "We're going to need more than dry napkins."

"I'll take him to the kitchen and get some paper towels."

"I'll grab a burp rag."

We walked to the kitchen together, then I left Kerrigan by the sink while I went down the hallway to the room where we'd left the car seat and diaper bag.

I was just on my way back to them when her voice carried down the hallway. "Mom, stop."

I slowed, not wanting to intrude.

"Honey, I'm trying to save you some heartache here," Madeline said. "He's just looking for a mother for this baby."

Ouch. This family of hers wasn't holding back, were they?

"No, he's not," Kerrigan insisted.

"How do you know? You don't really know the man."

"Please just . . . trust my instincts."

"Your instincts landed you in trouble with that man in the first place. You've spent the last six months living on next to nothing. Your house has been a construction zone and until last month, you've had to borrow my car to drive anywhere outside of a ten-block radius."

I cringed.

That was not the life I'd wanted for Kerrigan. The last thing I wanted was for her to struggle.

"Mom, can we not have this argument? Again?"

"Again? What's again?" Madeline's voice grew louder. "You show up here with this man and his baby. Of course we're going to have questions."

"You're right. I should have called and explained first. But Pierce is a good man. And I have feelings for him. So would it be so hard for you guys to just support my decisions?"

"What about Jacob?"

"What about Jacob? I dumped him. He's as condescending as Zach, and I should have dumped him weeks ago."

"I don't like this." Madeline sighed. "I'm worried he's using you to parent his little boy. Where is the mother, by the way?"

Fuck. Did Kerrigan think this was about me finding a mother for Elias? Because that was most definitely not the case.

"It's complicated," Kerrigan said. "And now is not the time to talk about it."

"But—"

"Madeline?" a female voice called into the kitchen. "We're ready for the cake."

"Okay. I'll be right there." There was a long pause as the door closed. "Kerrigan—"

"Mom, let this go. You have a cake to cut."

I waited until Madeline's footsteps disappeared before entering the kitchen.

Kerrigan had Elias lying on a stainless-steel table while she worked to clean the spit-up from his clothes. "Did you hear all of that?"

"Yes."

She sighed and picked up my son. "How about some cake?"

Before I could stop her and explain, before I could tell her that my trip to Montana had nothing to do with needing a mother for Elias and everything to do with her, she was heading for the door.

We walked into the common room just in time to pick up the beginning verses of "Happy Birthday."

"Ready to make a break for it?" Kerrigan asked as the crowd lined up for the cake table.

"Lead the way."

She turned, ready to dart into the kitchen, but our escape was thwarted when Kerrigan's father appeared.

"You're not leaving, are you?" Colton asked.

"Um . . ."

He frowned down at his daughter. "We're cleaning up afterward. Mandatory attendance."

Shit. "We're going to duck in the back and let Elias take a nap," I said. "But we'll be here for cleaning."

Colton nodded once, his scowl deeper than it had been earlier, then left to join the cake line.

256

With my hand on Kerrigan's back, I steered her away and to the sitting room. I wanted some time alone to talk about that discussion with her mother. But the moment we walked through the door, we found Larke sitting on the couch.

"What are you doing?" Kerrigan asked.

"I tried to leave but Dad stopped me."

"Us too." She plopped down beside her sister.

"I hate these family functions. Grandma doesn't remember half of the people out there, me included. And if I get asked one more time why I'm not married yet, I'm going to scream."

Kerrigan giggled. "Well, you've got company. I'm not going back out there until everyone is gone."

So much for my quiet conversation.

Elias began to fuss so I picked him up and while Kerrigan and Larke talked quietly, I fed him a bottle and walked him around the room until he finally fell asleep in my arms.

"You can take him back to the motel if you want," Kerrigan said. "I'll stay to clean up and Larke can give me a ride home."

I shook my head. "I'm staying."

"I like you, *Mr. Sullivan*," Larke said with a smile.

I chuckled. "She told you about that, huh?"

"She did. Though my darling sister still hasn't told me everything about what happened when you two got snowed in."

"I might have left a few details out," she said.

"The good ones," Larke muttered.

Kerrigan pulled in her lips to hide a smile.

If the party could have ended with the three of us

visiting in the sitting room, I would have called it a win. But an hour later, Kerrigan's brother opened the door and sucked the joy from the air.

"We're cleaning up," he said. "Come and help."

We did as ordered, returning to the hall, where most of the people had cleared out. After putting Elias in his car seat, I began stripping tablecloths. Once those were done, I helped fold tables to haul into the storage room.

I was stowing an armful of chairs on a rack when Kerrigan's voice rose from the main room.

"*What?*"

Rushing out, I found her standing in front of her brother, her hands on her hips and her face red.

"What's going on?" I asked as I joined them.

Larke came and stood at my side.

"Tell them what you told me," Kerrigan barked.

Zach's jaw clenched. "Jacob told me the reason you called it off with him was because you're broke. And you're picking up with this guy"—he nodded at me—"because he's the only way you can avoid bankruptcy."

What the actual fuck?

"Apparently, he heard it at the coffee shop this morning," Zach added.

"Bullshit," Kerrigan snapped. "If he heard it at the coffee shop, it was because it came from his own damn mouth."

"You said yesterday you were selling your place." Zach crossed his arms over his chest.

Fuck this guy for not defending his sister. Instead, he came here and spewed an obvious lie. Was he threatened by her?

"I'm selling my house to buy another one," Kerrigan said

through gritted teeth. "I'm not broke. But thanks for your support of my business."

Their parents came over from where they'd been packing away the gifts.

"What's going on?" Colton asked. "Kerrigan, stop shouting."

I opened my mouth to defend her, but I should have remembered it was unnecessary. Kerrigan could hold her own. Once, not all that long ago, she'd read me the riot act on First Street, and that day had changed my life.

This argument was headed down a different path.

"What is your problem, Zach?" She mirrored his stance, her legs planted wide and her arms crossed. "You throw my mistakes in my face every chance you get. When your friend suggests that I am dating a man for his money, instead of defending me and my reputation, you ask me if it's true. You should know I'd never do that."

"There's a rumor going around?" Madeline asked. "Oh lord."

Was she upset that Kerrigan's morals were being called into question? Or that her daughter was being gossiped about? It infuriated me that I even had to wonder.

Kerrigan had told me that her family wasn't overly supportive, but this was ridiculous.

"Jacob started that rumor." Kerrigan's nostrils flared. "His ego was bruised because I didn't want to date him."

Colton sighed. "I'll talk to him at work on Monday."

"Don't bother." Kerrigan shook her head. "I don't care if people talk about me. I don't. That ship sailed a long time ago. What I do care about is that my brother might actually believe it's true. That he actually thinks I'd be with a man for his money. I didn't realize you thought I was a whore."

I flinched. Larke flinched. Everyone in the room flinched, even Zach.

And then she was gone.

Kerrigan stormed past him toward Elias in his seat. I joined in step, collecting my son and marching out the door. The moment they were both loaded in the SUV, I climbed behind the wheel and drove out of Calamity.

"Where are we going?" she asked as I hit the highway.

"Nowhere. Just thought you might want a little breathing room."

She sagged, then leaned forward, dropping her face into her hands. When her shoulders began to shake, I pulled over to the side of the road and put my hand on her back. She didn't cry for long but even one tear was enough to rip me apart.

With the exception of her sister, the rest of her family could fuck off.

"I'm okay." She sniffled and sat straight, wiping her face.

"What can I do, babe?"

She gave me a sad smile. "You're doing it."

"Want me to drive you home?" I took her hand from her lap and brought her knuckles to my lips.

"Not really. But how would you feel about some company at the motel for a while?"

I didn't have to answer.

Elias let out a wild, happy shriek like he understood too.

My kid was damn smart.

CHAPTER NINETEEN

KERRIGAN

THE CHIME of my phone jolted me awake, and I scrambled to shut it off before it woke up Elias.

"Dad?" I whispered, pressing it to my ear.

Pierce sat up behind me, his arm still around my waist from how we'd fallen asleep.

"Hey, honey." Two words and I knew something was wrong.

"What is it? What happened?"

"Sorry to wake you up but I didn't want you to hear it from anyone else."

My heart stopped. "What? Is it Mom?"

"No, we're all fine. But Zach had a fire at his house tonight."

"A fire?" I sat up completely, pushing my back against the headboard.

Pierce sat up too, twisting to turn on the lamp on the nightstand. Beside it the clock showed it was four in the morning.

"When?" I asked Dad. "Is he okay?"

"He's fine. Shaken up, as expected. He's here. The fire started around midnight."

I scooched to the end of the bed and stood, searching the floor for my shoes. "Okay. I'll come over."

"You don't have to. But I wanted you to know what's going on. It'll be all over town by six."

"I'm coming over." Maybe Zach struggled to support me, maybe I was pissed at him for how he'd acted at the party yesterday, but he was still my brother. I ended the call and swiped up my shoes.

"What's happening?" Pierce stood.

"My brother had a fire at his house. Around midnight, Dad said. I didn't get more details than that, but he's at my parents' place so I'm going over."

"Give me ten to get Elias packed, then we'll come with you."

"You don't—"

The look he sent me was one I imagined silenced many boardrooms. Pierce was coming.

"I'll get the bottles."

While he readied the car seat, I refilled the diaper bag from the supplies scattered around the room. Then I carried it to the Mercedes while he strapped a sleeping baby into his car seat.

Elias whimpered but, by some miracle, stayed asleep. Probably because he'd woken up hungry at two.

The drive across town was quiet other than the directions I gave Pierce. My parents lived on the outskirts of Calamity, their house in the middle of three acres. Their private lane was bordered by lilacs, something Mom had insisted on when I was a kid. What had started as tiny green bushes that we used to weave our bikes around like an obstacle course was now a wall of shrubbery.

"In the spring, all of these are in bloom and sometimes I'll come over just to walk up and down this road to smell the air."

Pierce reached over and took my hand.

"Thanks for coming with me."

"I'm here, Kerr. No matter what."

I squeezed his hand as we approached the house.

After the party yesterday, we'd gone to the motel room and ordered delivery from the café for dinner. Calamity was embracing the future and had recently approved DoorDash. We'd eaten our sandwiches and played with Elias and after he'd fallen asleep for the night, I'd borrowed a pair of Pierce's sweats—the same pair I'd worn during our snowstorm. They were mine forever now, something I'd told Pierce as I'd settled into his side for the night. He'd kissed me once, then held me close as I'd fallen asleep to the TV.

We hadn't spoken about my parents or my brother. And as we parked beside Larke's car in the driveway, I worried that maybe I should have argued in the motel.

"I can't promise they'll be kind." The fact that I had to put a voice to that thought made me ache.

Before Pierce, I'd been frustrated with my family. Irritated. That was normal, right? All families had a dynamic. But yesterday, after the way they'd treated him and me at the party . . .

"I don't have a lot of faith in them right now."

"Hey." Pierce leaned over, his hand sliding up my neck to cup my cheek. "I'm not here for them. I'm here for you. After enough years, they'll realize we're a package deal."

"Years?" My breath hitched.

"I'm not going anywhere."

He'd said as much before, but tonight, it was starting to sink in. "People will think we're crazy. That this is too soon."

"And I don't give a shit what people think."

I leaned into his touch. "We have a lot to talk about." Namely, the accusations my mother had thrown his way yesterday.

"Later." He kissed my forehead.

My sister stepped out of her car, giving a little wave before she headed to the front door. We were right behind her, hurrying inside.

My parents' house had been built in the eighties. We'd moved in when I was a toddler and it looked the same as it had then. At the time, it had been one of the nicest homes in Calamity. It was still a beautiful home, but with the honey oak cabinets, brass fixtures and popcorn ceilings, it was dated. Oh, what I could do with this house and $50,000. I'd offered once at a family dinner.

After Zach had scoffed and rolled his eyes, I hadn't brought it up again.

We walked down the tiled entryway to the sunken living room, where my brother was on the couch. His eyes were red and his hair disheveled. He wore a pair of Dad's sweatpants and a borrowed Hale Motors T-shirt.

"Hey." I went straight for the space beside him on the couch. Mom and Larke were crowded in on his other side.

"Hey." His voice was hoarse. His hair was damp from a recent shower, but the scent of smoke clung to his skin and it wasn't the scent of cigarettes.

Pierce came into the living room and took one of the leather recliners, setting Elias beside him.

"So what happened?" Larke asked. Her hair was a mess

on top of her head, and she was in a pair of green flannel pajama pants paired with a hot-pink hoodie.

Zach stared at the floor as he spoke, his elbows on his knees. "I went to Jane's after the party. Had a few drinks. The band was playing and that friend of yours was singing. It was busy."

Most nights were when Lucy was at the microphone.

"I called a cab. Didn't think I was that drunk but I knew I shouldn't drive. Got home. Turned on the TV. Woke up in my bed. I must have stumbled in there. The house was full of smoke and when I tried to leave the bedroom, I hit a wall of flames. I had to crawl out through the window. By the time the fire truck showed up, the whole place was just . . . there was fire everywhere."

He rubbed at his eyes, then dropped his face to his hands.

"Did they say what caused it?" I asked.

"They'll investigate but after the fire was out, they did a walk-through. The worst of the damage was in the living room."

"What was in the living room?" Larke asked.

Zach hesitated to answer and a tear dripped down his cheek. He brushed it away, then choked out, "Probably a cigarette."

No. I closed my eyes and put my hand on his shoulder. "I'm sorry."

"My own damn fault." He shook his head, then shoved to his bare feet, pacing the room.

Dad was standing at the mouth of the room, where he'd been during the explanation. He and Mom must have already gotten Zach's story because neither of them looked surprised. Just . . . sad.

"What can we do?" Larke asked.

Zach shrugged and kept pacing.

"Was anything saved?"

He shoved his hands in his pockets and shook his head.

Everything he'd owned had been in that house.

"I think I'm going to lie down for a while," Zach muttered, then stalked past Dad and disappeared down the hallway that led to our childhood bedrooms.

"Shit," Larke said when he was out of earshot. "I can't believe this."

"How many times have I told him to quit smoking?" Mom wrung her hands in her lap.

"That's not helpful right now, Mom."

She shot me a glare. "The only reason he went to the bar was because of the fight you two had at the party."

My jaw dropped. "Wait. Are you saying this is partly my fault?"

"No. Of course not. It's just . . ." Her shoulders fell and her eyes flooded. "He lost everything."

"The important thing is that he's okay," I said.

Dad nodded. "Yes, it is."

The room went still. The magnitude of what had happened was settling. My brother could have died tonight. Had he not woken up in time, he might have suffocated or worse.

Mom must have been thinking the same because she started to weep, quietly at first, until a cry escaped and Larke pulled her close.

When Elias made a little mewl, Pierce unbuckled him from his seat. "Is there a place where I can change him?"

"Sure." I stood and motioned for him to follow me down the hallway to my old bedroom.

Mom and Dad had turned it into a guest room years ago, but it was still the same shade of lavender I'd painted it at sixteen.

"I'm going back out to sit with Mom and Dad," I said.

"Okay, babe." He pulled me in for a quick hug and kiss on the forehead, then let me go.

"Thanks for coming with me. I know it's awkward but—"

"I'm here."

He had no idea how much that meant.

When I was in fourth grade, one of my uncles had had a heart attack. It had happened in the middle of the night and when Dad had gotten the call, he'd woken us all up to go to the hospital. When we'd arrived, the waiting room had already been packed with my aunts and other uncles and cousins.

In an emergency, the Hales showed up in numbers.

I knew from friends that it wasn't normal to show up en masse. Most parents probably would have left their kids behind.

But sometimes support simply meant showing your face. Even if it was awkward. Even if it was hard.

And Pierce was here.

I gave him a small smile and eased out of the room, shutting the door behind me. Then I walked quietly down the hallway, only to run into my dad.

He opened his arms and I walked right into them. "Thanks for coming over."

"Of course."

"Not sure it was a great idea to bring him though."

Every muscle in my body tensed and I wiggled out of his embrace. "Seriously?"

"We're worried about you too, you know. What happened at the party was not good."

"Are you blaming me for the fire too?"

"What? No." Dad raked a hand through his graying hair. "I don't like it when you kids are fighting. You were right about what you said to Zach. He should have defended you."

Some of my anger eased. "Thank you."

"But was that party really the time to bring along Pierce?"

"I'm not going to hide him, Dad." Not anymore. "He's important to me. Which should be enough for you guys to be kind. The fact that he came here with me tonight, that he insisted on it even after how you all treated him, should be proof enough for you to give him a chance."

Dad sighed. "It's just . . . how do you know he's not looking for a woman to raise that baby?"

Oh, for fuck's sake. "I see you've talked to Mom."

"Yes, we've talked, and it's a valid concern."

"He's worth billions of dollars. Billions. Pierce doesn't need me to raise that baby. He's got a nanny. He can hire a team of nannies."

"But—"

"I want Kerrigan because I'm in love with her."

I whipped around at Pierce's voice, stunned to see him striding down the hallway with Elias in the cradle of an arm.

His gaze was locked on Dad as he came to stand by my side. "In your shoes, I'd be wary too. But I don't need your approval because in time, I'll earn it. Treat me however you like. That said, I've seen Kerrigan cry more tears tonight than she should have. So I'll warn you, Colton, she doesn't need me to defend her, but I will. Make no mistake about it, if you cause her any more pain, you'll answer to me."

I blinked, stunned.

There was a lot to unpack in all of that, and I wasn't the only one rendered speechless.

"I forgot the diaper bag." Pierce strode past us for the living room. When he returned, a diaper in hand, he didn't say a word as he marched down the hallway and into my old bedroom.

"If you don't marry him, I will." Larke came up behind Dad. She looped an arm through his and dragged him away.

I stood there and let Pierce's statement sink in.

He loved me. I'd wondered if he did, or at least, I'd thought he might. But hearing it chased away whatever lingering doubts I'd been silencing for the past day and a half.

Pierce really wasn't going anywhere.

He was here.

For me.

Spinning on a heel, I rushed down the hallway and slipped into the bedroom. Pierce was just buttoning up Elias's jammies.

"Hi," I said, closing the door behind me.

"Hi." His jaw clenched as the last snap clicked into place. Then he moved some pillows so that in case Elias rolled, he wouldn't fall off the bed.

"About what you said . . ."

"Not exactly how I'd planned to say that. Especially to your dad. Shit." He stood and raked a hand over his bearded jaw. "How about you forget I said it?"

"Nope."

Pierce came over and dropped his forehead to mine. "This is not about Elias."

"I know," I breathed.

"You do? Earlier today, when you were talking to your mom, I worried you'd think she was right."

"Maybe if you had stayed." I hated that we'd spent time apart. That he'd gone through so much on his own. But what he'd told me the other night had struck a chord.

If he'd been busy falling in love with me, he wouldn't have given Elias his all.

"You were right to leave," I told him. "You were right to put Elias first. And I know you're not here because you're searching for a mother. I know you're here for me."

"Thank fuck." His sigh of relief filled the room. Then his mouth was on mine, his tongue diving deep. He kissed me breathless as I poured everything I had yet to say into the kiss.

Maybe people would think we were crazy. But like he'd told Dad, we'd show them in the years to come.

We had time.

A noise from Elias broke us apart.

I gazed into Pierce's sparkling brown eyes and felt these roots take hold, this invisible tie between us. For months, I'd wondered if I'd imagined these feelings for Pierce. If I'd built him up in my head. If our fling had meant more to me than it had him because of my broken engagement.

I wasn't alone in this. Not in the slightest.

Across the hall, a door opened. It had to be Zach.

"I should go talk to them," I said. "See if I can do anything."

"You go." Pierce jerked his chin to the door. "I'll stay here with my boy."

I smiled at the baby, then went over and dropped a kiss to his smooth cheek before returning to the living room where my family was sitting.

"You can move in here," Mom told Zach.

He shook his head. "I'm thirty-two. I'm not moving in here. I can find a rental or something. I doubt insurance is going to cover my house if the fire was started by my cigarette. Fucking hell."

Mom cringed at the language but didn't correct him.

I went to my purse, bending to retrieve my keys. Then I twisted off a silver one from a ring, bringing it to Zach. "Here."

"What's this?"

"A key to the loft above the gym. You can stay there for as long as you need. It's furnished too."

He stared at the key but didn't take it. "You don't need to rent it out?"

"It's covered." Now that I'd paid off my loan with Pierce, the income from the gym was enough to pay the utilities and taxes on the building. Any rent on the loft was simply a bonus.

Zach took the key, turning it around in his fingers. "No, thanks."

"But ... why?"

"It's hard to be around someone who never fails. Everyone would choose you over me in a blink. I don't need your charity." He tossed the key in my direction.

I didn't even try to catch it. It landed on the shag carpet beside my feet. "Excuse me? Just yesterday at the party, you reminded me that I'd gone broke. How is that not a failure?"

"This is not the time to get into an argument." Mom stood from the couch and shot me a look. It said, *Shut up, Kerrigan.*

Maybe the problem was that as a family, we showed up. But we shut up.

"I give up." I threw my hands in the air. "I give up. I'm trying to help Zach, but instead, he tells me it's hard for him to be around me. I won't apologize for my success. I won't apologize for my ambitions. I won't apologize for going to college when he had the same opportunity and chose to stay in Calamity. I am tired of tiptoeing around my achievements because they make my brother feel insecure."

I took a step back. It was awful of me to put this all out there tonight. My brother had just lost his home. But as the words bubbled free, there was no pulling them in.

"I'm sorry about your house," I told Zach. "You're welcome to the loft. Take it or leave it, but I don't want to fight with you anymore."

Without another word, I strode down the hallway and to the bedroom. Pierce was sitting on the end of the bed, his phone in hand.

"Time to go."

He gave me a sideways glance. "What happened?"

"Nothing good."

That was all I had to say. He turned, swept Elias into his arms and led the way toward the front door.

Zach was gone when we returned to the living room.

The key to the loft was still on the carpet.

Pierce picked up the car seat. I grabbed the diaper bag. I was determined not to say a word, but as I moved to leave, I paused and shifted to face my parents.

"You never liked Gabriel. Maybe our relationship was odd. I can understand how you'd see it that way. But he believed in me. So does Pierce. He doesn't tell me not to look at a new house. He doesn't tease me about my blog. He doesn't continue to offer me a job I don't want. He doesn't wait for me to fail with an *I told you so* on the tip of his tongue. He'll watch me jump off a cliff because he believes I'll fly. And I will. I will fly. But you're so busy standing at the bottom, waiting to pick up the pieces, that when you finally look up, I'll have already flown away."

I left Mom and Dad with guilty faces as I took Pierce's outstretched hand. It was only when we were in the SUV that I finally breathed.

"Where to?" he asked.

"I don't know." My limbs were shaking. I was on the verge of hysterical tears. Had I ever spoken to my parents that way? Maybe as a teenager. At the moment, I couldn't remember.

Since I'd moved back to Calamity, I'd worried too much about rocking the boat and tipping them over the edge.

But I'd forgotten that they knew how to swim.

"Maybe the motel," I said. "If I go home, my sister will show up and I just . . . I need some space. From all of them." I wasn't mad at Larke but I knew her well enough to know she'd try to calm the waters.

"I've got a better idea." He held my hand as we drove through town to the motel. Then after a quick stop at my place to pack a bag and pick up Clementine and her things, we were on the road.

Two hours later, we walked into the cabin.

It smelled like pine trees and cedar planks.

Pierce had Elias in his arms and a grin on his handsome face. "I missed it here."

"Me too."

Maybe it wasn't mine, but for today, it felt like coming home.

CHAPTER TWENTY

KERRIGAN

"THIS IS NOT GOING TO WORK." Pierce glared at the situation on the kitchen island.

Elias was in his bouncer, staring at the mobile's monkeys hanging from the attached arm. And beside him was Clementine, seemingly content to rest on the smooth granite surface. Except every time Pierce reached for his son, my cat would pop up on all fours, hiss and swat his hand away.

"She's deemed Elias hers." I shrugged. "It's better to just accept it."

He frowned, reaching in again.

Clementine's hiss was so loud it filled the kitchen.

"You know, you had her in a couple of your Instagram posts," he said. "She looks like such a sweet, innocent ball of fluff. Then we picked her up yesterday morning and I realized she's actually possessed by Satan."

I laughed and went back to stirring the scrambled eggs. "She has her sweet moments."

"When?"

I turned the stove off and went to his side, sliding an arm around his waist. "Look at her protecting him. That's sweet."

"I'm his father. *I'm* the protector."

Standing on my toes, I kissed his bearded jaw.

Beyond the windows, the sun was shining white gold. The snow-capped mountains in the distance stood proud in the clear blue sky. Spring hadn't quite hit at this high of an elevation, but a hint of green grass was sprouting on the lawn and buds would soon follow on the trees.

It was as gorgeous as it had been this winter. So was the man at my side.

Pierce's hair was damp from his shower, and he looked insanely handsome in a pair of faded jeans. A long-sleeved, navy T-shirt stretched across his broad chest, and as his hand drifted down my spine to my hip, a heat wave spread over my skin.

Pierce in a suit was devastating but I'd come to love this version of him more. The barefoot, unbuttoned Pierce who'd been touching me constantly but still hadn't *touched* me.

I really needed him to touch me.

Except after yesterday's drama, he'd let me lean on him. I had. But the constant caresses over my shoulders and the brushes of his lips against my temples had lit a fire I was ready to let blaze.

Maybe after breakfast, while Elias was napping.

I went to the counter and swiped up Clementine, earning a hiss of my own as I set her on the floor. Then I kissed Elias's cheek and went back to making our eggs.

"How's it going this morning, pal?" Pierce asked as he unbuckled Elias from the bouncer.

Elias answered with a giggle and kick of his legs as Pierce picked him up.

One glance over my shoulder at the two of them and my ovaries exploded.

"Do you like the cabin?" Pierce asked him. "Pretty fun here, isn't it?"

"When you were in the shower, I had him on a blanket in the living room. He was screeching and yelling as loud as he could because I think he likes the echo. Then he was squirming and kicking. He even tried to roll over."

Pierce chuckled. "He's almost got it figured out. Maybe while we're here, he'll get it."

I wasn't sure how long we'd stay, but at the moment, I was in no rush to go home. In the past forty-eight hours, I'd become so entirely disappointed in my family that I didn't have the energy to deal with them. Not yet.

"Need some help?" Pierce asked, coming over to inspect my scrambled eggs, sausage, peppers, onions and cheese.

"No, I've got it."

I'd forgotten just how nice it was to have a fridge stocked for us.

On our way up yesterday, Pierce had called Nellie to tell her we were headed to the cabin. It had been barely after sunrise as we'd pulled out of Calamity, but in the two hours it had taken us to get here, the club had cleaned the entire house and filled the refrigerator and pantry.

The man who'd met us here had said not everything was available immediately but then just yesterday afternoon, he'd returned with more supplies that would last for the rest of our stay. We'd told him a week, but if it was longer than that, I wouldn't complain.

The Refinery was covered. When I'd called each of my employees yesterday, every one of them had jumped at the chance for more hours. I had my laptop in case I needed to do any other work, but for the moment, I simply wanted some time alone with Pierce and Elias.

"How are you feeling?" he asked as we sat down to eat at the island. Elias was back in the bouncer with his lioness Clementine by his side.

"Raw. But I'm glad to be here."

"So am I."

"Thanks for bringing me here." I'd told him that three times since we'd arrived yesterday.

His eyes softened, crinkling at the sides. "This is your place now too."

"Well, I don't know about that," I muttered, filling my mouth with a huge bite.

"There's a lot to talk about."

Yes, there was. Like the fact that Pierce had told my father he was in love with me. The fact that he hadn't mentioned it again. The fact that I hadn't either.

"But not today," Pierce said. "Today, we're just going to chill. Tonight, we'll talk."

"We chilled all day yesterday."

"One more day."

"Okay," I whispered.

Since we'd arrived yesterday, we'd mostly busied ourselves with settling in. Our bags had been unpacked in the master bedroom. Drawers filled. Clothes hung in the closet. Pierce had known that he'd be coming here and the guest room closest to the master had been turned into a nursery.

"Have you been here since December?" I asked.

He shook his head. "No. When I left Denver, I went straight to Calamity."

Straight to me.

"Are you okay staying in the master?" I should have asked him last night, but when he'd steered me to bed, I'd been so exhausted that I'd crashed not ten seconds after hitting the pillow.

"It's the biggest room."

"We could stay in the guest suite."

"No, it's okay. Besides . . ." He grinned. "I bought new beds. For the entire house."

I laughed and now it made sense why the bedding was all different. "So the beds. The nursery. Everything else looks the same unless I'm missing something."

"That's all for now. In time, I'm sure we'll add stuff. Our own pictures. Clothes we want to leave here. Skis for the winter. Hiking gear for the summer. Different furniture if you want to redecorate."

The fork nearly fell out of my hand. He was talking like this was ours. Together. That this monstrosity of a mountain lodge was as much mine as his.

"What?" he asked, his own fork freezing midair as he took in my face.

"Maybe we need to have that talk right now."

He chuckled and took a bite. "Today is for relaxing."

"And this conversation won't be relaxing?"

Pierce set down his fork and swiveled in his seat to lean in close. "After this conversation, I'm going to want to reinforce my words by tearing off your clothes and making good use of the new beds. Plural. It's not going to be fast. It's not something I'm willing to squeeze in during Elias's nap time."

"Oh." My cheeks flamed and a throb settled between my legs. I pulled in my lips to hide a smile.

"Today, we relax. Tonight, we'll talk."

As long as talk meant stripping him out of those jeans, I

was ready. Four months without sex had never been an issue before Pierce.

There was a lot I'd gone without before Pierce.

Elias turned out to be the perfect entertainment to pass the day. We played on the living room floor after breakfast. Pierce had to spend some time working while I fed Elias his midmorning bottle. Then we returned to the kitchen, where I decided to take advantage of the high-end appliances and make grilled paninis for lunch.

During Elias's afternoon nap, I wandered around the house, taking some photos for Instagram. I posted a video of me standing on the property's edge, the mountains at my back and the breeze in my hair.

It all served as a distraction to the conversation coming.

My nerves started to get the best of me as we gave Elias his bath.

Clementine was locked in her bedroom—the laundry room—because we didn't want her sneaking into Elias's room at night and climbing into his crib.

I knew what the discussion would entail. Well, sort of. I had a vague idea. Pierce had been very forthcoming about his feelings—to me and Dad. But I hadn't ever said those three words to any man besides my ex.

The fear of saying them again wasn't one I'd had to deal with.

I hadn't loved anyone since him. And if I was being honest with myself, I hadn't really loved him either.

"You okay?" Pierce asked as I put Elias in his pajamas on the changing table.

I'd never bathed a baby before. I'd never put a kid in pajamas. Maybe Pierce realized that I'd needed the tasks to keep my mind occupied because he let me take the lead, offering suggestions along the way.

"I'm good." I kept my attention on the baby, like I had all evening. Even through dinner. "Can I rock him to sleep?"

"Of course." He bent to kiss his son's cheek, then he did the same to mine before slipping out of the nursery.

"Okay, little one." I picked Elias up and carried him to the glider in the corner, settling in with the bottle Pierce had prepared earlier. Then we rocked, me and this sweet boy who was stealing my heart.

"I'm in love with you too, you know," I confessed. "You are precious, my darling."

Elias was the happiest baby I'd seen in my life. He drank his bottle in silence, his big brown eyes never looking away from my face.

It wasn't hard to tell him that I loved him. Not in the slightest.

"I was thinking about what my mom said. Not all of it was kind, but she was partially right. You need a mother, not just a nanny. I don't know if I'm equipped for it. I don't know if your real mother would have chosen me, or even liked me for that matter."

I blew out a deep breath, resting my head on the back of the chair. "Today when we were playing and I was taking those videos of you squawking at the ceiling, I thought about someone else being there with you. Someone else with the camera, listening to you. Watching you roll over. I got so jealous I could barely see straight."

This all-consuming envy had washed over me so fast that it had taken me aback. "The only other time I've ever felt that level of insane jealousy was over your dad. He was in Denver, taking care of you, not that I knew that. But every now and then, I'd picture him with another woman, and I'd get so jealous that it would ruin my entire day."

Elias grunted and when I looked down, the bottle was empty.

"Done already?" I shifted and put him against my shoulder to pat his back.

Three pats and the belch that came from his tiny body was loud enough to rival a grown man's.

"Whoa." I laughed. "Nice one, bud."

I rubbed his back, continuing to rock him until his body went limp and he was out. *Time to talk.* It would be fine, right?

Right.

And I'd likely get an orgasm or two afterward. I just had to tell Pierce how I felt. Three little words.

My heart raced as I put Elias in his crib, careful not to wake him, then snuck out of the room.

The door to the master was open. I sucked in a fortifying breath, then padded down the hallway to find Pierce on the bed.

His legs were crossed at his ankles. His back was to the headboard. And on his lap was the baby monitor.

From the serious look on his face, he'd heard that whole one-sided confession I'd given his son.

My stomach dropped. "Uh, you heard all of that, didn't you?"

"I did."

"And?"

He set the monitor on the nightstand, then stood from the bed and crossed the room. "And it changes our conversation some."

"It does?" Oh, God. I'd gone too far admitting that I'd

happily step in as Elias's mother. Heidi was his mother, not me. What the hell was I thinking?

"It does." Pierce lifted a hand to my face, cupping my cheek. Then his mouth was on mine and the fears racing through my mind took a backseat to the sweep of his tongue and the taste of his lips.

I melted into him, sinking into the kiss I'd been craving from the moment he'd returned to Calamity. Because though he'd kissed me, this one was going somewhere. This was the kiss I'd been craving for months.

My hands skimmed up and under his shirt, roaming across his hard chest. I dragged my nails against his taut skin, savoring the strength of his body beneath my palms. When my fingers tangled in the dusting of hair on his chest, he let go of my face and his hands dove into my hair.

Then he tilted my face, holding my head at a slant so he could plunder my mouth.

I moaned and stood on my toes, wanting more and more. But Pierce broke away, still holding me in place as he leaned back to study my face.

"God, I love your mouth. You are beautiful, Kerr." There was so much emotion shining through his eyes that it stole my breath. "I missed you. Fuck, but I missed you."

"I missed you too."

"Never again. No more time apart. For the rest of our lives, where we go, we go together."

My heart skipped. I thought there'd be more words, but then he kissed me again and there was no indication he'd ever stop.

This man delivered so much pleasure with his lips and tongue, I was shaking when he tore his mouth away to drag my sweatshirt up and over my head. He sent it sailing to the floor along with my bra. Then he shuffled me to the bed, laying me down and pulling off my jeans and panties. Whoosh. I was completely bare.

Pierce, fully clothed, stepped back and drank me in.

His Adam's apple bobbed as he raked his gaze over my naked skin. Then as quickly as he'd divested me of my clothes, his joined mine on the carpet.

When his hard cock bobbed free, I gulped, having forgotten just how big he was. I let my own eyes wander, traveling up his washboard abs and down those sculpted arms. But when I took in his face, he looked . . . well, miserable.

"What's wrong?" I asked.

He gritted his teeth. "I haven't been with anyone since you. But . . . do I need a condom?"

"No." I sat up on my elbows. "There's been no one else."

"Oh, thank fuck." He dove for me, taking us both deeper into the bed. One hand trailed down my ribs as the other wrapped around my neck.

He shifted so one side of his body had mine pinned to the bed. And that hand—that damn hand—drove me wild. It glided over my skin, torturing me as it moved in a lazy trail over my stomach. Then up again to the swell of my breasts.

"Pierce," I warned. "Save the foreplay for round two."

He ignored me, bringing those fingertips higher. Around the top, then under the areola. He circled my nipple, never touching the hard bud, but the tingles beneath his touch spread straight to my core.

I arched into him.

"Are you wet for me?" he asked, grazing my nipple before dropping his hand to my ribs. His fingers stayed in a constant state of motion.

"Find out for yourself." I spread my legs wider.

He grinned but did he move lower? No. The bastard brought his hand to my face, tracing the line of my nose, my cheek, my mouth.

Touch after touch, he played with my skin like it was his own personal instrument. It was by far the most erotic foreplay of my life. To be only touched by a man. To have him worship me. To have him memorize every line, every crease, every curve.

Two could play that game.

I raised my free hand, about to touch the veins in his sinewed forearm, but the moment I brushed his skin, he captured my wrist and raised my arm above my head, trapping it against the pillows.

"No touching." He ran his lips along my cheekbone.

"That's not fair."

"You should know by now that I'm not all that interested in fair." He dropped his mouth and sucked on my earlobe. After a nip, he shifted faster than I could blink.

One of my arms was trapped beneath his ribs, the other in the pillows held in his grip. And since he had a hand free, he continued his touch torture.

"Pierce."

"What do you want, babe?"

"You."

"Where?"

"Inside," I breathed.

Did he listen to me? No. He gave me a devilish grin, and this time as he traced my skin, he did it with his tongue instead of his fingers.

Minutes passed. Hours. I was drenched and on the verge

of an orgasm when he finally shifted into the cradle of my hips.

I was sure he'd make me suffer through more, but when I felt the tip of his cock drag through my folds, I opened my eyes to his.

He hovered above me, his arms bracketing my face. Then with one smooth, long stroke, he buried himself to the root.

"Oh, God," I cried out, savoring the stretch as I adjusted to him.

"Christ." He clenched his jaw. "Fuck, you feel good."

"Move."

He shook his head.

"Pierce, move." My arms and legs were trembling. I ached for release. My orgasm was right there, so damn close, but I needed him to move.

"Kerr," he whispered, the playfulness gone from his voice. "I'm in love with you."

I locked my eyes with his and whatever fears I'd had earlier were . . . gone.

There hadn't been a time in my life when I'd wanted to say it. Not like this.

"I'm in love with you too."

He dropped his lips to mine and then we were just us. Moving together. Bringing each other to the peak and holding on as we both tumbled over the edge.

I cried out his name as I broke, as he thrust in and out, holding me close as he poured inside me. Our legs were tangled. My arm was trapped in his and the other banded around him so tightly I never wanted to let go.

The stars in my eyes turned to tears, startling me so much my breath hitched.

"Why are you crying?" he asked.

"I'm . . . happy. I didn't even know that this happy existed."

"Neither did I," he whispered.

I fell asleep in his arms, the two of us tangled together in the sheets. I jerked awake at Elias's cry through the monitor. The clock on the nightstand read a bleary two.

I sat up, but Pierce touched my shoulder, urging me into the bed.

"I'll get him."

I dozed off, and when Pierce settled in behind me, I startled awake once more. "Is he okay?"

"Back to sleep."

I snuggled into his arms, but this time when I relaxed into the pillow, my brain decided I'd slept enough. I did my best to lie still, to let Pierce rest. I squeezed my eyes shut. I counted sheep. I sang a mental lullaby. Nothing would get me back to sleep.

"What's going on in your head?" His arms tightened.

"I can't sleep." I sighed. "Sorry to wake you."

"I can't sleep either." He rolled me, spinning me to face him. "Guess we'd better have the conversation we didn't earlier."

Everything that had needed to be said was said. The important parts, anyway. "Do we really need it?"

"Yes." Pierce nodded. "Because I have a proposal for you."

CHAPTER TWENTY-ONE

PIERCE

EVEN IN THE DARK, I saw the fear on Kerrigan's face.

I laughed. "Not that kind of proposal."

Not yet anyway. We needed more time, and if she agreed to my idea, we'd have it.

Kerrigan relaxed and sat up, bringing the sheet with her to cover her chest. "Okay, I'm listening."

"Thirty days."

"Thirty days for what?" She narrowed her gaze. The last time I'd told her thirty days, she'd torn up a letter and thrown it in my face.

"Thirty days together."

"And then what?"

"Then another thirty more." I grinned. "But let's take this one month at a time. Thirty days here."

"In this house?"

"Yeah. You. Me. Elias. We'll make this home base. If you need to go to town to be at The Refinery, it's only two hours away. We can spend however many days there that we need for business, but the majority of our time, we'll be here."

We'd be home.

"I know it's a big ask to put your projects on hold," I said.

"They're done." She shrugged. "I haven't decided what to start on next. Trips back and forth might mean a lot of driving."

"We'll make it work."

"What about your job?"

I shifted, turning to flip on the lamp and then sat up beside her, putting an arm around her shoulders and pulling her to me. "I've already arranged to work from here for the next month." *Or longer.*

"You set this all up before you came here?"

"I told you, babe. I'm here. For as long as it takes."

Elias wasn't due to check in with his pediatrician for another two months. That was the only reason I'd need to go back to Denver, and even then, there were doctors in Montana. I'd need to find one if this area became our permanent home.

But that was another decision we'd make in a month.

Kerrigan blew out an audible breath, staring across the room to the dark windows.

I knew it was a big ask. Her family would probably think I'd abducted her. But a month together would do us all some good. A month to come together and just be us.

There was time to make up for.

"Why?" she whispered. "Why here?"

"Because it's our place. At least, it could be. Maybe after some time, it won't feel like Grandpa's."

"Will you think about *them* here?"

"It's getting easier. Especially with you and Elias here."

And not just because the beds had been replaced.

The rooms were beginning to have new memories.

When I saw the couch, I thought of Kerrigan, naked with her legs draped open wide. When I walked into the kitchen, I saw her at the stove and Elias in his bouncer with the demon cat as his personal bodyguard.

If we filled up the house with baby toys and the sound of his laughter mixed with Kerrigan's, real memories would chase away the imaginary ones of Grandpa and Heidi together.

Real, lasting memories.

"You can pick some rooms and redecorate. Paint, lighting and whatever else you can think of. If you want to do a larger remodel, then we'll tackle it too. We'll take one of the guest rooms downstairs and turn it into your own office. Or you can have the main office and I'll take a guest room. Whatever you want. But we'll spend thirty days and see if we can make this place ours."

And at the end of that month, I'd have a different proposal for her too.

This morning, I'd snuck away for ten minutes to call my mother's favorite jeweler. One sizeable deposit later and I'd commissioned him to design a custom ring.

A crease formed between Kerrigan's eyebrows. I'd seen that expression a few times, whenever she was working through something in her head. Then the line disappeared, and I held my breath, waiting for her answer.

"The nursery," she said. "We should make it an actual nursery. Maybe paint a mural or find a unique, little boy wallpaper. Or we could—"

I slammed my mouth on hers, my tongue sweeping inside her open lips.

She giggled and put her hands to my face, holding me to her as we kissed.

I pulled her into the bed, yanking the hem of the sheet up and over our heads. Her laughter died on a gasp when I parted her legs and slid inside her tight, wet heat.

Neither of us slept the rest of the night. I kept her awake until the early morning hours when my son's babbling roused us both from bed.

Kerrigan pulled on her sweats and beat me to the crib.

When I came in wearing sweats of my own, she was in the rocking chair with my son.

"Thirty days," she said, smiling at me and Elias.

I nodded. "Thirty days."

Those beautiful brown eyes sparkled. "You've got a deal, Mr. Sullivan."

———

"WILL you add heavy cream to the list?" Kerrigan asked, pointing to the notepad I was writing on. "I want to try making some homemade ice cream in that machine I found in the cupboard."

I scribbled it down below *Pampers Swaddlers, Size 2*. "What else?"

"That's plenty for now. Are you sure they don't mind getting all of this for us?"

"I pay the club a hefty monthly fee to run our errands." There were quite a few celebrity members and when they came here, the last place they wanted to go was out in public. "They expect to go to the grocery store for us. They have staff exactly for that purpose. I promise."

"Okay. It still feels weird."

"You'll get used to it."

In time, she'd realize that what was mine—billions

included—was hers. If that money could make her life easier and earn me more smiles, I'd spend every cent.

She sighed, stroking Clementine's head. The two of them were curled up on one side of the couch while I was on the other. "I guess if we forgot anything, I can swing by the store when we go to town on Wednesday."

"Or we could send the club on another errand run."

"That's silly. I'll just go myself."

This morning, after we'd had breakfast and played with Elias for a while, we'd decided to head back to Calamity later in the week.

Kerrigan wanted to spend some time at the gym with her employees and hammer out this month's schedule now that she wouldn't be there as often. She wanted to check on her own house and pick up more clothes to bring here. And though she hadn't said it, I suspected she also wanted to see her family.

None of them had contacted her since we'd arrived. It infuriated me, but so far I'd managed to keep my mouth shut. I'd caught Kerrigan checking her phone a few times yesterday and each time it had turned up with no notifications, there'd been a flash of hurt on her face.

I was giving Colton Hale one more day to get his family in line. And then I'd be stepping in. The brother could go fuck himself for all I cared, but her parents needed to support her.

"What do you want to do today?" I asked, setting the notepad aside.

She shrugged. "Maybe poke around and see if I can find a tape measure. I was looking at wallpaper and found the cutest green and gray mountain pattern."

"There's a toolbox in the garage. I suspect you'll be handier with its contents than I will."

Kerrigan smiled. "When I first started remodeling places, I'd get some supplies from Bozeman on my trips there. The variety was better than Calamity's hardware store. The checkout clerks would always ask if I was buying tools for my husband or boyfriend."

"It's hot, babe. You know that picture you posted on Instagram where you're wearing that toolbelt?"

"Yeah."

I winked at her. "I like that picture. It came in . . . handy during my months without you."

"Oh my God." She laughed and poked her foot into my ribs, nodding to Elias as he played on the floor.

We'd turned on a cartoon for some background noise and with the way his eyelids drooped as he watched, I suspected he'd be out for a morning nap in minutes.

"When we go to your place, let's remember to grab that toolbelt."

She rolled her eyes but the sexy flush in her cheeks said she'd remember. "Are you sure you don't mind if I decorate the nursery?"

"Not at all." Sooner or later, she'd realize this place wasn't mine, but ours. Probably not in the next thirty days, but eventually.

She reached to the end table, taking the remote and turning down the volume on the TV. Then she stood, setting Clementine down on the floor. The cat instantly went to Elias, settling at his side. The cat shot me a glare.

"She didn't hiss at you this morning," Kerrigan said. "I think she likes you."

I scoffed. "She's just plotting how to break out of the laundry room at night and smother me in my sleep."

Kerrigan moved across the couch to settle into my side. "She'll warm up to you. Just wait."

"I was thinking about something." I twisted a lock of her hair around my finger.

"What?"

"What your mom said about Elias needing a mother. About what you said over the monitor last night about Heidi. She would have liked you. She would have been jealous of you. Completely." Even after the divorce, if Heidi had seen the way I looked at Kerrigan, she would have envied Kerrigan's beauty and smile. "But if she put that aside, she would have liked you."

Kerrigan leaned away, staring up at me.

"I want Elias to know who she was. The good things, at least. But she's gone. And he can't say it, but he loves you too."

One look at my son and anyone could tell he adored Kerrigan.

"What are you saying?" she asked.

"We're lucky to have you. Both of us." And he'd be lucky to have her as a mother.

"I'm lucky too." She planted a kiss on the underside of my jaw, then stood. "I'm going to put him in his crib."

"Okay."

She had my son in her arms and was halfway out of the living room when the doorbell rang.

"Must be someone from the club." I swiped up the list to pass it along and walked through the entryway for the door.

But it was not a club employee on the porch.

It was the Hale family.

Colton and Madeline stood side by side. Zach was behind his mother. And Larke hung back with a smirk on her face, like she was simply here to enjoy the show.

How had they gotten through the gate? Or known where the cabin was?

"Hi." Colton cleared his throat. "Sorry to intrude but we were hoping to talk to Kerrigan."

I crossed my arms over my chest. "If by talk you mean apologize, then you're welcome to come in. But if this talk doesn't include a variation of *I'm sorry*, then have a safe drive home."

Madeline's eyes widened.

Larke's smile did too.

"Mom? Dad?" Kerrigan came up to my side with Elias in her arms. "What are you doing here?"

I didn't budge, forcing her to look past my arm. I stood there, statue still, until Colton gave me a nod. Then I moved aside, waving them in.

"What's going on?" Kerrigan asked Larke.

Larke kept her smile in place and nodded to Elias. "May I?"

"Uh, sure." Kerrigan handed him over to her sister.

"Hey, sweet pea. I'm your auntie Larke. How about you show me around your fancy house?"

"Wait. Where are you going?" Kerrigan asked as Larke strode down the hallway, past her parents and brother.

"Exploring," Larke answered, still walking away.

"The nursery is on the second floor," I said.

"Excellent. Thanks, Pierce." Larke waved at me, then disappeared around the corner to the living room.

"What are you guys doing here?" Kerrigan asked her parents.

Colton gave his daughter a sad smile, but it was Madeline who stepped up, wrapping her arms around Kerrigan, and whispered, "We're sorry."

My shoulders sagged. Thank God. We would have been fine without their support, but I wanted more for Kerrigan than *fine*.

"We thought a lot about what you said on Saturday." Colton stepped up, putting his arm around Kerrigan's shoulders. "We didn't realize that you felt unsupported. That's not what we want. Those job offers for a spot at the dealership were because you're so smart. I'd love to work with you. And we're just trying to take care of you. You're our girl."

"We promise to do better," Madeline said.

"Thank you." Kerrigan leaned into their huddle, sending me a smile over her shoulder. It fell when she glanced at her brother.

Zach cleared his throat. "I'm sorry too."

"You're an asshole," Kerrigan said.

He nodded.

"Why?" She stepped away from her parents and stood in front of her brother, her arms crossed over her chest.

"I don't know," he muttered.

"You're jealous," I said.

His eyes flew to mine. There was surprise on his face that I'd blurted it out, but there was some truth there too. We all knew it.

"Jealous?" Kerrigan huffed. "Of what? Me?"

"People talk about you all the time. How great you are. How smart you are. How driven you are. How you're going to run the town one day. All I've ever done was go to work for Dad."

"You're going to take over the dealership," Colton said.

"Your dealership. Granddad's dealership. He started it. You grew it. It's yours, Dad. Not mine. I didn't even go to college."

"Then make it yours." Kerrigan held up her chin. "If you want to prove yourself as more than Dad's fill-in, do it. But don't criticize me in the process. And you can always get your degree. If it means so much to you, go to school."

He dropped his gaze, his shoulders slumped. "You're right."

"I know I'm right." She stared at him, shaking her head. Then, because my woman had a heart of gold, she threw her arms around him and hugged her brother. "I'm so sorry about your house."

"So am I." He relaxed, pulling her close. "If the offer still stands, I'd love to live in the loft for a while. I'll pay rent."

"I already told you that you could."

"I thought maybe my invitation got revoked."

"Not yet." She laughed. "But you're on notice."

He chuckled and let her go. Then he squared his shoulders and walked to me, hand extended. "Hi, I'm Zach. Kerrigan's brother. It's nice to meet you."

I shook his hand. "Thanks."

"This is quite the place." Madeline looked around the entryway. "Is this where you were snowed in? I wouldn't mind getting stranded here myself."

Kerrigan waved her family into the house. "Come on in."

I joined them in the living room. A few minutes later, Larke came down alone with the baby monitor in her hand.

And then I spent the day getting to know her family. They got to know me.

When Elias woke up from his nap, he became the center of attention. Madeline drooled over the kitchen and insisted on cooking lunch. Colton inspected the grounds and helped Kerrigan measure the nursery for the wallpaper order. And Zach mostly hung back, still carrying a weight on his shoulders.

It would pass in time. Homes could be rebuilt. And all he had to do was ask because his sister would design him a dream house.

Colton admitted over lunch that after we'd left on Saturday, they'd wanted to find us but with the fire, they'd stayed in Calamity with Zach. The fire department had identified the cause of the blaze. It had been a cigarette that had fallen to the carpet and ignited the home.

As soon as the report had come in, they'd talked and decided that a face-to-face visit here would be better than a phone call. Larke had done some research and called Nellie, who'd gladly offered up my address and gate code.

I owed her another bonus.

Because one day here with her family and there was a lightness in Kerrigan's gaze I hadn't seen before.

"You're going to stay here?" Madeline asked after dinner as we all sat in the living room. She'd stolen Elias from Larke and was bouncing him on a knee. "For how long?"

Kerrigan gave me a smile. "A month or so."

"I can work at the gym," Madeline said.

"It should be covered but maybe we could put you down for emergencies."

"Oh, I'd love to. It gets me out of the house and gives me something to do to feel useful."

"I can keep an eye on it too," Zach said. He hadn't ventured too close to Elias but that damn cat had been on his lap for hours. "Since I'll be around."

"That would be great," Kerrigan said.

"Well, we'd better hit the road." Colton slapped his hands on his knees and stood from his chair. "Early day tomorrow."

"Thanks for coming up," Kerrigan said, getting hugs from everyone as we shuffled for the door.

"Come by and visit when you pop into town later," Madeline said, handing Elias to me. "Oh, you are a perfect baby. I'm going to spoil you rotten."

"Get in line, Mom." Larke moved in to kiss my son's cheek, then she opened the door, shivering at the gust of cold wind.

Zach and Colton followed the women outdoors, shaking my hand before they left.

The moment the door closed behind them, Kerrigan sighed.

"Feel better?" I asked.

"I hate fighting with them, but maybe it was overdue. Maybe I should have told them how I was feeling a long time ago."

"It's done now." I pulled her into my arms, Elias sandwiched between us. "Early bedtime?"

"Yes, please."

I chuckled and kissed my son's hair. I hadn't held him hardly at all today, though sharing him wasn't such a bad thing.

Kerrigan must have sensed that I'd missed him today because she left me alone to do his bath, feed him his last bottle and rock him to sleep.

When I found her naked in bed, I sent up a silent thanks to the heavens before taking off my own clothes and joining her. Three orgasms for her, two for me, and I fell asleep, totally dead to the world until a sunbeam woke me the next morning.

The bed beside me was empty. When I dressed and walked to the nursery, Elias wasn't in his crib either.

I found them downstairs, Elias in Kerrigan's arms. The two of them were staring out one of the large windows.

"Hey." I walked up behind her and wrapped my arms around them both. "Would you look at that."

Beyond the glass, a heavy blanket of snow was falling. It wasn't the angry storm from December, but the white came down in such fat flakes that we couldn't see twenty feet beyond the house. White covered the shoots of green grass and dusted the trees.

"So much for spring," I said. "I wonder if we'll get snowed in."

"I hope so," Kerrigan whispered.

So did I.

With my family in my arms, we watched the snow fall.

And neither of us complained when the road was closed six hours later.

EPILOGUE
KERRIGAN

TWO YEARS LATER...

"Mommy! Here I go!" Elias flew down the slide, landing with his feet on the wood chips at the base. Once his legs were steady, he threw his arms in the air and did his booty-shake victory dance. "I dit it. I dit it."

"You did it!" I clapped. "All by yourself."

He'd been nervous to go on the biggest green slide at the park alone, but there was no way I could climb up there and squeeze myself through the various holes at the jungle gym these days. Just tying my shoes took a small miracle.

Elias ran over to me, colliding with my knees.

I reached past my belly and ruffled his dark hair. The mop of thick waves was becoming a creature of its own, but every time Pierce suggested we cut it, I'd convince him to wait one more week.

The last time we'd cut it, Elias had looked instantly older and I'd cried at the hair salon. Granted, I'd been in the early stages of this pregnancy and a hormonal mess about everything. At nearly nine months along, that hadn't changed.

"Okay, bud. Time to go meet Daddy."

Pierce had texted me an hour and a half ago that they were leaving the airport. By the time I made it to The Refinery, they should be back in town.

I held out my hand, taking Elias's in mine as we set out across the park. My white floral sundress swished above my knees. With my free hand, I pushed the stroller as he walked, and when walking became too much, I let him climb into his seat as I eased it along Calamity's quiet neighborhood streets.

It was a hike from the park to First Street for a woman whose ankles were twice their usual size and whose lower back was in constant pain, but I'd wanted to do some spying today.

Pierce and I had built our current home after he'd officially moved to Montana. My old house, the one I'd remodeled a couple of years ago, we'd sold because it wasn't big enough for both Pierce and Clementine to coexist under the same roof in peace.

Earlier this week, Mom had seen the new owners outside with ladders, rollers and paint buckets. She'd raced to The Refinery, livid that they'd paint what she still considered my house.

Why would they paint it? What color could possibly be better than the creamy white you picked?

"Black, apparently," I muttered as it came into view. Seriously? Black? Yes, it was trendy, but that house was too small for such a dark shade. My heart sank as I passed it by.

"We're not walking down this street anymore," I told Elias.

"Doggie!" He pointed to a golden retriever in a yard ahead. "Mommy, wook at da doggie!"

"Should we get a dog?" I kept my voice low because I

knew my son's answer. Pierce would be all for it, but another animal might send Clementine over the edge. Maybe after she had two babies to protect, we could think about a puppy.

When we hit First Street, the road was crowded with cars, and out-of-state license plates marked most as tourists. Memorial Day weekend in Calamity was always busy, and unlike most members of the older generation, I loved seeing the sidewalks full of people. This foot traffic would be fantastic for the new brewery we'd opened in March.

This past fall, another one of the older buildings at the end of First had gone on the market, and we'd bought it from the previous owner, who'd decided to shut down his wild-game-processing business and retire. So after washing the building with ten rounds of bleach to get the smell out—even after a complete remodel I swore there were days when I could still smell the blood and tallow—we'd converted it into a brewery.

Our menu was small, focusing on small plates for people who just needed a quick bite while they drank a beer. We'd hired a brewer from Bozeman who'd been wanting to move to a smaller community, and for the most part, we let him run the show.

There'd been some grumbling around town about another bar in Calamity, this coming mostly from Jane, because for years she'd cornered the booze market on First with her own bar. But after a couple of months, she'd realized that there was enough demand in Calamity for two popular hangout spots.

I smiled at the full parking spaces in front of the brewery and kept on walking toward the gym. The moment Elias spotted Pierce's Land Rover, he squirmed out of the stroller.

"Daddy!" Elias pumped his chubby arms as he ran down the sidewalk.

"Hey, pal." Pierce swept him up, tossing him in the air, then hugged him like they hadn't seen each other in weeks, not five hours.

Pierce stood in nearly the same place he had years ago when we'd had our first face-off. I laughed, thinking back to how handsome he'd looked in that suit. Entirely out of place, but utterly magnetic.

He didn't wear suits as often these days. He favored jeans like the ones he wore today, ones that fit his strong thighs and long legs. But he was just as magnetic. Just as irresistible.

When I reached them, I moved the stroller out of the way and leaned into Pierce's side.

"Hi, babe." He kissed my hair. "How are you feeling?"

"Good." I rested my hands on my belly. Tired, but good. There wasn't much to complain about these days.

After our thirty days at the lodge, Pierce had given me another proposal, this one including a diamond ring. One month later, we'd been married in a small ceremony at one of my favorite places in the foothills outside of town with our family and close friends watching on.

As soon as the attorneys had the paperwork ready, I'd adopted Elias. Then we'd begun construction on our new house. The cabin was just too far from Calamity and in the winter, there was too much risk of getting stranded.

Our home here was in the country, surrounded by trees to give us some privacy. Given that Pierce had wanted to put in plenty of rooms, we had space to expand, and I'd already captured enough blog and social media content for a decade.

Not that I had a lot of followers.

Two years later, it was still a hobby more than an income stream, but I loved it enough not to give up. If I gained ten followers a week, I was happy. Besides, my businesses were flourishing and a healthy bottom line, along with my family and a few DIY projects, was enough to keep the smile on my face.

Construction on the satellite office for Grays Peak had just wrapped. It sat on the outskirts of town and was going to be my next feature for the blog. Most of his employees would remain in Denver, but twenty people had opted to move to Calamity.

Twenty new faces, plus their families, would be calling this home.

Including Nellie.

She'd moved here two weeks ago. Which was good, because if she'd realized who else was moving here, she probably would have changed her mind. As it was, she had a mortgage and was committed for a bit.

"Where's Cal?" I asked.

Pierce jerked his chin at The Refinery. "I was telling him about the gym on the drive over from Bozeman. He wanted to check it out."

Cal had visited us in Montana a few times since we'd moved here, including the wedding. But we'd always gone to the cabin and he had yet to spend much time in Calamity.

Though apparently enough to move here.

"I'm sure it's a locker room compared to the huge gyms he's used to," I said. "If he makes one snarky comment . . ."

"Give him a chance." Pierce always defended Cal, and though I'd heard plenty of stories that made the retired football star seem almost human, I'd also heard plenty of stories from Nellie, and hers were anything but flattering.

"I'm on Nellie's side." A declaration I'd made countless times since Cal's decision to relocate.

Nellie and I had become great friends over the past couple of years, and I was not going to lose her from Calamity. With Nellie, Lucy and Everly, I had my very own girl gang. No one, not even a former NFL quarterback, was going to fuck it up.

And it wasn't just Nellie's horror stories about Cal that I'd heard. Turns out, this wasn't just a small town, but a small world. Not only did Pierce and Nellie know Cal from high school, but Everly and Lucy knew Cal from their days living in Nashville. Everly had even gone on a couple of dates with Cal until she'd called it off.

Nellie loved having someone to commiserate about the awfulness that was Cal Stark.

I'd spent enough time around Cal that I wouldn't go straight to awful. He was a different person around Pierce. He'd only ever treated me kindly and he loved Elias. He wasn't really awful.

Not that I'd ever admit that to Nellie.

"Let's not get stressed about this," Pierce said. "Calamity is big enough for them both."

"I don't know about that," I muttered. Pierce gave us too much credit.

The community was currently kissing Pierce's ass because not only was he bringing his billions here, but he'd also given sizeable donations to every local charity. When the gossip about you was positive, life here was roses and rainbows.

But some day—it was inevitable in a town this size—someone would say something nasty and he'd realize just how small this town was.

"Where's Unka Cal?" Elias asked.

Elias, like Pierce, loved Cal. Probably because Cal spoiled my son with anything and everything football, which was Elias's favorite thing beyond his teddy bear.

"He's in Mommy's gym."

"Should we go find him?" I stood straight, wincing at a pain in my side.

"What's wrong?" Pierce set Elias down immediately and his hands shot to my belly.

"Nothing." I waved it off. "Everything is just tight."

"Are you sure?"

I laughed. "I'm sure."

Pierce's fretting and hovering had been a constant companion to this pregnancy. There'd been a lot of nerves at first given both of our histories, but as the months progressed and this baby girl grew with only healthy checkup reports, I'd calmed considerably.

Pierce? Not even a little bit.

"Kerrigan!" My name rang out from down the sidewalk and we all turned as Nellie rushed our way.

"Oh shit," Pierce mumbled.

"Still think the town's big enough?"

"I'd hoped to avoid this for a day or two. And break the news before they actually saw each other."

Nellie's white-blond hair streamed behind her as she ran our way with a huge smile on her face. A smile that would vanish the minute she spotted Cal.

"Nellieeeee." Elias skipped over to her, holding out his hand for a high five.

"Hi, buddy." She ruffled his hair.

"Hey." I waved and did my best to steer her so that her

back was to the gym. Maybe if Cal spotted her, he'd stay inside. "What are you up to?"

"I came to find you."

"You did? Why?"

She dug her phone from the pocket of her jeans and pulled up TikTok. "You are going viral."

"What?" I crowded close to her screen as she pulled up the video I'd posted this morning. I'd been working in my new garden shed, installing this antique window. The shed had been a pet project and something fun to do in my limited spare time. It was shabby chic and adorable and when it was done, it would become my summer greenhouse-slash-hangout.

The video was of me with a nail gun, my pregnant belly on display in a pair of overalls. My hair was a mess and my safety glasses were filmy, but I was smiling as I put in the window.

"Oh my God." I blinked at the views on the video, then studied them again. "Does that say three point four million?"

"Yes!" Nellie put her arm around my shoulders and then Pierce was there too, holding me up because my knees had gone weak.

"Oh my God." I'd been so busy with Elias all morning that I hadn't checked my social media. I'd posted the video, expecting the same two thousand followers as normal to watch this one too.

I took my phone from the cupholder on the stroller and opened my apps. My eyes bugged out at my follower count on TikTok. Then I opened Instagram and I nearly fainted.

"Easy, babe." Pierce was there to hold me up again.

"Fifty thousand. There are fifty thousand people following me." I looked up at my husband and just stared.

His smile was blinding. "What did I tell you?"

"To keep going." He'd been my biggest supporter from the beginning. Every time I mentioned giving up, he'd tell me not to quit. He'd tell me my ideas were fresh and unique. That I had something others would want to see, but it would take time.

A laugh bubbled free as Elias came over and wrapped his arms around my leg.

"Mommy, where's Unka Cal?"

"Um . . ." Leave it to the two-year-old to bring you right back to reality.

"Uncle *Cal*?" Nellie's smile disappeared. "Please tell me he's in Tennessee where he belongs."

"Oh, look. It's my favorite bottle blonde." Cal's deep voice echoed from over Nellie's shoulder as he came striding out of The Refinery.

Her face transformed from sunshine to ice as she turned to face him. "Well, if there's anyone in the world who should understand fake, it's you. Fake it till you make it. That's like the model for your career, right? Oh, sorry. Former career. I heard you got fired. Ouch."

His jaw clenched. "I was a free agent and retired."

"Sure," she deadpanned.

"Can you two save it for another day?" Pierce asked. "We need to celebrate my wife."

"Unka Cal!" Elias went racing for Cal, who picked him up and tickled him mercilessly.

Both man and boy laughed and the affection on Cal's face was as clear as the big sky.

I couldn't put my finger on Cal. Some moments, I liked him. A lot. Others, I'd be right behind Nellie as she slapped him in the face. He could be such a dick to her but the way he loved my son was adorable. His loyalty to Pierce was unwavering.

"How about we all go to the brew—" A stream of water trickled down my leg.

"What the fuck is that?" Cal asked.

"Language," I snapped. Elias would repeat anything Cal said. "And that would be my water breaking."

So . . . not a side ache today.

Pierce flew into action, taking my arm and steering me to his SUV. "Nellie—"

"I've got Elias," she said. "We'll walk to my place."

"He hasn't had lunch," I told her as Pierce helped me into the passenger seat.

"We've got him," Cal said.

We? I didn't need my son in the middle of their next battle. "Maybe you should just let Nel—"

Pierce closed the door on me before I could finish my sentence.

"I've got him," Nellie called loud enough for me to hear.

I nodded as a new pain spread. "Oh, that is . . . weird. Breathe."

"Okay." Pierce climbed behind the wheel.

I'd been talking to myself but as he drove and the color drained from his face, I realized that we both needed the reminder.

"Hey." I reached over and put a hand on his arm. "I love you."

"I love you."

"We get to meet her today."

He gave me a shaky smile, barely glancing over as he tore through town for the hospital. "We get to meet her today."

Today turned out to be tomorrow.

At four thirty the next morning, our daughter, Constance May Sullivan, was born.

When they released us from the hospital, Pierce had already gone to our house to pick up Elias and our bags.

Because the first place we wanted to take her was to the cabin.

BONUS EPILOGUE
PIERCE

"Again. Again!" Constance demanded, swimming across the hot tub at the cabin.

We'd lowered the temperature so the kids could play in here without it being too warm, and it had become their personal swimming pool.

"Ready?" I picked her up under the arms and launched her into the air, sending her crashing into the water. At two, she didn't make much of a splash. The inflatable pink wings around her biceps popped her right out of the water so I could hear her giggle.

"It's my turn, Daddy." Elias swam over, positioned himself on my knees and plugged his nose before I sent him into the air. My son was huge at four—hello, ninety-fifth percentile—and when he landed, the water sloshed out and onto the snowy patio.

"There's not going to be any water left in there," Kerrigan said from the doorway.

I chuckled and grinned over my shoulder. "Are you coming in?"

"Dinner will be ready in twenty minutes. But maybe we can have a little hot tub time later." She winked at me before disappearing inside.

Damn, but I loved our vacations here. Not that Kerrigan and I didn't have a great sex life, but my wife relaxed at the cabin. Really relaxed. And it made our nights in the bedroom unforgettable.

We'd come up for Christmas and decided to stay through New Year's. Kerrigan's family had joined us but left earlier this afternoon before dark as a cluster of dark, ominous clouds had drifted in. Maybe we wouldn't make it home by Friday. Snow was in the air.

Getting stranded at the cabin was never a bad thing. That was how we'd conceived Constance.

I smiled wider, tossed my kids one more time, then hurried them inside to dry off and change into warm clothes. Dinner was followed by our nightly s'more-fest at the fireplace. Then as Kerrigan went to put them to bed, I ducked into the office to send a quick email that I'd forgotten earlier.

Grays Peak was taking on a new investment in San Francisco, a sports complex for underprivileged kids. The VP in charge of the account had sent me the pitch but there were a few numbers that didn't jibe.

I went in search of a pen and some paper to jot down a few quick figures, but when I tried to pull open the desk's drawer, it stuck.

"What the hell?" I pushed it in, reaching my fingers inside to feel for whatever was caught.

A thick piece of paper had gotten wedged in the top, so I yanked it out.

Except it wasn't a piece of paper. It was a photograph.

I smoothed out the wrinkled picture and took it in. "I'll be damned."

My grandfather's face greeted me. So did a much younger version of mine. I was in his arms, laughing. A smile stretched across his mouth as he stared at me. I had to have been around the same age as Elias in this photo, maybe four or five.

"What's that?" Kerrigan asked, coming into the room.

She was wearing a red bikini, clearly ready for some time in the hot tub.

"I found this in the drawer." I handed it over and pushed my chair away from the desk, making room for her to sit on my lap.

"Look at you." She smiled. "You and Elias look almost exactly the same."

"Crazy, right?"

"And Gabriel." Her face softened. "He was so young."

I nodded, taking him in.

"Does it bother you? Seeing him?"

"No, not anymore." I wrapped her in my arms. "You were right. I just needed time."

The hate and anger I'd had for my grandfather had vanished long ago.

If not for Grandpa, I wouldn't have Kerrigan. If not for Heidi, I wouldn't have Elias. I hoped that from wherever they were watching, they could see how grateful I was for these gifts they'd left me.

Forgiveness was powerful. Without any lingering resentment, my life had been consumed by love. Mostly for this woman and our children.

"Ready for a quick swim?" A naked swim.

"I can't." She set the photo aside and smiled. "I put on my suit but stopped in the bathroom."

"Okay. And why does that make you unable to go in the hot tub?"

"Because I failed a test. Or rather, I came back with a positive."

My heart skipped. "You're pregnant?"

Her beautiful face came closer, her lips a whisper against my mouth. "I'm pregnant."

I didn't need the hot tub to love my wife. I stripped her out of that red bikini and made love to her right there on the desk while beyond the walls, a snowstorm raged.

We were snowed in for a week.

And once again in early spring.

Then later that summer, in Calamity, our son Gabriel was born.

ACKNOWLEDGMENTS

Thank you for reading *The Brazen*! Writing in the Calamity, Montana, world is an absolute joy, and I am so grateful you picked up Kerrigan and Pierce's book.

Special thanks to the incredible team who contributed their talents to this book. My editor, Elizabeth Nover. My proofreaders, Julie Deaton, Karen Lawson and Judy Zweifel. My cover designer, Sarah Hansen.

To the fantastic bloggers who take the time to read and post about my stories, thank you! And a huge thanks to the members of Perry & Nash for loving my books whether they are from Devney Perry or Willa Nash. I am so very grateful for your support!

And lastly, thank you to my wonderful family. Bill, Will and Nash—I'm so lucky to have you three in my corner.

ABOUT THE AUTHOR

Willa Nash is *USA Today* Bestselling Author Devney Perry's alter ego, writing contemporary romance stories for Kindle Unlimited. Lover of Swedish Fish, hater of laundry, she lives in Washington State with her husband and two sons. She was born and raised in Montana and has a passion for writing books in the state she calls home.

Don't miss out on Willa's latest book news.
Subscribe to her newsletter!
www.willanash.com